THE
SILENCE
OF
MURDER

THE
SILENCE
OF
MURDER

DANDI DALEY MACKALL

Alfred A. Knopf
New York

THIS IS A BORZOI BOOK PUBLISHED BY ALFRED A. KNOPF

Visit us on the Web! www.randomhouse.com/teens

Educators and librarians, for a variety of teaching tools, visit us at www.randomhouse.com/teachers

Library of Congress Cataloging-in-Publication Data
Mackall, Dandi Daley.
The silence of murder / Dandi Daley Mackall. — 1st ed.
    p. cm.
Summary: Sixteen-year-old Hope must defend her developmentally disabled brother (who has not spoken a word since he was nine) when he is accused of murdering a beloved high school baseball coach.
ISBN 978-0-375-86896-2 (trade) — ISBN 978-0-375-96896-9 (lib. bdg.) —
ISBN 978-0-375-89981-2 (ebook)
[1. Brothers and sisters—Fiction. 2. People with mental disabilities—Fiction. 3. Selective mutism—Fiction. 4. Trials (Murder)—Fiction. 5. Mystery and detective stories.] I. Title.
PZ7.M1905Sk 2011
[Fic]—dc22
                              2010035991

The text of this book is set in 11.5-point Goudy.

Printed in the United States of America
October 2011
10 9 8 7 6 5 4 3 2 1

First Edition

To the memory of my dad,
Frank R. Daley, MD, who taught me to love words,
wit, and a good mystery. I have been blessed with
two fantastic parents, who gave me
a much better start to life than I deserved.

1

The first time Jeremy heard God sing, we were in the old Ford, rocking back and forth with the wind. Snow pounded at the window to get inside, where it wasn't much better than out there. I guess he was nine. I was seven, but I've always felt like the older sister, even though Jeremy was bigger.

I snuggled closer under his arm while we waited for Rita. She made us call her 'Rita' and not 'Mom' or 'Mommy' or 'Mother,' and that was fine with Jeremy and me. Pretty much anything that was fine with Jeremy was fine with me.

We'd been in the backseat long enough for frost to make a curtain on the car windshield and for Rita's half-drunk paper cup of coffee to ice some in its holder up front.

Jeremy had grown so still that I thought he might be asleep, or half frozen, either one being better than the teeth-chattering bone-chilling I had going on.

Then came the sound.

It filled the car. A single note that made it feel like all of the notes were put together in just the right way. I don't remember wondering where that note came from because my whole head was full of it and the hope that it wouldn't stop, not ever. And it went on so long I thought maybe I was getting my wish and that this was what people heard when they died, right before seeing that white tunnel light.

The note didn't so much end as it went into another note and then more of them. And there were words in the notes, but they were swallowed up in the meaning of that music-song so that I couldn't tell and didn't care which was which.

Then I saw this song was coming from my brother, and I started bawling like a baby. And bawling wasn't something you did in our house because Rita couldn't abide crying and believed whacking you was the way to make it stop.

Jeremy sang what must have been a whole entire song, because when he closed his mouth, it seemed right that the song was over.

When I could get words out, I turned so I could see my brother. "Jeremy," I whispered, "I never heard you sing before."

He smiled like someone had warmed him toasty all the way through and given him hot chocolate with marshmallows to top it off. "I never sang before."

"But that song? Where did you get it?"

"God," he answered, as simply as if he'd said, "Walmart."

I'd just heard that song, and even though it seemed to me that God made more sense than Walmart for an answer, I felt like I had to say otherwise. I was the "normal" sister, the one whose *needs* weren't officially *special*.

"Jeremy, God can't give you a song," I told him.

Jeremy raised his eyebrows a little and swayed the way he does. "Hope," he said, like he was older than Rita and I was just a little kid, "God didn't give it to me. He sang it. I just copied."

The door to the trailer flew open, and a man named Billy stepped out. Rita was breaking up with Billy, but I don't think he knew that. We'd stopped by his trailer on our way out of town so Rita could pick up her stuff, and maybe get some money off her ex-boyfriend, who didn't realize he was an ex. Billy stood there in plaid boxers, his belly hanging over the elastic like a rotten potato somebody'd tried to put a rubber band around. If I hadn't been so cold, I might have tried to get Jeremy to laugh.

Rita squeezed up beside the potato man. She tried to slip past him and out the door. But he took hold of her bag and grabbed one more kiss. She laughed, like this was a big game. Then she stepped down out of the trailer, wiping her mouth with the back of her hand.

I would have given everything I had, which I admit wasn't so very much, just to hear Jeremy and God's song again.

The tall heels of Rita's red knee-high patent-leather boots crunched the snow as she stepped to the car, arms out to her sides, like a tightrope walker trying to stay on the wire. She jerked open the driver's door, slid into place, and slammed the door hard enough to shake the car worse than the wind.

Without saying a word, she turned the key and pumped the pedal until the Ford caught. Then she stoked up the defrost and waited for the wipers to do their thing. I figured by the scowl on Rita's face that Billy hadn't forked over the "loan" she'd hoped for.

Jeremy leaned forward, his knobby fingers on the back of the seat. "Rita," he said, "I didn't know God could sing."

She struck like a rattler, but without the warning. The slap echoed off Jeremy's face, louder than the roar of the engine. "God don't sing!" she screamed.

That was the last time Jeremy ever spoke out loud.

Sometimes I think if I could have moved quicker, put myself in between my brother's soft cheek and Rita's hard hand, the whole world might have spun out different.

2

"Your Honor, I object!"

The prosecutor stands up so fast his chair screeches on the courtroom floor. He has on a silvery suit with a blue tie. If he weren't trying to kill my brother, I'd probably think he's handsome in a dull, paper-doll-cutout kind of way. Brown hair that doesn't move, even when he bangs the state's table. Brown eyes that make me think of bullets. I'm guessing that he's not even ten years older than Jeremy, the one sitting behind the defense table, the one on trial for murdering Coach Johnson with a baseball bat, the one this prosecutor would like to execute before he reaches the age of nineteen.

The prosecutor charges the witness box as if he's coming to get me. His squinty bullet eyes make me scoot back in the chair. "The witness's regrets about what she may or may not have done a decade ago are immaterial and irrelevant!" he shouts.

"Sit down, Mr. Keller," the judge says, like she's tired of

saying it because she's already said it a thousand times this week.

Maybe she has. This is my first day in her courtroom. Since I'm a witness in my brother's trial, they wouldn't let me attend until after I testified. So I can't say the whole truth and nothing but the truth about what's gone on in this courtroom without me.

"I'll allow it," the judge says. "Go ahead, Miss Long."

I smile up at her, even though she's not looking. I'm thinking there just might be a nice regular person under that black robe. I try to imagine what she has on under there and decide cutoffs and a T-shirt that reads GRATEFUL DEAD. That's what I remember seeing on the black shirt of one of Rita's girlfriends during her trial for solicitation, which is one fancy way of looking at that job. "Thank you, Judge," I tell her.

Raymond Munroe, attorney for the defense, smiles at me now, but it's a half smile, the kind a ninety-pound weakling might risk if a bully decided to walk on by instead of pounding him into the sand. Poor Raymond, our court-appointed attorney, looks more out of place than I do in this courtroom. He looked out of place in our house when he made Rita and me practice our testimonies. And he looked out of place when he stood up next to my brother in the Wayne County Courthouse and helped Jeremy plead "not guilty and not guilty by reason of insanity." Raymond's voice cracked.

I glance over at the table where Jeremy is sitting all by himself. He's in a constant state of motion—like a hummingbird—his hands patting the table, his knees bouncing, his arms twitching. He's not like this all the time, only when he gets upset. When Jeremy was little, his face was handsome. Then it took on angles, like his skull rebelled because it couldn't hold on to the thoughts Jeremy kept inside.

"Hope," Raymond says, looking at the jury instead of me, "have you always suspected there was something . . . well, let's say 'wrong' . . . with your brother?"

My brother is staring hard at me, his mouth slightly open, showing too much gum on top. I know Jeremy's waiting for me to tell the truth, the whole truth, and nothing but the truth because that's his way.

But it's not mine. And it hasn't been for a long time.

So even though I have never even once thought there was something "wrong" with my brother, I nod.

"You'll have to speak up," the judge says, leaning over her desk. You can tell she's not mad, though. "We can't record gestures," she explains. "Answer the question with words, please." She leans back in her big chair and waits for words.

"Sorry," I say, making sure not to look at my brother again. "Jeremy's always been different. I guess, like Raymond says, 'wrong.'"

I try to remember the way Raymond and I rehearsed this part of the testimony. This is not how it went. I remember that much.

I have a good memory, but it doesn't work with words. Just pictures. Like I can picture Raymond sitting at our sticky kitchen table, a pile of papers and a yellow pad in front of him. A full glass of Rita's too-sweet ice tea is sweating a water ring to the side of Raymond's notebook. Raymond's trying to tell me how to support his strategy, which is to convince the jury that Jeremy's too crazy to be killed by the State of Ohio just because he murdered Mr. Johnson. Raymond wants to make sure we understand that Ohio can give the death penalty to anybody eighteen or over, unless they're really, really out of it.

I can picture Raymond, Rita, and me at that table as if we were still there. Jeremy's the same way. He notices details. He can tell when I'm getting a migraine headache even before I feel it, just by seeing the lines on my forehead change. Jeremy used to say God wired us alike, loaded us with the same film. That was before he stopped talking. Jeremy, I mean. But God too, I guess. At least to me.

Raymond's frowning at me, waiting for me to say what we practiced. I notice the shiny lining of his suit and his skinny black belt. I glimpse Jeremy swaying at his table, his skin drawn too tight over the angles and bones of his face. Two rows back sit three of my teachers from high school, not together but in a blur of other town faces, including T.J., a guy in my class and about the only friend I've got in this town. Behind T.J. a row of reporters lean into each other.

And I see Chase, Sheriff Wells's son, who stands out in this crowd, in any crowd. Even here, with life and death dangling from the courtroom rafters, his face—I notice every line in that face—makes it real hard for me to look back at Raymond.

Raymond clears his throat and glances at the jury, then at me again. "Would you mind giving us an example of how your brother is *different?*"

I do mind. I know exactly what Raymond wants me to say.

He wants me to tell the jury about something that happened when Jeremy was ten. That's what we rehearsed. Only I don't want to tell this story. I know it will hurt Jer.

But if *I* don't tell it, Rita will. And she'll get it all wrong, and Jeremy will hate that worse than having me tell it right.

Besides, it's important to tell it right. Because if I don't, if the jury doesn't understand Jeremy, then the State of Ohio will give my brother a shot that will put him to sleep forever. And even if they don't do that, they'll put him in a prison with grown men who will crush all the Jeremy out of him, or kill him trying.

3

"Hope, will you tell us about an incident that took place in Chicago when Jeremy was ten?" Raymond Attorney for the Defense asks. It's the exact question he made me answer half a dozen times at the kitchen table.

"I was eight, and Jeremy was ten," I begin. I close my eyes and remember. I can see Rita's hand reaching for something. I know it's her hand because she's wearing the big green ring she used to have. Jeremy's behind her, and I'm behind Jer. I have straggly blond hair and big blue ghost eyes, and I'm bundled into a quilted ski jacket a size too small. Steam rises from a loaf of bread. Plastic forks are piled at one end of a long, skinny table with a yellow-and-green-checked tablecloth.

"It was our first night in Chicago," I continue. "Rita decided we needed a change of scenery from Minneapolis, although the snow looked the same to me. She told us she'd always wanted to see the Windy City. Plus, there was this guy named Slater who was looking for us, and Rita didn't want him to find us. I kept thinking how Windy City was a real good name for this place because we could see snow blowing everywhere, like it wanted to get out of town fast as it could.

"Jeremy and I held hands and trailed behind Rita." I can see her in her pale pink wool coat and red high heels, but I don't bother telling the jury that. "We'd ridden all night on a bus from Minneapolis. Rita had struck up a conversation with a man who said he was a salesman."

Raymond steps in closer to the witness box. He glances at the clock, then at the judge, and finally back to me. "Get to the part where the police were called in."

That makes the prosecutor bounce up again. "Your Honor! He's leading the witness."

I can't imagine Raymond leading anybody, but the judge nods, agreeing with Mr. Keller. "Sustained." She turns to Raymond. "Just ask your question, Mr. Munroe."

I feel kind of sorry for Raymond because he looks like a kid who got his hand slapped for reaching where he shouldn't have.

"Would you tell us what happened when you arrived at the shelter?" Raymond asks.

I tell myself I need to cut to the chase. But thinking this reminds me that Chase, *the* Chase, is sitting in this very room, listening to and watching . . . me. And I have to talk about going to a shelter to get a meal.

I clear my throat. "There was a long line of people waiting to get their dinner for free. It was a good dinner too, with fresh bread and everything. Rita gave us plates and told us to fill them up. She and the salesman did the same thing. I think

I forgot to tell that part, that the salesman came with us from the bus station. He was the one who knew about the free-dinner place."

My mind is jumping ahead, and I see Jeremy's hand reaching for that bread. I remember being glad about that because my brother had started looking skinny as a shoelace.

"Please go on," Raymond urges.

I take in a deep breath and let out the rest of the story without taking in another. "Jeremy kept piling bread onto his plate, even when Rita tossed him a dirty look not to. And there were drumsticks too, and he piled those up. Then, instead of eating his own food, like he should have done, he walked around that room and handed it out."

"Handed it out?" Raymond repeats.

I nod, then remember about using words instead. "Yeah. He gave drumsticks to old men and little boys and other kids' mothers. And he gave bread to people right off his own plate, even if they already had some. When his plate was empty, he went back and filled it up again and then handed out the food all over again. It was like he couldn't stop giving it away."

"How did people react?" Raymond asks, right on cue.

"At first, people took the food without saying anything, just giving him a funny look. Then they got into it. They hollered, 'Over here! I can use some of that!' And Jeremy kept it up until there wasn't anything more to give out."

"And then what?" Raymond asks.

"And then he took off his shoes."

"His shoes?" Raymond looks all surprised when he turns to the jury. But he knows what's coming, which is why he wanted me to tell this story.

"He took off his brand-new snow boots, and he gave them to a kid who wore beat-up tennis shoes. Then he took off his socks, and he gave those away too."

"Where was your mother during all this?" Raymond asks. As if he doesn't know.

"Rita was yelling at him to stop. She kept saying she paid good money for those boots, although it was really Slater who did, and I'm not so sure the money was all that good."

"And what did your brother do when your mother yelled for him to stop?" Raymond asks.

I answer just like we practiced. "It was like Jeremy didn't hear her. He gave his coat to a red-haired girl with a long braid down her back. He unbuttoned his shirt. Rita took hold of his hand, but he kept going, unbuttoning with his other hand. So she smacked him."

"Smacked him?" Raymond says, like he's never heard of such a thing in his whole life.

"Just the back of his head," I explain. "But it didn't stop him. He gave the shirt off his back. And he kept going. He was down to his boxers when security got him. I don't like to think what might have happened next if they hadn't stopped him when they did." I deliver that line exactly like Raymond and I practiced it.

But I feel like a traitor bringing up this story this way. I can't look at Jeremy, but I can imagine the look he's giving me. I've seen it enough to know. Not mad. Disappointed. Like he thought I'd understood that day and now he sees I didn't and it's too bad—for me, not for him—that I don't.

The truth is, when the security officers stopped him, Jeremy didn't look crazy. I don't think a single person in that room thought he was crazy. They'd all grown quiet by then. All except me. I shouted for them to get their hands off my brother.

Then this little boy walked up to Jeremy and held out his own jacket for Jer to put on, and Jeremy did. And then a very large woman took something out of a grocery bag, and it turned out to be shoes exactly Jeremy's size. And not only did she give him those shoes, she put them on his feet. But not before a little girl ran up and gave my brother her own white socks that had little yarn balls on the back of them so they wouldn't fall down. Somebody else came up with a pair of jeans for my brother. One of the security people helped Jeremy get those jeans over his new shoes because by then guards had his arms behind his back.

When we left that place, people said goodbye and waved. And Jeremy was better off than when we'd come in.

We all were.

I feel sick inside my bones. My whole life I've fought anybody who said Jeremy was crazy, or treated him like there was something wrong with him. And now I've done that and worse, here in front of everybody and after swearing about it with my hand on the Bible.

"It's getting late," the judge says. "We'll adjourn until nine o'clock tomorrow morning." She turns to the jury and gives them orders not to talk to each other or anyone else about this case. Then she bangs her gavel on her desk. We all stand up to go home.

Only not Jeremy.

4

I stumble down from the witness box because I have to get to Jeremy fast. He and Raymond are standing up at the defense table, and an officer is heading for Jer. I don't know what the rules are here, but I need to talk to my brother.

"Jeremy?" I rush over to him before anybody can stop me, but the table is between us. I can't touch him. I want to hug him, to feel his stiff arms fold around me, to have his chin on my head. "I'm sorry. I had to tell it that way." I want to shout to Jer that I don't believe he's crazy, but I can't. Raymond told me I can't ever say that to anybody, especially not in court.

"You need to leave, Hope," Raymond says. He's tossing papers and files into his briefcase.

I ignore him. It's Jeremy I want. "Jeremy, you have to tell them you didn't do it. Write it out. Please? Just write down what happened." He can write. Until this . . . until Coach died . . . Jeremy wrote notes all the time, in beautiful, pointy, swirling letters, his own brand of calligraphy.

Jeremy turns and gives me a sad, disappointed smile filled with forgiveness. Bile spouts from my belly to my throat, but I gulp it back down. His eyes widen as the officer slaps on handcuffs. His wrists are bruised, and his forearms have blue-and-yellow fingerprints. I'd be horrified if I didn't know firsthand how easily my brother bruises. It was Rita's curse when Jeremy was young because the world could see her temper spelled out on Jeremy's skin in purple and blue. She made him wear sweatshirts and jeans, even in Oklahoma summers. Most of the bruises came from Jeremy's clumsiness, though. I used to call them nature's decorations.

"Wait!" I beg. "Please let me talk to him."

I watch my brother's hands, his long, knotted fingers twisting frantically in the cuffs.

"Settle down, son," says the officer of the court, a burly man with tiny wire-rimmed glasses. Except for his soft eyes, he looks like the bald bouncer Rita fell for in Arizona, right after she quit her waitress job. "Come along now."

Jeremy's wrists spin faster and wilder. The metal cuffs clink together. He stares over his shoulder at me, intense, desperate.

"Take it easy, Jer," I urge, angry at myself for making him worse, for upsetting him, for calling him crazy in front of God and everybody.

Then I get it. He's not trying to wrestle out of the cuffs. He's doing charades, mimicking the motion of turning a lid on a jar. Jeremy wants one of his jars. He collects empty jars, and he wants—*needs*—one now.

"I'll try, Jeremy. I promise. And I'll take good care of your jars. Okay?"

His hands stop twisting. His body goes limp.

The officer takes him by one arm. "There's a good boy," he says, leading him away. "Time to go."

I stare after Jeremy for a solid minute after he disappears behind a side door. I don't want to think what's on the other side, where Jeremy will spend one more night.

I wheel on Raymond. "This is wrong, Raymond. He didn't do it."

Raymond doesn't look up from his overstuffed briefcase. "Hope, we've been all through this. Your mother and I settled on a trial strategy."

"But you pled not guilty by reason of insanity *and* not guilty?" I sat through as many of Raymond and Rita's trial talks as they'd let me. I'd wanted them to come out and say Jeremy didn't do it, but they wouldn't listen to me. Rita is convinced Jeremy did it but didn't mean to, so she was all about the insanity plea. Then Raymond told us that in Ohio, you can plead both things, "not guilty" and "not guilty by reason of insanity." So that's what we did. He said it was like covering your bases, like telling the jury: "My client didn't do it, but if he did, he was insane and didn't know what he was doing."

Raymond sighs like he's losing patience with me. "Yes. We pled NG and NGRI, not guilty and not guilty by reason of insanity. At the insanity hearing, Jeremy was deemed capable of standing trial and helping in his own defense. Hope, I thought you understood that."

"I did! But if they've already said he's *not* insane in that insanity hearing, why are you trying to make out like he's crazy now?"

"One has nothing to do with the other," Raymond explains. "That hearing was separate from this trial. The jury wasn't there. Here, in this court, we can still go for not guilty by reason of insanity."

"But what about proving he didn't do it? Period! Why aren't you doing that?" I'm shouting now, but I can't help it.

Raymond glances around, then whispers, "Because there's no evidence for that."

That shuts me up. No evidence, except the evidence piling up *against* my brother. I haven't been allowed in the courtroom before now because I had to testify, but I've read the newspaper articles about the state's witnesses, who claim they saw Jeremy running from the barn with a bloody bat, *his* bloody bat.

I sense someone behind me before he speaks. "I'm sorry. You need to clear the courtroom." Sheriff Matthew Wells has the gravelly voice of an old-time Wild West sheriff.

I turn to face him. He's about Rita's age, tall with a beer gut. The sleeves of his light brown shirt are rolled up to the elbow, showing a purple tattoo of a star, or maybe a badge. His black hair has a circular dent where his hat must belong when he's not in court. There's a gun in his holster. "Need to move along, folks."

"Of course," Raymond says. "Sorry, Sheriff." He snaps his briefcase shut and looks over at me. "Hope, I'll see you tonight, all right?"

I nod. But that sick feeling in my stomach comes back. Raymond wants to prepare me for tomorrow. More testimony, including the prosecutor's cross-examination. How do you rehearse for that?

"Miss?" Sheriff Wells touches my arm, and I automatically pull away. "You really do need to leave now."

I hear footsteps and wonder if he's called in reinforcements. A posse? A SWAT team?

But it's only T.J., coming to my rescue. "She was just trying to talk to her brother's lawyer, Sheriff." Thomas James Bowers is a couple of inches shorter than I am, about half the size of the sheriff. Everything else about T.J. is too long—his nose, his jaw, his hair, which flops over sturdy rectangular glasses. He swore he'd stick with me through this whole trial, and he has.

"She can talk to her brother's lawyer outside the courtroom," Sheriff Wells snaps.

Shouts flood the courtroom as the main doors open and Raymond exits. He's swarmed by reporters. Before the doors close again, I see Raymond duck, like he's dodging tomatoes.

"Let's go, Hope," T.J. says. "I got us a ride home."

I nod, grateful. Rita dropped us off this morning, but she's not coming back for us. I don't feel much like walking seven blocks to the station to catch a bus back to Grain, especially since buses don't leave that often.

Following T.J. to the big doors that swallowed up Raymond, I feel Sheriff Wells's gaze on my back. It's the same invisible shove Rita uses to make sure I do what she tells me to.

As soon as I step out into the hall, cameras click. I keep my head down and rush through the courthouse. Half a dozen reporters follow me, shouting questions: "Hope, why won't your brother speak?" "Did you know he did it?" "What did he—?"

I try to block out their voices and focus on the clatter of

our footsteps on the hard floors, the echo that reaches the high ceiling and bounces off marble walls. I make it to the front doors and am amazed how dark it is outside. And the temperature must have dropped twenty degrees. August should be dry-bones hot, and usually is around here, but the gray clouds and west winds are promising rain.

I stop on the top step of the courthouse and glance around for T.J. He must have gotten lost in the crowd of reporters. A couple of them close in on me. One has beautiful red hair, which she pushes behind her shoulders while signaling to the cameraman beside her. "Hope, Mo Pento, WTSN. Can you tell us if you think—?"

I push past her. My head feels like it's floating off my shoulders. I think I might vomit. *How'd you like that, WTSN?*

A horn honks. A blue Stratus is parked at the foot of the steps. A window lowers, and Chase Wells peers out. Green eyes, sun-blond hair. He doesn't look a thing like his dad. Everything about him screams East Coast, from his khaki pants to his navy polo shirt. Chase is not just cute; he's beautiful.

I feel a hand on my back. "Sorry." T.J. guides me down a step or two. "They had me trapped back there. You okay?"

"Where are we going, T.J.?" I shout because it's too loud out here. Reporters are crowding in again. I smell sweat and perfume and cigarettes.

"There he is!" T.J. exclaims, pushing too hard from behind. I have to struggle to keep from falling down the steps.

"There *who* is?" I know he's trying to help—he always tries to help. But I think I should have made a run for it on my own. I could have been at the bus station by now.

Chase's car is still at the bottom of the steps. He honks his horn again and shoves the back door open. T.J. waves at him and keeps pushing toward the car.

I stop short on the bottom step. "Wait. Who did you—?"

"I—uh—I talked Chase into giving us a ride back to Grain." He takes the last two steps down, but I don't follow him. "Hope?"

I shake my head.

T.J. tosses a smile to Chase and whispers up to me, "You know Chase. He plays ball with me." He lowers his voice. "His dad's the *sheriff*!"

Do I know Chase Wells? I've watched him for two summers and thought about him in between.

"Hope?" That reporter with the hair sticks a microphone in my face. "Can you tell us why your brother—?"

I reach for T.J.'s hand. We make a dash for the car, dive into the backseat, and shut the door as Chase Wells takes off, tires squealing like they're in pain.

5

The second Chase pulls away from the courthouse, I know I've made a big mistake. I have to get out of this car. "Listen, we . . . I can walk to the bus station from here. Thanks."

T.J. elbows me and makes a face. We're in the backseat, being chauffeured.

Chase doesn't slow down. "That's okay. I'm headed to Grain anyhow. I can drop you guys off."

"Thanks again, man. I didn't know who else to ask. Dad's stuck at work." T.J. fastens his seat belt and nudges me to do the same.

"I really want to walk," I insist. There's an edge to my voice, like metal on metal. I reach for the door handle.

"You want to walk fifteen miles?" T.J. says, trying to make a joke of it.

"I get it," Chase says. He lets up on the gas. "Sorry about that."

But it's not speed that terrifies me. It's definitely not his driving, which could never be worse than Rita's after half a bottle of vodka. It's him. Chase Wells. The guy I've worshipped from afar—or at least watched from behind my bedroom curtains—as he's jogged by every summer morning, regular as sunrise.

"My dad's always on me about driving too fast," he admits.

Dad. As in *Sheriff Dad.* I didn't hear the sheriff testify, but Raymond said he did a lot of damage to our side. So what am I doing in a car with his son? What was T.J. thinking?

"Pretty sure you two know each other from Panther games," T.J. says, reaching across me to fasten my seat belt. I let him. His voice is thin, with that tinny laugh he gets when he's nervous. "Hope, Chase. Chase, Hope."

I'm thinking Chase knows my name. He just heard me swear *on a Bible* that I'm Hope Leslie Long.

As for him, there's not a human being in Grain who doesn't know who Chase Wells is. I've sneaked peeks at him while waiting for Jeremy to collect bats and balls for Coach Johnson at games and practices. Chase was hard to miss, with Bree Daniels hanging all over him, and guys like Steve and Michael and half a dozen of their crowd cheering him on.

Chase glances at us in the rearview mirror. Smiles. His eyes are framed, deep-set, the color of green sea glass, like the smooth, translucent chunks in my desk drawer at home.

I collect sea glass, or at least I used to. It's how I met T.J.

I stare out my window and remember a rainy day just like this one, when T.J. and I first got together. It was about three years ago, a month after I'd started school at Grain. T.J.

brought in some pieces of sea glass he'd found by Lake Erie, near Cleveland. He used them for a science project. I knew all about sea glass because Jeremy and I used to walk the Chicago shoreline hunting for it. We called the pieces mermaid tears. T.J. had reds that came from the lanterns of old shipwrecks. And pink from Depression-era glass. Broken pieces of history worn smooth by years of violent waves and rough sand. I had to gather all my courage to go up to T.J. after class and ask him about his collection. When I told him I made jewelry out of sea glass, he wanted to see it. Before long, he started bringing me pieces to work with. He still brings me some now and then, even though I've stopped making jewelry.

"Seriously, man," T.J. calls up to the rearview mirror, "we appreciate the rescue. That was pretty crazy back there. I actually used to want to be a reporter. Not now. Huh-uh." He elbows me again.

"Yeah. Thanks." I settle into the seat and stare out the window again. Tiny drops of rain speckle the windshield, but Chase hasn't turned on his wipers. A splat of rain trickles down the glass, shaking and splitting into streaks. The car smells like oranges, unless that's the way Chase Wells smells.

"Not a problem," Chase mumbles.

"So, now I guess we're even," T.J. says.

I frown over at him because I don't understand.

"I told you how I convinced Coach to give Chase a shot pitching the Lodi game, didn't I?" T.J. explains. He lets out his tin chuckle again. "If it hadn't been for me, Chase would still be stuck on second base. Right, Chase?"

"Mmm-hmm," Chase answers, without a glance in the mirror.

I want T.J. to stop talking. I'm still not sure why he pushed Coach into letting Chase pitch that game. It's not like he and Chase are buddies or anything. I used to think it was because T.J. thought Chase might be his ticket to the "cool guys." If that was it, it hasn't worked out.

I tune in to the whir and whistle of the wheels on black-top, the steady splatter and patter of rain picking up.

"Hope?" Chase says, breaking our silence with my name. "I've been wanting to tell you that I'm sorry for what you're going through—you and Jeremy. Your family."

He's sorry? What am I supposed to do with that? I shrug.

"I know my dad—well, he's not the most sensitive law enforcement officer in the world."

I can think of a million comebacks. If it weren't for Sheriff Wells, Jeremy might not be where he is right now, behind bars, on trial for murder. I'll never forget the way the sheriff barged into our house and arrested my brother.

We turn onto a one-lane road I've never been on. The only sounds are the rain tapping gently on the roof, a rumble of thunder, and the hum of the windshield wipers starting up. We pass a dozen black-and-white cows huddled under a tree in spite of the threat of lightning.

Our silence has turned uncomfortable, awkward. I wish T.J. hadn't asked Chase for a ride.

I sneak a glance at Chase in the rearview, and he catches me. Before I can look away, he grins.

"You don't talk much, do you, Hope?" he says.

"More than Jeremy," I answer before I can stop myself. I want the words back. It feels wrong to talk about my brother with the son of the enemy. Besides, people like Chase Wells

25

don't get Jeremy. They don't get me either. Whenever we move somewhere, it's almost funny how popular I am right off. From day one, guys try to sit by me in class. The cool girls invite me to eat with them. They think I'm like them because I look like them—blond hair, blue eyes, pimple-free heart-shaped face, and a figure that made me self-conscious in elementary school because I developed earlier than everyone else.

But I'm not one of them, and it only takes a couple of weeks for them to figure that out.

"So, Chase, bet you miss Boston, right?" T.J. asks, changing the subject with the grace of a hippopotamus.

"I don't know. Maybe I miss Mom and Barry sometimes. But after three summers, Grain's home too, I guess."

"You play ball there too, don't you?" T.J. says. "Must be where you learned that wicked curve. I wish you'd teach me that one."

We come up over the crest of a long hill, and an Amish buggy appears in front of us. "Look out!" I scream. Chase slams his brakes, then swears and swerves to pass. I look back and see a mother and three little boys. "You can't drive like that around here." I keep staring out the back window to make sure they're all right.

"Man." He's breathing heavy. "I know. I'm sorry." He slows to about ten miles an hour.

"That's the worst part of driving around here," T.J. says.

"No kidding," Chase agrees. "I love seeing the buggies, but I'm always scared I'm going to hit one, especially at night. Aren't you guys?"

"Yep," T.J. answers.

Taking his eyes off the road, Chase turns back to look at me. He's waiting for me to answer.

"Hope doesn't drive," T.J. says.

"You mean she doesn't drive at night?"

"Hope doesn't drive, period," T.J. explains.

"Why not?"

I answer for myself this time. "Rita doesn't want to share the Ford."

"Ah," Chase says. "I get that. I thought it would be tough sharing the Stratus with Dad, but it's worked out. He's got the squad car. And in a pinch, he can borrow one of the impounded cars at the police lockup."

"Cool," T.J. mutters.

"The what?" I smooth my skirt and wish I were wearing jeans. Raymond picked out my court clothes—white shirt, gray skirt.

"Impounded," T.J. explains. "You know. Cars they lock up from drug busts or three-strike drunk drivers."

Chase continues, "The sheriff's office really isn't supposed to use the vehicles, but Dad's deputy, Dave Rogers, took me for a spin in a silver BMW they found drugs in last summer. I don't think my dad would take anything out for a joy ride, though. He's not exactly into joy."

"He looked pretty happy watching you pitch for the Panthers at that Lodi game," T.J. says.

I'm not so sure I'd call it *happy*. Chase's dad screamed at Coach and shouted to Chase for every play. I remember I didn't know whether to be embarrassed for Chase or jealous. I

27

played T-ball one summer, and Rita didn't attend a single game. She's never come to Panther games either, except for the big Wooster-Grain game. Everybody in both counties goes to that one. At least they used to . . . until this summer.

"Dad definitely gets into it," Chase admits.

T.J. leans forward. "Man, can you imagine what he'd do if he watched you pitch the Wooster game? He played in that game 'back in the day,' right?"

"Yeah. Still, I don't get why everybody around here makes such a big deal over that one game."

"Are you kidding?" T.J. grips the seat in front of him. "Wooster and Grain have hated each other since, like, forever! It's the biggest summer-league rivalry in the state. The *Cleveland Plain Dealer* covers the game. Even people who don't like baseball come for the fireworks, and the picnics and tailgate parties. You know what I'm talking about. There's nothing like the Wooster-Grain game. I was almost relieved when Coach said you'd be starting pitcher. Too much pressure for me. The whole state would have turned out for that game if—"

He stops short of saying "if Jeremy hadn't knocked off Coach," but the words are there, invisible, in the air of the car. We hear them.

In silence, we cross the railroad tracks, where I don't think trains have passed in years, and enter Grain, population 1,947, give or take. Cornfields flank the blacktop on the left all the way to the Dairy Maid, a tiny white shack with a single serving window. BEAT WOOSTER! is still printed on the side window in big black letters. Half a dozen girls are eating ice cream cones while they sit on—not at—the wooden tables outside. As we pass, Bree Daniels looks up. Her gaze follows us, her expression unchanged.

"I think you may have some explaining to do," T.J. says when we're past.

Chase turns around to look behind us. There's something about his jawline and the way it hits his chin. Boys from Grain don't have faces like this. "Bree and I aren't talking anymore. I just wish we'd broken up two days earlier than we did."

"How come?" T.J. asks. This time I elbow *him*.

"Then I wouldn't have this to remember her by." He lifts the short sleeve of his shirt and leans forward to show us the back of his shoulder, tanned and muscled. I can see something tiny and green moving with his skin. I think it's a four-leaf clover.

"Lucky," I mutter.

"Lucky I didn't get the idiotic clover tattooed on my forehead, I guess." He lowers his sleeve. "She got one on her ankle. I have a feeling she's regretting it too. It was a dumb impulse. We were at her cousin's house, and he does tattoos on the side. One minute we're looking at patterns. The next we've got these clovers drilled into our skin forever. One second of stupid, a lifetime of tattoo."

My throat burns, like it's being tattooed. Because I'm thinking that life is like that. In one single moment, things can change forever—like Rita's hand smacking Jeremy's cheek and mine not lifting to stop hers. Like the bat picked up and swung, and Coach Johnson's life leaving his body forever.

I need to get out of here. "Listen, Chase. Thanks for the ride and all. You can let us out now. I can walk from here."

"That's okay. I'll take you home. I know where it is. I run by there every morning. T.J., want me to drop you off first? Unless you're going home with Hope?"

T.J. turns to me, his bushy eyebrows raised. I shake my head. I just want to get home and be by myself. "Just let me out at the intersection." He points to West Elm, his street.

Chase pulls over, and T.J. climbs out, thanking our driver two more times, then leaning into the back before shutting the door. "I'll call you about tomorrow."

I nod. "Thanks, T.J." Amazing how much thanksgiving is going on in this car.

In dead silence, with me still in the backseat, Chase drives through town and turns onto my block. I should feel embarrassed by the house we're renting. It's pretty awful. But I guess I'm past being embarrassed. Having a brother on trial for murder will do that to you.

"Uh-oh." Chase takes his foot off the gas.

"What?" I look up to see a blue van with *WTSN* on the side. It's parked in front of my house.

6

I don't say anything, but I'm grateful when Chase drives past my house. I slump down in the backseat as he passes the minicrowd hanging out on our front lawn. "Stay down," he commands.

After they arrested Jer, it was like this for a week or two, but they've mostly left Rita and me alone since then. "If you let me off at the next block, I can circle back and go in through the kitchen."

Chase stops where I tell him to, and I get out. "Thanks, Chase," I say through the window. Only I mean it this time. Maybe he's not Jeremy's and my enemy just because his dad is. I suppose I'm the last person who ought to judge a kid by his parent.

He nods and drives off. I watch his car until it turns the corner—I'm not sure why I do that. Then I hightail it through Old Man Galloway's yard and backtrack to my house.

I guess I haven't walked through our backyard in a

while—that, or Jack Beanstalk sprinkled seeds out here last night. Some of the weeds are almost as tall as I am. I pick up the beer cans, empty potato chip bags, and candy wrappers on my way through, then dump everything into the smelly trash bin by the back door.

The second I step inside, I'm smothered by a blanket of humidity. The after-rain freshness hasn't touched this house, where a musty onion smell hangs in the air. It takes a few seconds for my nostril cells to die so that I can breathe again.

Heavy metal blares from the bedroom radio, and canned laughter cackles from the TV in the living room, where lights and shadows battle.

I make it as far as the hallway when Rita steps out of her bedroom. She's wearing a denim skirt that's too tight and too short, but I'd never say so to her face. Her red checkered shirt is unbuttoned for maximum display. There's never been the slightest question of where I got my own cleavage. Other than that, we don't look a thing alike. We're about the same height, five six, but I don't think Rita has ever been thin like me. Her eyes are big and brown. Her hair is bleached blond now, frizzy and overpermed, but she's a natural brunette. The dark roots have grown a couple of inches out from her scalp. I can tell she's heading off to waitress at the Colonial Café because she's caught up her hair in a rhinestone clip—a safety pin snapped around a haystack.

She squints up the hall at me. "Where the devil have you been?" In other families, like T.J.'s, mothers greet their kids with "Hi, honey. How was your day?" This is Rita's version.

"I've been in court." Suddenly I'm dying of thirst. I head back to the kitchen.

"I know that," she snaps, following me.

"And you didn't drive me home, so—"

"I know that too. What I want to know is why that TV van is parked out front. What did you say in that courtroom?"

"I said Jeremy was crazy. Isn't that what you wanted me to say?" I open the fridge. Nothing to drink but beer and out-of-date milk.

"You better have said that." She checks her watch. "Raymond called and wants you at his place at seven."

I step back so I can see the pear-shaped kitchen clock that hangs above the toaster. It's six-fifteen. The sooner I get out of this prep-school skirt and blouse, the better. I need my jeans. I head for my room, which is just off the living room. Jeremy's bedroom separates Rita's and mine. "Can you drop me off on your way to work?" I ask.

"No. I'm leaving now. I was supposed to be there at six. I hate this shift." She says this like it's my fault she's working tonight. It probably is. If I didn't have to get coached by Raymond, Rita would likely make me work for her.

Coached by Raymond. I don't even want to think the word *coached.* Suddenly a picture pops into my head of Coach Johnson straightening Jeremy's Panther hat before a game, as if my brother would be stepping up to the batter's box and had to look just right. Jeremy's tongue is hanging out, like a puppy that's been patted on the head.

I shake my head to get rid of that image. As if my brain is an Etch A Sketch, the tiny gray crystals of Jeremy and Coach together break up and slide down. But they're both still on my mind.

Rita hasn't left yet. I trail back to the living room, where she's reapplying dark red lipstick, making a fish face in the mirror. "Rita," I ask, leaning on the back of the sofa, "what was he like?"

"Who?"

We're six feet apart, a body's length. Coach was about six feet tall. "Coach Johnson. What was he like?"

She shoves a pack of cigarettes into her purse. "You saw him more than I did."

"But you and Coach went to high school together, right? What was he like then?"

Still not looking at me, she stands on one foot and slaps a two-inch-heeled sandal onto her other foot. "He was like every high school boy—girl-crazy. And not a one of them knew what to do with a girl when they got one." She sticks her other foot into a sandal and stares at her red-tipped toes. "Jay Jay wasn't quite like the rest, though. He was all right."

This is a lot for Rita to say about any male. I try to imagine both of them at my age, but I can't see it.

"It was a long time ago." She grabs her purse off the back of the chair and opens the front door. "The TV van's gone." I can't tell if she's disappointed or relieved. She takes our umbrella and closes the door behind her.

By the time I grab a sandwich and change into jeans, I have to leave for Raymond's. I know where his house is, even though I've never been inside. All of our other meetings with Raymond have been at our house, or in his tiny law office on Main, next to the Subway shop.

Since Rita took the umbrella, I have to hope the rain holds off for now, and that Raymond can drive me home when we're done. The shortest route is straight up Main

Street, but I don't take that. Instead, I circle the back lot behind the IGA and go across the street to the thrift store, behind the post office, through the bank drive-through to the sidewalk by St. Stephen's Catholic Church, then across the damp grass of the practice field behind the high school, where Ann, who used to be kind of a friend at school, told me couples go to make out.

From here, it's about a ten-minute walk. It gives me time to think. And to plan. Since day one, Raymond and Rita have gone with the insanity plea for Jeremy. I went along because it scared me to think about what would happen to Jeremy if the jury found him guilty. Raymond's lined up doctors to talk about what's wrong with Jer, and I'm supposed to help with the "human side." But I hated telling those stories in court. My brother isn't insane. He's innocent.

So far, the rain is holding off, sticking to the air like it's afraid to hit earth. A girl younger than me is mowing her lawn with a push mower. She's wearing a tank top and shorts and listening to her iPod. When she looks up and sees me, she wheels the mower around and cuts a strip through her lawn all the way to her front porch.

Seconds later, a car pulls beside me. The driver gawks like I'm a traffic accident, then drives away. At the next intersection, an Amish buggy crosses. I close my eyes and listen to the clip-clop of the horse's hooves on pavement, the squeaky jiggle of the buggy. I'd trade places with any of the four kids piled into the back of the buggy, or the mother driving. I could disappear into the black dress and white bonnet, the sensible shoes, and the sensible family.

Raymond's house is set on a hill, back from the road. It's a brick one-story, really nice by Grain standards. Flower beds flank both sides of the walk. He must take a lot of real cases, not just freebies for the state, "pro bono," like ours.

I ring the doorbell, and the door is opened by a tall woman with thin brown hair and a big belly under a spandex top and cotton sweats. Raymond is going to be a daddy.

"You must be Hope." She stands on tiptoes to gaze out at the road. "Isn't your mother coming in with you?"

"No."

She motions for me to step in, so I do. Her smile makes her pretty. She puts one arm around her belly, like she's protecting her child. "Come and sit down. Ray will be out in a minute."

I take off my soggy sneakers and wish I'd worn socks.

"You don't have to do that, Hope," Mrs. Munroe says.

"It's okay." I take a whiff of the house and wish Jeremy were here to breathe Munroe air. There's nothing stale or musty here, just a hint of vanilla and maybe lemon. The white carpet looks new, and it makes me nervous to walk on it, even in bare feet. The furniture matches, and the only mess is on the dining room table, where papers are spread out all over.

"Becca, is that Hope?" Raymond comes out of the hallway, wiping his face with a little towel. He tosses it into a room I'm guessing is the bathroom. "Hey, Hope. We better get down to business. We have a lot to cover."

"If you'll excuse me," Mrs. Munroe says to both of us, "I think I'll go lie down for a while."

Raymond stops in his tracks. "Are you okay? Are you nauseous?"

"I'm just tired, Ray. Offer Hope something to drink, will you?" She smiles at me.

"I'm good, thanks." I feel as if I'm watching one of those TV family shows, where people are nice to each other even though they're related.

She kisses Raymond on the forehead and disappears down the hall. He watches her go before settling us at the table.

Soon as we sit, he gets serious. "What happened after court adjourned today can't happen again, Hope." He doesn't raise his voice or sound mad, but I know he means business. I think Raymond Munroe might make a good dad. "You and your mother, and Jeremy and I, have to present a united front, whether court is in session or out."

"I know, and I'm sorry. But . . . but I don't agree with you and Rita about Jeremy."

"I realize that, Hope. But even if we have differences, we have to appear as though we're on the same team." He reaches into his briefcase like this discussion is over.

"Please, Raymond? Could I just say something?"

He sighs. I think he's going to say no, but he puts down his pen. "Two minutes. That's all I can give you. We have to prepare the rest of your testimony *and* your cross."

My heart thumps, and my head feels dizzy. This is my chance, and I know it. "Jeremy didn't murder Coach Johnson. He liked Coach. I think he may have loved him. And anyway, Jeremy couldn't kill anybody, even if he hated them. And he's never hated a living soul. You don't know Jer like I do."

"Trials aren't about what happened. They're about what either side can prove. You haven't been in court to hear the prosecution's case, Hope," Raymond says.

"You wouldn't let me," I protest.

"The judge wouldn't let you. When you're done testifying, you might be allowed in the courtroom as a spectator. But that's not the point. The point is, you didn't hear the evidence that the prosecution has against Jeremy. And evidence is all the jury can consider."

"Then we need to get our own evidence!" I insist.

"What evidence? Keller put Sarah McCray on the stand, the woman who discovered the body. She came to the barn a little after eight that morning, and Jeremy almost knocked her over running away. He got blood on her, Hope. John Johnson's blood."

I try not to picture this. "He was scared. That's why he was running away."

"He was carrying the murder weapon," Raymond continues. "She saw the bat in his hands."

I know these facts. I read the papers. "There's an explanation. I'm sure there is."

Raymond shakes his head. "Jeremy certainly hasn't given it. He won't talk to me."

"He doesn't talk!"

Raymond doesn't lose his cool, even with me shouting. "All right. He hasn't written. He could write the explanation."

"Maybe he's scared! Maybe he . . . he saw it happen. He saw who did it, and he's afraid to say."

"His are the only fingerprints on the bat. And Mrs. McCray would have seen if somebody else had been there."

I'm breathing hard. If I cried, ever, I'd be crying now. "He didn't do it. Jeremy didn't do it."

"I'm not saying he did." Raymond's voice is softer, less lawyerly. "I'm just telling you what the jury's heard up to now. The prosecution's case is strong. I'm the only lawyer your brother has, and I have to look out for his best interest. Right now, that means going after the insanity plea as hard as I can. If I don't, and if the jury finds him guilty . . ."

Raymond doesn't finish his sentence . . . because he doesn't have to.

7

Raymond sits up straight and pulls over a file from the stack on the table. "So, are you ready to get down to some serious work?"

I nod. I want to keep trying to convince Raymond that Jeremy couldn't murder anybody, but I'm all out of arguments. I wish Jeremy had somebody smarter for a sister.

"Okay." He's already jotting things on his yellow notepad. "Tomorrow, I have to let Dr. Brown, the psychiatrist, testify before I recall you. I don't like breaking up your testimony, but I don't have a choice. Dr. Brown is testifying in a big case in New York and has to get back. She's good, though. She won't take long, and we need her to explain Jeremy's condition to the jury."

People have been trying to explain Jeremy for as long as I can remember. I keep this thought to myself. "Then maybe you don't need me again?" I'd give almost anything not to have to get back up on the witness stand.

Raymond smiles at me. "I need your testimony, Hope. You give a human face to the clinical analysis."

I nod.

"Good," he says, shuffling papers. "We should still be able to finish your direct testimony with no problem. I want you to tell the jury about Jeremy and his empty jars."

I've already agreed to this, but I don't like it. Everybody else thinks it's weird that my brother collects empty jars, but I don't. I tell Raymond a bunch of stories, like how Jer always carries a couple of jars in his backpack and sometimes gets them out and opens and closes them. Then I tell him about the time we were in the IGA and Jeremy loaded up his backpack with Mason jars, then threw a fit when I took the jars out and put them back on the shelf.

"Good," Raymond says, scribbling notes. "You can tell that one—just like that, Hope. What else?"

It feels like I'm tattling on my brother, but I keep going. "Most of the time, he uses regular jars that are empty. He peels off the labels. I have to wash them fast, when he's not looking, before he puts them in his pack or squirrels them under his bed. They can really stink if I don't."

"What does he do with all those jars?" Raymond asks, still writing.

I don't know if he's asked for real or for practice, but I answer anyway. "He saves them. Sooner or later, they end up on the shelves in his bedroom. I've never counted, but he probably has a couple hundred in every shape and size."

"Keep talking, Hope."

I have so many memories of Jeremy and his jars. It's hard

to settle on a single story. "Sometimes, if a jar of mayonnaise is almost empty, he'll dump out what's left—usually into the wastebasket, but not always."

I remember a day about four years ago. I can almost see Jeremy in his jeans and a gray sweatshirt I got him at the Salvation Army thrift store. His whole body is wound tight, and his eyes bulge. He's in the kitchen, with the refrigerator door open. At his feet is a pile of long, sliced dill pickles swimming in a sea of yellow-green pickle juice.

"Once," I begin, "Jeremy came running into the house, dashed to his room, then darted out again. He was pacing the kitchen floor and refused to stop long enough to write me what was wrong. For whatever reason—and we never know the reason—Jeremy needed a jar. A fresh jar. Before I could stop him, he took out a giant jar of pickles and dumped the whole thing onto the floor. I just stood there, staring, while he tucked that jar into his chest like a football and ran back to his room, closing the door behind him. He didn't come out the rest of the night."

"What did you do?" Raymond asks.

"I cleaned up the kitchen. The next day I took a lot of flak from Rita for eating a whole jar of newly bought pickles."

We keep talking about the jars. I tell Raymond about the elderly neighbors we had in Oklahoma who saved their empty jars for Jeremy, no questions asked. They even washed the jars out first. I bring up every jar story I can remember, including the time Jeremy went through the garbage to get a mustard jar. That jar sat in his room for weeks before I found it.

Raymond settles on the pickles, the mayo, and the mustard.

He makes me tell him each story two more times, prepping me on what to cut and what to draw out. Finally, he puts down his pen and squeezes the bridge of his nose. "Hope, tomorrow the prosecution gets to cross-examine you. I've got to warn you that Prosecutor Keller won't go easy on you just because you're a young girl."

"I didn't expect he would."

"You didn't see him in action all month, Hope. He's a pit bull at getting what he wants out of witnesses. He's even tough on his own witnesses."

"Well, he can't get anything out of me. There's nothing to get."

"Don't kid yourself, Hope. He's earned his nickname, Killer Keller. Keller has been at this a long time, a lot longer than I have anyway."

"I think you're doing great, Raymond," I say, although I don't have any idea how he's doing.

Raymond looks grateful. "So, we better start preparing you for the state's cross-examination. Remember that Keller can only take side doors if we open them. Let's get started."

Footsteps patter up the hallway, and Mrs. Munroe scurries into the bathroom. She tries to shut the door, but I can hear her hurling.

"Honey?" Raymond gets up so fast his chair tips. "I'm sorry, Hope. I'll be right back." He joins his wife, and they close the bathroom door, but I can still hear them—her puking, him murmuring to her. If I listen to her, I'm in danger of hurling too. Whenever Jeremy has the flu, I throw up worse than him.

I turn back to the table, where Raymond has every last folder out of his briefcase. Thumbing through loose papers, I spin a couple of the folders so they face me. One is labeled "Cases—Precedents." Another says "Crime Scene."

I slide the crime scene folder over and open it. The top photo is of a woman in the stable. I recognize her. It's Mrs. McCray, but it looks like a much older version of the woman who let Jeremy ride her old pinto. She kept two horses at the Johnson Stable, an expensive bay gelding for dressage and the old mare Jeremy fell in love with, Sugar. Coach taught Jer how to ride on that horse. Sometimes I'd come by the barn and see Jeremy riding that spotted horse bareback through the pasture, his backpack of jars clinking like angel chimes.

In the crime scene photo, Mrs. McCray looks like she's seen a ghost, or worse. Her back is to the sun, which peeks through gray morning clouds and lights the barn entrance. Her arms are wrapped around her like she's keeping herself from splitting into pieces. She's the one who found Coach dead in front of her bay's stall. She's the one Jeremy bumped into.

I glance back at the hallway. The bathroom door is still shut. I hear dry-heaving.

I slide Mrs. McCray to the side to see what's under-neath . . . and there's Jeremy. I guess this is what they call a mug shot—Jeremy looking forward and to both sides. In each shot, he's smiling for the camera. The photos look like every school picture Jeremy ever posed for—that same goofy grin he'd get when the photographer told him to say "cheese."

Shoving Jeremy's mug shots to the side, I take a look at

the next photograph. It's Coach Johnson, lying on his side, curled up like a baby inside its mother's womb. His hands are drawn over his ears, like he doesn't want to hear his own cry. A circle of darkness pools beneath his head and shoulders. If I didn't know better, I'd think it was a shadow. I know better.

How can a single blow do that?

I can almost hear the horses screaming, a rumbling thunder, life bubbling out into sticky dark pools. I can smell manure and blood mixed with sweat and flies and fear.

The person on the ground isn't just "the victim" anymore. Tears are trickling like early rain down my cheeks, but I don't know how they got there because I don't cry. This is Coach Johnson, the nice man who gave Jeremy a job mucking stalls at his stable and paid him twice what he should have paid, the kind coach who made Jeremy feel part of the team, who gave Jer a Panther uniform that he would have worn every day, all day, if I'd let him.

I can't stop staring. Coach is not so much a dead person as he is a person without life. I take in all the details of this picture—sawdust and a dark pool of blood, a hoofprint partially covered by Coach's foot, a cell phone inches from his hip, fallen from his pocket. Coach—faceless, lifeless John Johnson.

My brother could not have done this.

The toilet flushes, and the bathroom door opens. I shove the photos back into the folder and push the file away from me.

"Sorry, Hope," Raymond says, returning to the table.

"Is she okay?" I ask.

Raymond runs his fingers through his hair and looks about twelve years old. "The doctor says not to worry about the nausea, even though it's late in her pregnancy. But I can't help it."

"You'll make a good dad," I tell him.

"You think so?" he asks, like it matters what I think.

"I do."

We go at it for another thirty minutes. Raymond does his best to prepare me for cross-examination. But when it's time to go, I'm pretty sure I'm a whole lot less prepared than your average Boy Scout.

Raymond follows me to the door, where I put on my shoes. It's raining pretty good now. "Isn't Rita here yet?" he asks.

"I'm meeting her." I don't add that I'll be meeting her at home, though, and not out on the street.

Raymond frowns. "Are you sure you don't need me to give you a lift?" He tosses a nervous glance down the hall. I can tell he's worried about his wife.

"Nope. But thanks."

"Here. Take an umbrella. That's the least I can do." He hands me a giant black umbrella, leaving three just like it in a tall white can by the door.

"Thanks, Raymond. I'll see you in court."

"You'll do fine, Hope!" he calls after me. But I know neither of us believes him.

8

When I crawl into bed, I'm too tired to sleep. In every
other apartment where we've lived, I slept on the couch. This
is the only bedroom I've ever had. It's the smallest room in
the house, but I'm not complaining. I should paint the walls,
but one wall has a cracked wallpaper mural of a green forest,
and I love it, even though it curls at every seam. I keep the
room picked up, except for books I've checked out of the
library, books I almost never finish. I jump to the end after a
few chapters and then lose interest. Near one wall, half a
dozen books are spread out in tepees that mark my quitter
pages. But I'm too tired to read.

I close my eyes, and my mind fills with images from the
courtroom. I can see Jeremy, wearing a suit that could never
fit right. And Chase, leaning forward, elbows on his knees, his
green eyes staring up at me.

Other images of Chase flip through my brain too. The
tighter I shut my eyes, the faster they go—Chase driving, the

back of his head, his golden hair thick but not coarse, his broad shoulders and strong back. Chase, his neck craned to see something out the rear window. His arms are muscled without being gross, the arms of a runner.

I can see each line and curve of Chase's classic features, the angle of his chin when I thanked him for the ride. Thinking about him makes me feel . . . what? Content? Peaceful? Maybe a moment, just one moment, of good?

Then I stop. Because mixed in with the joy of that picture of Chase Wells is the mug shot of Jeremy. And the crime scene photo of Coach Johnson.

And I wonder what kind of a person can feel even a piece of good in the middle of so much bad.

When I wake up at six the next morning, my first thought is of Chase. I guess I really can't help myself. I roll out of bed and head for the window, where I always watch for him. Dust and dirt cling to the windowpanes. Sunrise is officially past, but I have time to get a cup of instant coffee.

I take up my lookout post again. And before I finish my coffee, Chase comes running up the street like somebody's after him. He's tan and fit in his running shorts and looks more like a California surfer now than a Boston preppy. I can see the muscles of his legs twist and tighten as he gets closer.

This is the moment when every other morning I duck into the shadow of my musty curtains. But today I stay where I am, watching, willing Chase to look this way.

"Morning, Hopeless."

Rita startles me so bad I spill coffee on my T-shirt.

"Hopeless" is her little joke. Hope Leslie. Hope-Les. Hopeless. Funny as ever.

"What are you looking at?" she asks.

I turn back to the window, but Chase has already passed. He's halfway up the street.

Raymond leads off with his expert witness, who couldn't look less like a psychiatrist if she tried. If I didn't know she came in on an airplane this morning, I'd swear she left her Harley and biker jacket, size extra large, parked out back. Her hair is shaved so close to her head I can see her skull from where I sit. The only doctorly things about her are the thick black glasses, and even they are strapped to her head like she's off to play ball instead of testify in another case.

Raymond starts out slow, getting her to list all her college and doctor degrees. I guess the jury has to believe her, since she swore on the Bible and all, but if I were Raymond, I would have made her bring in her framed diplomas to prove what she's saying about being so smart.

RAYMOND: Please tell the court your current position and title.
DR. BROWN: I'm senior advisor for NORD, based currently in New York.
RAYMOND: Please explain NORD, Dr. Brown.
DR. BROWN: The National Organization for Rare Disorders is an American nonprofit group that provides support and advocacy for people with rare diseases. I meet with individuals all across the United States and help in any way I can.

RAYMOND: Were you able, from your experience and expertise, to discover what might be Jeremy Long's particular disability?

PROSECUTOR KELLER: Objection! Lack of foundation.

JUDGE: Overruled. Answer the question, Dr. Brown.

DR. BROWN: I can't state it unequivocally, but the boy certainly has a disability along the spectrum of autism. He has impaired social skills, yet high-functioning splinter skills—which is to say, he has overall developmental delays and lacks certain ordinary skills, such as dressing himself appropriately and interacting appropriately in social situations, yet he excels at writing and organizational endeavors. This, coupled with certain repetitive gestures, would lead one to suspect a diagnosis of Asperger's syndrome. I personally believe the boy may also be suffering from Landau-Kleffner syndrome. One of the symptoms of the disease is the inability to verbalize language. It's often misdiagnosed as pure autism because the patient tends to rock back and forth, or side to side, and focus in unusual ways. And there are often tantrums associated with the disorder.

RAYMOND: Tantrums. I see. When a person has one of these tantrums, is he aware—in your opinion—of what he's doing while he's doing it? And again, I'm only asking for your expert opinion here.

DR. BROWN: I would say that, in general, a person is a victim of his own tantrum. Tantrums are not malicious. Toddlers have tantrums. We're all familiar with the behavior; most of us outgrow it. Some do not. However, no one *wants* to have a tantrum.

RAYMOND: You say you can't be one hundred percent certain of the diagnosis. Is there any diagnosis you can testify about with absolute certainty before the court today?

DR. BROWN: Yes. Jeremy definitely suffers from SM.

RAYMOND: SM?

DR. BROWN: Selective mutism. He is able to speak, but he chooses not to.

RAYMOND: Tell us more about this selective mutism, if you will.

DR. BROWN: Of course. Let us start by defining our terms, shall we? A mute is one who cannot talk; a selective mute elects not to talk. Originally identified in 1877 as aphasia voluntaria, selective mutism presents itself most frequently in children around the age of five but can develop at any age. Over the past two decades, more and more American children have decided to stop talking. Due to the lack of funding and research for this disorder, it is a daunting task for those of us in the field to determine whether the child is simply shy, extremely shy, or if something more serious underlies the behavior—drugs administered to, or by, the mother during pregnancy; early childhood trauma; displaced hostility. One hypothesis suggests that the absence of speech results from biological deficiencies combined with psychological and social abnormalities. We may never know with absolute certainty, although future funding would help us find the answers we need to help children like Jeremy.

RAYMOND: Thank you so much for enlightening us, Dr. Brown. We appreciate your taking time out of your busy schedule. I have no more questions for the witness, Your Honor.

Prosecutor Keller is scribbling so much in his notepad that all of the rest of us, including Dr. Brown, have to wait for him to get up and take his turn. When he does stand and head for the witness box, he's frowning, like he has no more idea than I do what the expert psychiatrist really said.

KELLER: Hello, Dr. Brown. I have a few questions I hope you'll help me with. I admit that I'm not familiar with Landau-Kleffner syndrome, but I've done a bit of research on Asperger's and on selective mutism. Perhaps you could help us understand the nature of these tantrums you talk about. Would it be correct to say that many individuals with selective mutism—the one diagnosis you're certain of—have tantrums?

DR. BROWN: Of course. As I explained, there are cross symptoms with L-K, SM, Asperger's, and autism—the focus, the mannerisms, and, yes, the occasional tantrum.

KELLER: I see. And is temper generally associated with the tantrums?

DR. BROWN: That's correct. We believe that in selective mutism especially, the frustration of self-imposed silence fosters a temper, and thus the tantrums.

KELLER: I see. And how many of these selective mutes, in a sudden burst of insanity, have murdered another person?

RAYMOND: I object!

JUDGE: Overruled.

DR. BROWN: Well, no one that I know of.

KELLER: No one has given in to the insanity and committed murder, in spite of himself?

DR. BROWN: You can't equate selective mutism or Asperger's or autism with insanity.

KELLER: I can't? Ah. So let me be sure I'm understanding you correctly, Doctor. You're saying that just because someone is selectively mute, or has Asperger's or autism, we should not assume he is insane. Have I got that right?

DR. BROWN: Yes, technically, but—

KELLER: Thank you, Doctor. By the way, Dr. Brown, how long has the defendant been a patient of yours?

DR. BROWN: What? No. He's not my patient.

KELLER: Oh? I'm sorry. You must have interviewed him, then?

DR. BROWN: That's right. I was able to meet with Jeremy Long this morning.

KELLER: I see. For how many hours?

DR. BROWN: Well . . . we had to be in court. I suppose I was with Jeremy under an hour.

KELLER: Under an hour? And you were able to get him to tell you enough about himself to diagnose him? You must be quite an expert psychiatrist.

DR. BROWN: He didn't actually tell me about himself, per se, of course. By definition, selective mutes don't answer questions. I was, however, able to observe the boy and—

KELLER: Observe him? Like the jury is doing now? Only . . . for a much shorter length of time?

DR. BROWN: Well, I wouldn't say—

KELLER: That's all right, Doctor. I think I've gotten all the information you're able to give. No more questions for the witness.

9

It's afternoon before I'm called back up to the witness stand. I guess swearing must have lasted overnight because I don't have to do it again. My palms are so sweaty they slip when I grab the wooden railing.

I try to get Jeremy to look at me as I take my seat. He's wearing another suit I've never seen, and I figure Raymond must have bought it for him. It's a nice suit, gray and brand-new. I'm grateful, but Jer looks like he's playing dress-up in it. His hair is cut short and close, which looks neat and everything, but makes his ears stick out. He won't look at me. And then I remember I promised him I'd see if I could get him an empty jar, and I didn't even try.

"Good afternoon, Hope," Raymond says.

"Afternoon." My voice sounds thin, like a little girl's. I clear my throat.

"I won't take very long today, Hope. Just a few more questions for you. The court has heard expert testimony concerning Jeremy's mental condition. I just want you to tell the court about your brother in your own words. Is that all right with you?"

"Yes."

"Good. Hope, can you tell us if Jeremy has had any hobbies like other boys his age?"

This is how we practiced getting into the glass-jar stories, so I tell the first one. Then I wait for Raymond to ask me about Jeremy dumping all the pickles on the kitchen floor so he could have the jar, and I tell that one, glad that Rita's not allowed in the courtroom until after she testifies.

When I'm done, Raymond smiles at me. I think he winks, but it might be a twitch. "Thank you, Hope." He turns to the judge. "That's all, Your Honor."

I'd like to get up and follow Raymond, but the prosecutor is already out of his chair and heading for me.

"Good day," he says. He unbuttons his jacket and walks so close I think I smell the sweat that's left dark circles around his armpits. It's hot in the courtroom, even with the fans going. "My name is Mr. Keller. Can I call you Hope?"

"Okay."

"Good. Thank you." I keep thinking how Raymond called him a pit bull. And I guess he was kind of hard on the doctor. Still, I don't see him as a pit bull. Not yet anyway. On the other hand, people who get bitten by pit bulls are always saying how the dogs were so sweet until that minute before the bite.

"I just have a few questions for you, Hope," Mr. Keller begins. "Then we'll let you get out of here and go home."

I wish he could say that to my brother.

Raymond warned me to keep my answers short and not volunteer information not asked. So I wait to be asked. Only Keller is flipping through his notes. My knee starts bobbing all by itself, and my heart is pounding so loud I wonder if the prosecutor can hear it. I look past him to the crowd of reporters in the back row, to the jurors on my left, to Jeremy on my right. T.J., wearing a red T-shirt with a gold dragon on it, is sitting as close to the front as he could get. Then my gaze passes over the gallery in the little balcony, and I see him. Chase. He's sitting in the front row, leaning forward, his hands on the rail.

And instantly, I feel better.

I don't know why Chase shows up every day, but T.J. says he's been here for the whole trial. A lot of Grain citizens have. Maybe they come for the same reason rubberneckers gawk at highway accidents.

"Hope," Mr. Keller says, turning his side to me so he can smile at the jury, "what was your brother's relationship with Mr. Johnson like?"

Raymond jumps up. "Objection! The witness isn't qualified to answer. She isn't an expert in relationships."

Raymond's right about that.

But the judge disagrees. "Overruled. Proceed, Mr. Keller."

He turns to me this time. "Why don't you just tell us from your own observations how your brother got along with the deceased?"

"They got along fine."

"Could you explain your answer for the court, please?"

I'm trying to keep my answers short, like Raymond said, but I can't see how it would hurt for the jury to know how much Jeremy liked Coach. "Coach Johnson gave Jeremy a real good job at the stable. Jer mucked the stalls and all, but he got to ride and brush the horses too. He loved his job. And the pay was great."

"Did they see one another outside the stable?"

"On the ball field," I answer quickly, eager to make the jury understand how much Coach meant to Jeremy. "Coach let Jeremy be his assistant for the summer games. Jeremy was the first one to show up on the ball diamond and the last to leave. He was in charge of the bats and balls, the game equipment."

Keller looks like he wants to ask another question, but I'm not done yet. "Plus," I add quickly, "Coach gave Jeremy a Panther uniform. Jeremy loved that uniform. He would have worn it every day if I'd let him. And—" But I stop myself just in time because I was going to say how Jeremy carried his bat with him to the barn every single morning.

Mr. Keller nods, like he's taking it all in. "Did Coach Johnson ever give Jeremy a bat?"

I bite my lip so hard it hurts. I try to glance at Raymond because we didn't practice for this question, but the prosecutor's standing in my way.

"Do you need me to repeat the question?" Keller asks.

"No. I mean, yes. Coach gave Jeremy his bat."

"Thank you. Now, Hope, I'd like to go back to the day of the murder."

I wouldn't. It's the last day I'd like to go back to.

"I'm hoping you can help us fill in a few time gaps," Prosecutor Keller says. "Where were you on the morning of June eleventh?"

"Asleep. In my bed."

He nods, like he knew this already. "Did you see your brother that morning? Before the police knocked on your door, that is?"

"No." I add quickly, "But I saw Jeremy when I went to bed the night before. He was in his bed sound asleep."

"Okay. Let's talk about the next day. What woke you that morning?"

"Pounding on the door. The front door. It woke Rita and me both up."

"But not Jeremy?"

I shrug, then remember I'm supposed to use words. "I wouldn't know about that."

"Of course," he says, like he agrees with me. "So what did you do when you heard this pounding on the door?"

"I answered it."

"Go on, please, Hope."

The facts. Just the facts. Raymond's coaching throbs in my head, along with a headache that better not turn into a migraine. "Sheriff Wells was standing there, with a couple of others behind him. He asked me where Jeremy was, and I told him Jeremy was asleep."

Keller nods for me to continue, waving one arm while he takes a couple of steps toward the jury.

"Sheriff Wells started to come in, but that's when Rita took over."

"That would be your mother and the defendant's mother, yes?"

"Yes. Rita shoved in front of me and stood in the doorway so they couldn't get in. 'What do you want with Jeremy?' she shouted." I figure it's okay to leave out some of the four-letter words Rita used. "'We need to talk with him. There's been an accident, Rita,' Sheriff said.

"So Rita asked what kind of accident. And the sheriff told her that Coach Johnson had been found murdered.

"Rita gasped, and tears filled up her eyes. I thought she was going to pass out, so I took hold of her. But she shook me off and glared back at the sheriff and told him to stay right where he was unless he had a search warrant. He said he was waiting on one right now, and she said he would just have to wait then, wouldn't he.

"Then she slammed the door right in Sheriff Wells's face and told me to go and check on Jeremy while she kept an eye on the police. So I ran to Jer's room and knocked and hollered and knocked. Only he didn't come. And I got so scared that I went in anyway." I stop then because my mind is flashing back to my brother, sitting on the floor, in the corner, in nothing but his boxers, rocking back and forth and staring at the wall as if he were watching a movie, which I suppose he was in a way.

Keller turns to me, and his voice is soft. "I know this isn't easy for you, Hope, but would you please tell the court what you saw when you entered Jeremy's room?"

I take a deep breath. "I saw Jeremy, but I'm not sure he saw me. He wouldn't look at me, so I sat down on the floor

59

with him and tried to hold him. I sat there with him until Sheriff Wells got his warrant and barged into the room."

"What happened next?"

"They tore up his room. They searched under the bed and took photos of everything, including me and Jeremy. Then they searched his closet."

"And what did they find in your brother's closet?"

I know this whole courtroom, except for me, has probably already heard exactly what they found. They've probably seen pictures. Maybe they've even seen it for themselves. "A bat."

"Was it a wooden bat?" Keller asks.

I nod. "Yes."

"And even though most of the Panthers use metal bats for the league, what kind of bat did Jeremy own? What kind of bat had Coach given him?"

"A Louisville Slugger."

Keller bows his head. "Metal or wooden?"

"Wooden," I admit.

Keller is silent for at least a minute, probably letting that answer soak in. I wish I knew if the jurors were picturing everything in their heads the way I am. I hope not.

"Hope," Keller asks at last, "do you love your brother?"

"Yes!" I exclaim, looking directly at Jeremy now. He gazes up at me, the touch of a grin on his bony face. "I love Jeremy more than anybody in the whole world."

"I'll bet you'd do just about anything for him, wouldn't you?"

I lock gazes with Jeremy and will him to take this in.

"I would do anything in the world for my brother. He's the most important thing in my life."

"I can see that," Keller says, like he understands. "Let's go back to your earlier testimony, if you don't mind."

I'm grateful to go back, to go anywhere that's not June eleventh.

"When did Jeremy start collecting jars? Can you remember?"

"I'm not sure. Maybe when he was nine."

"And were you upset by your brother's troubling hobby?"

"I wasn't, but Rita was. If I missed a jar under his bed, it could smell up the whole room pretty quick."

Keller wrinkles his nose as if he can smell sour mustard right now. "Empty jars . . . You have to admit it's a pretty unusual hobby."

"No. I don't admit that at all. People collect all sorts of things."

"Like . . . ?"

"Like stamps and spoons and bells, for example. Like sea glass." I finger my necklace. I made it out of a tiny, smooth piece of glass T.J. gave me two years ago.

"True," Keller mutters, agreeing with me.

"Or even Barbie dolls. People pay hundreds of dollars for old Barbies, don't they? If you ask me, I'd say *that's* crazy."

Keller laughs a little, and so do a couple of the jurors. I'm thinking my testimony today is going better than it did yesterday.

"What do you admire most about your brother, Hope?"

I can't believe it's the prosecution asking me this. Raymond should have asked this a long time ago. "A lot of things." I smile at Jeremy. He's smiling back at me, and I see the old Jeremy peeking out. "My brother is the kindest person I know. He loves the little things, like watching ants carry bits of food on a trail, or hearing people laugh, or seeing the sun go down every single evening. He gets excited when an acorn falls from a branch and lands at his feet, or a leaf spins in the air. He calls them God-gifts. That's what he writes on his pad for me when he sees a butterfly or a deer, or whenever he makes out a cool shape in a sky full of clouds."

"Jeremy dropped out of school in the eighth grade, didn't he?" Keller asks.

"That was more Rita's doing than Jeremy's. Jer never caused any trouble, except with teachers who were too lazy to read his writing instead of getting the answers out of his mouth. Have you seen Jeremy's handwriting?"

"No, I haven't," Keller says, as if he'd really like to.

"It's beautiful. Jer's own brand of calligraphy."

"Why do *you* think your brother can't talk, Hope?"

"He *can* talk. I know because I heard him when we were younger. He just stopped one day. That's all. But he doesn't really need to talk because he communicates just fine—with his notes and his gestures. Jeremy can say more with his eyes than most people can in a whole speech."

Keller laughs. "I know exactly what you mean. We lawyers hear a lot of those speeches. We even give a few ourselves." He gets some chuckles from the spectators. "Do you have anything else you want to tell us about your brother, Hope, before I let you go?"

Raymond was wrong about this guy. I think Keller *gets* Jeremy. Maybe *he* should have been Jeremy's lawyer. "Thanks," I tell him. "There are a lot of things I could tell you about my brother. Jeremy is trustworthy. He took good care of the team equipment. And he was so responsible at the stable—he never missed a day of work or complained about the messiest stalls or anything. He has a sense of humor, and . . . and he loves me. I'd do anything for Jer, and he'd do anything for me. I know that."

Keller smiles at me. "Sounds like a normal brother to me." He turns from me and repeats this to the jury. "Absolutely and completely normal."

And that's when I see what he's done. What *I've* done. What I've done to Jeremy. "No! Wait! I didn't mean—!"

"I have no more questions for the witness, Your Honor."

"But—!"

"You may step down now, Miss Long," says the judge. "The court will take a short recess." She bangs her gavel. All I can think is that it sounds like a hammer, the hammer that nails Jeremy's coffin shut.

And it's all my fault.

10

I don't know how long I sit in the witness chair while the courtroom clears. Finally, T.J. comes up and gets me. He leads me through the courtroom. The second we step into the hallway, reporters start shouting my name: "Hope, over here, honey!" "Ms. Long!"

I stare at them, their faces blurred, their words nothing more than static. I don't know whether to run through the mob or find a corner and curl myself into it and rock like Jeremy did that morning.

T.J. jerks me back into the courtroom and slams the doors shut. "There's got to be another way out of here." He glances at the little door that swallows my brother every day when he leaves the courtroom. "Besides that one," T.J. mutters.

Together, as if somebody's pointing a gun at us, we back farther into the courtroom. T.J.'s head swivels in every direction. Then he shouts, "Chase!" He's staring up into the gallery. I look too and see Chase, still sitting in his balcony seat. "You know another way out of here?" T.J. hollers up.

For a second, Chase doesn't answer. Then he pushes himself out of his seat, and I think he's going to leave without answering T.J. Slowly, he points to the side stairs that lead to the gallery.

T.J. takes my hand, and we climb to where Chase is, in the small balcony area, where it's even hotter and stickier than the witness stand. The gallery smells like sweat, smoke, and furniture polish.

None of us says a word as Chase leads the way, threading through the wooden fold-down chairs, pushing up each seat so we can get past. He stops at a skinny door. There's a big silver alarm on the doorpost. He takes out his pocketknife and does something to the alarm. His back is to me, so I don't see what he does. But he knows what he's doing. He's obviously done it before, somewhere. He turns around and sticks the knife back into his pocket. "We're going down the fire escape. Are you both good with that?"

I nod. Then I remember T.J.'s afraid of heights. If Jer and I sit on the top bleacher at a practice, T.J. won't come up. "You don't have to," I tell him.

"I'm fine," he says, but the pupils of his eyes are too big, and his voice too high.

I don't let go of his hand as we follow Chase, taking each black metal step, clang-clanging with every move on the rickety ladder. I expect to descend into a pool of reporters and spectators, who will swallow me whole.

But nobody's there when we reach the bottom. I glance back at T.J., asking, without words, if he's okay. He nods, his face cloud white, his glasses crooked. I squeeze his hand before letting go.

"I'm parked back here," Chase says. We haven't asked for a ride, but we follow him. The sun has already set, leaving the sky a mess of gray.

We get into the backseat like before, and Chase starts the car. He eases around the side of the courthouse, then away from the throng of people forming on the courthouse lawn.

When we're safely away, T.J. and Chase exchange words in low tones, but all I hear are empty voices. My mind is back in the courthouse, on the witness stand, going over all the things I should have said . . . and all the things I shouldn't have.

We're halfway to Grain before I try to speak. Even then, I'm scared I won't be able to hold back the tears that are so hot and thick they're clinging to my throat. "I can't believe I did that to Jeremy. I should have let those reporters tear me apart, piece by piece. I deserve it."

"Don't beat yourself up, Hope," T.J. says. We're sitting as far apart as possible. I'm gripping the door handle.

"You didn't say anything wrong," Chase whispers, so soft I'm not sure he really said it.

"Are you kidding?" I'm too loud, but my heart is pounding in my ears. "Raymond and I practiced, but not for that. Not for *those* questions. That prosecutor, Keller, he tricked me. He got me to say exactly what he wanted, that my brother is strange, but not insane. I'll never forgive myself if I—"

Nobody except Jeremy has ever seen me cry. I cover my face and try not to let out the sobs that rack my body. But I can't control anything. I hear the animal noises coming from me as if they're from someone, or something, else. T.J. reaches out his hand, but I don't take it. "I thought I was doing so great," I say between sobs. "I wanted the jury to know Jer the way I do. Then they'd have to see that he couldn't murder anybody. But all I did was make them see he's not insane."

"It's not up to you, Hope," T.J. says, sliding his fingers through his slicked-back hair. "And anyway, you did better than that fancy psychiatrist."

I know T.J. is trying to help. But it's not helping. My head's pounding, and I feel like I'm going to throw up. This is no time for a migraine attack.

"Hope?" Chase's voice is soft, but firm. He expects me to answer.

"What?"

"Did you say anything in court that you don't believe?"

"No!"

"Do you believe your brother's crazy?"

"Of course I don't!"

"Well, then, you couldn't say anything except what you did, could you? Not under oath."

I don't answer.

"What the jury saw today was a sister who loves her brother. That's it. Jeremy's attorney can still make a solid case for insanity."

"But Jer's not insane." The fire has gone out of my voice. Out of me.

"Okay," Chase says, not looking back at us, not glancing in the rearview. "But isn't that the best outcome of the trial? If they find Jeremy insane, they'll just send him to some kind of mental facility, right? And if he's okay, they'll see that and let him go eventually."

"He's right, Hope," T.J. whispers.

I'm shaking my head. "Jeremy wouldn't survive in a mental hospital. He needs to be with me. He needs me. We need each other."

"Great," Chase mutters. "That TV woman is there again."

When I look up, I can't believe we're in front of my house. The blue van is parked in the same spot as yesterday. "I can't face them. Not after what I did today. I don't even want to face Rita."

Chase does a one-eighty and heads north. "Where do you want to go?"

"We can go to my house," T.J. offers.

In a few minutes, we're walking up to the Bowers's two-story white house. There's not much of a front yard, but what there is looks like a green carpet. Impatiens hang in baskets from the front porch, and black-eyed Susans form gold-and-brown clumps big as bushes against the house.

T.J. goes in first. "Hey! Anybody home?"

His mother comes downstairs carrying a laundry basket. "That you, Tommy?" T.J.'s real name is Thomas James, but his mom is the only one who calls him Tommy. When she sees Chase and me, she balances the basket on her hip and pushes thin strands of brown hair out of her freckled face. "Well, how are you, Hope? Good to see you too, Chase." If she's surprised to see him, she doesn't show it.

I'm surprised he's still here, and I'm pretty sure I'm showing it. He tried dropping us off, but T.J. wouldn't have it. Chase is hanging back, close to the door, like he's ready to bolt first chance he gets.

T.J. takes the laundry basket from his mom. "We need

someplace to hide out for a while. Reporters are all over Hope's lawn."

"What a shame." She shakes her head, then smiles at me. "You know you're always welcome here, Hope." I thank her, sure that she means it. Her smile passes to Chase, who reaches for the doorknob. "You too, son. Say, are you kids hungry? I'd be happy to make you something to eat. Plenty of time before I have to get ready for the night shift." Mrs. Bowers has worked at the Oh-Boy cookie factory longer than any other employee, so she could have the day shift if she wanted. But T.J. says she started working nights the year they adopted him so somebody would be home all the time. She got used to the hours, and now she can't imagine working days.

"I'm not hungry, Mrs. Bowers," I tell her. "But thanks."

"I should be going," Chase says. His eyes dart around the living room. He looks like he's scared the house is about to blow up. He probably never hangs out with people like me and T.J.

"Don't go, man." T.J. nods to the basket he's holding. "Let me run this down to the basement. I'll meet you in the kitchen. Hope, get us something to drink, whatever's in the fridge." He slants his eyes at me, like he and I have some kind of secret that explains why he's making sure Chase sticks around.

I don't get it. But a lot of times I don't get T.J. "Sure," I say to his back as he heads toward the basement. Then I start for the kitchen.

Chase stays where he is a second, then follows me.

I love the Bowers's kitchen. It's the biggest room in the house. T.J.'s dad built all the cupboards, plus a cooking island in the center. Chase slides into the small corner booth, also built by Mr. Bowers. They have a dining room, but I've never seen them use it.

I pour three glasses of OJ and join Chase in the booth, taking the other end of the L. "You really don't have to stick around," I tell him.

Chase is fiddling with the salt and pepper shakers. He shrugs without looking up.

After a minute, I can't stand the silence. "I'll go see if T.J. needs any help." I make my way to the basement and find T.J. pulling clothes out of the dryer. "T.J., what's going on?"

He glances back at me. "Sorry this is taking so long. I'll be up in a minute."

"No. I mean, why are you trying to keep Chase around? It's weird."

T.J. sets down the clothes basket and walks over to me. "Hope, he can help us."

"Help us what?"

"Look," he says, like he's explaining a tough algebra problem to me. "Chase is an insider. He's going to know more than we do about your brother's trial."

"So?"

"So we can use him." T.J. grins and touches his glasses. "Why else would I want to hang out with Chase Wells?"

I can think of a couple of reasons, like becoming popular by association, like being part of Chase's crowd. But I keep my thoughts to myself.

T.J. puts his hands on my shoulders. "Hope, trust me. Okay?"

I take a breath of basement air filled with mildew and dust. If I can't trust T.J., who can I trust? "Okay."

He nods toward the stairs. "Go back up. I'll be there in a minute."

Chase is sitting exactly where I left him. I scoot into the booth. "T.J. will be right up."

Neither of us says anything else until T.J. gets back. "You guys sure you're not hungry?" He opens the fridge and takes out bologna, cheese, mustard, and bread. Who keeps bread in the fridge? "Bologna sandwich? I'm having one. Well, actually two."

"No thanks." Chase and I say this at the same time, exchange glances, then stare at the flowered tablecloth.

A sandwich in each hand, T.J. scoots in on my side, forcing me closer to Chase. The smell of bologna and mustard makes me think of Jeremy. "Jer likes bologna sandwiches," I say, more to myself than to them. "Not as much as peanut butter." I turn to Chase. "What do you think they're feeding him in jail?"

"I don't really know," Chase says. "I can find out . . . if you want."

Do I? Do I want to know? Chase could find out. Maybe this is what T.J. meant about Chase being able to help us. "All I know is that Jeremy has got to be going crazy locked up in a cell." I glance up because I didn't mean to say "crazy."

"They have to take good care of him, Hope," T.J. says. But he doesn't know. He doesn't know Jeremy either, not really. He's nice to Jer, but he never seems at ease around him. Most people are like that.

"Was Jeremy always like . . . like he is now?" Chase asks.

I frown at him and wonder if he really wants to know or if he's trying to change the subject. Or if he's working for his dad, the sheriff.

"Never mind," he says quickly. "None of my business. I just . . . I don't know. Seeing him in court every day, I wondered."

"So why *are* you in court every day?" The question's out before I can stop myself.

"You sound like my dad," Chase says. "He'd just as soon I never set foot in the courthouse."

"Yeah?" T.J. sounds surprised. "I thought he'd want you to be there. You know? So you two could talk over the case and how the trial's going and everything?"

"Yeah, right," Chase mutters. "I don't know. I've never been to a trial before. There wasn't anything else to do, so I went. I guess once I started going, I got hooked." The whole time, he's been staring at his fingernails. Now he looks up at me. "Sorry. I didn't mean to get personal, about Jeremy. You don't have to talk about him if you don't want to."

But the thing is, I do want to talk about Jer. Pretty much every thought I have goes back to my brother, so talking about anything else feels like a lie. "Jeremy has always been *special*. I know people say *special* so they don't have to say *different*. But for me, it means something wonderful, like full of wonder. That's what Jer's always been. My brother could sit for hours and listen to birds sing, but he couldn't sit for two minutes in most of his classes."

Chase smiles. "He likes birds?"

"He loves their songs. But I think what Jeremy loves most is when birds and man-made things get along."

Chase narrows his eyes. "You lost me."

"Like birds on telephone wires, the way crows and jays seem so comfortable on wire made by people. Or gulls hanging out at shopping malls in Cleveland because of those white stone roofs that look like a beach, but that it works out because people leave food for the birds."

"Only birds?" Chase asks.

"He loves our cat," T.J. says. Then, as if he's just realized his cat's not around, he says, "Speaking of which, I better see where Whiskers got off to." He slides out of the booth and heads for the door. "Be right back."

There's a minute of awkward silence with T.J. gone. I hear him in the backyard calling his cat. Finally, Chase breaks the silence. "I like dogs. Mom's husband number two had a cat when he moved in, and he got a dog for Trey and me the only Christmas we had with them. Trey was my stepbrother . . . for maybe a year. How about you? Any pets?"

I shake my head. "Jeremy and I begged Rita for a pet, but we've never had one, except a puppy I can barely remember. Rita said we called it Puppy. Apparently, we were exceptionally original and bright toddlers." He makes a low laughing sound that helps me breathe easier. "Puppy ran away, or got run over, or maybe found a family who'd give him a better name. When we moved here, there was a cat in the house we're renting, but Rita called animal control on it."

T.J. stumbles into the kitchen with his cat draped across both arms. Whiskers weighs more than a poodle. "She was eating the neighbor's dog food again." He sets the cat down and slides back into the booth.

Chase's cell rings. He checks the number. "It's my dad."

He glances at T.J. and me. "Do you guys mind not talking for a minute?" He puts the phone to his ear. "Hey, Dad. What's up?"

It's impossible not to eavesdrop, although we can only hear Chase's end of the conversation:

"Just hanging out with friends."

. . .

"Yeah, I did." He rolls his eyes. "Easy, Dad. Dial it down, okay? The way those reporters went after her, *you* should have given her a bodyguard. Somebody had to do something. I just—"

. . .

"Will you listen?" Chase's eyes are dark slits. "I said I—"

. . .

"I can't come home now."

. . .

"Because I'm in the middle of something." He holds the phone away from his ear.

I can hear his dad yelling, but I can't make out the words. I don't think I want to.

Chase puts the phone back to his ear. When he gets a word in, he doesn't raise his voice, but I get the feeling it's taking everything he has not to. "Sorry. You're right, Dad. I should have told you." He listens for half a minute, the only sound his heavy breathing as his chest rises and falls. "All right," he says. He flips his cell shut and squeezes it so hard his knuckles turn white. Then, without taking his eyes off the phone, he whips it across the kitchen floor.

11

Whiskers darts out of the kitchen. I can't blame her. T.J. and I exchange wide-eyed gazes. Neither of us says a word. Then T.J. gets up and retrieves the phone from across the room. "Still in one piece," he offers.

Chase rubs the back of his neck and looks kind of sheepish. "Guess that's one good thing, huh? Sorry about that. So now you've seen the famous Wells temper for yourselves. I'm really sorry . . . and embarrassed. It's just . . . Sheriff Matthew Wells isn't the easiest person in the world to live with, even for the summer."

"Wish you'd stayed in Boston?" T.J. asks, sitting down again.

"Not really. There are a lot of things I like about Grain."

"For instance?" I ask, glad the anger has gone back inside, where we can't see it.

"I love hitching posts, for one thing. And the Amish buggies. Nobody back at Andover believed me when I told them about the hitching posts everywhere—at the post office, the dollar store, even the car wash."

"Jeremy rolls down the car window whenever we pass a buggy, just so he can hear the clip-clop. I love it too. I really didn't want to move to Ohio. But when I saw those buggies tied out behind the thrift store the first day we got here, I changed my mind."

"Let's see. What else? I like that Dalmatian statue in front of the firehouse," Chase says. "No idea why."

I can't believe he said that. "Jer and I used to walk out of our way to church so he could pet that concrete Dalmatian."

Chase grins. "My dad is always on me about being too much of a city boy to be a real Panther. Guess this proves I'm not so different from you Grain guys after all."

"Yeah, right," T.J. mutters. He laughs, but it doesn't sound real.

"Come on," Chase says. "I'm into birds, cats, dogs, hitching posts, and buggies. And fire station Dalmatians. What more does a guy need to be a real Panther?" He looks at me to back him up. "Right, Hope?"

"Maybe," I admit.

Chase turns to T.J. "See? Even Hope agrees I'm a regular Panther."

T.J. still won't go for it. "Yeah? Well, she must not have seen you at batting practice. None of the *regular* Panthers work that hard at it."

T.J.'s got a point. I have seen Chase at practice. Jeremy and I watched him at the batting cages too. Talk about intense.

"I have to work hard," Chase answers. "I don't have your natural swing."

"I don't know about that," T.J. says, obviously pleased.

"Do you play sports, Hope?" Chase asks.

T.J. laughs. I glare at him. "Sorry," he says. "I didn't mean you *couldn't* play sports. You'd probably be great, if you ever stuck with anything long enough."

It's true, the part about not sticking with things. "So I'm a born quitter," I admit.

"I find that hard to believe," Chase says.

I stare over at him, wondering why he'd find that hard to believe.

"And regardless," he continues, "I still say I'm no different from you two, or anybody else in Grain."

I tilt my head, sizing him up. "I'll bet you're a morning showerer."

"I shower in the morning, after my run."

"But you'd shower in the morning even if you didn't run," I guess.

"Yeah. Is that important?"

"It is where we come from. Right, T.J.?" He nods, agreeing with me. "White-collar workers shower in the morning because they can," I explain. "Blue-collars shower at night because they have to. They need to get the dirt and grime of the mine or factory off. I'm a night showerer by birth."

Chase narrows his eyes at me. I couldn't look away if I wanted to. "Hope Long, you may be the most interesting person I've ever met."

I have nothing to say to that. Neither does T.J. Nobody

has ever told me I was interesting, much less the most interesting person they've met. Maybe it's a line he hands out. If it is, it's a good one. Without thinking, I tug the rubber band out of my hair and free the ponytail Raymond wanted me to wear in court. My hair follicles tingle, thankful for the freedom.

Mrs. Bowers shuffles into the kitchen, a giant purse over one arm. "I'm sorry I have to leave." She sets her purse down in the middle of the floor and reaches into a cupboard. "You children have to try these." She brings down a box of cookies and takes out a plate. "They just came off the line last week— Monster Nuts and Chips." She dumps the whole box onto the plate and sets it in front of us.

"Thanks, Mrs. Bowers." I take one, even though I don't like nuts. "That's really nice of you."

"It is," Chase agrees, taking a big bite. "It's great."

T.J. keeps staring at the table. "Bye, Mom. Thanks. See you in the morning." His voice is strained. His fingers clench and unclench.

The second his mother leaves, T.J. springs to his feet, grabs the plate of cookies, and takes them to the counter, where he puts every cookie back into the box.

"T.J.? Are you okay?" I've never seen him like this.

For a second, he doesn't answer. Then, without looking at me, he says, "I'm tired. It's pretty late. I don't think the TV van will still be at your house."

I glance at the clock, amazed it's almost ten. "I didn't realize it was so late." I scoot out of the booth. "I've got to go. Thanks for letting us come over."

He nods, still not looking at me.

"I'll drop you off," Chase says, moving for the door. "Bye, T.J."

T.J. doesn't return the goodbye. Something's going on, and I don't know what.

When we're outside, I turn to Chase. "What was that back there?"

He doesn't answer until we're in the car, pulling away. "I guess T.J. knows how to hold a grudge."

"What are you talking about?"

"He didn't tell you? It was stupid. At the last practice, Mrs. Bowers showed up with cookies—you know, from the factory? She said it was to get us ready for the big game with Wooster. People were bringing us all kinds of things, like we were headed for the Olympics. Anyway, soon as she left, one of the guys broke out laughing. We were all dead tired from practice. Before we knew it, we were all laughing—the cookies really are pretty bad. Then Coach said, 'Let's save the cookies and give them to the Wooster team. All's fair in love and war.' That did it. Everybody cut loose. I kind of thought T.J. joined in, but I guess I was wrong. We didn't mean anything by it."

I feel bad for T.J. He loves his family, and so do I in a way. More than once, I've shown up on the Bowers's doorstep after a bad fight with Rita. They always welcome me, feed me, and ask no questions. But I guess I'm not that surprised that T.J. didn't tell me about what happened with his mom and the team. We're both pretty private. We know what subjects to stay away from. We don't talk about Rita. Or Jeremy, really.

But T.J. is always there when I need him. And it's just good to have somebody to eat lunch with at school and do homework with sometimes. T.J. gets A's, and he deserves them. He works hard. I'm fine with B's, but he's always up for helping me if I want to shoot for more.

Chase punches the radio on and station-hops until there's loud music pouring out of the front and back speakers. I don't know the songs, but I'm grateful to have music blaring in my head, drowning out thought. This is Rita's kind of music. I'm not about to tell Chase, but my kind of music is way different. I love old songs from the forties, especially the ones written during the war, when people pined for each other—"I'll Be Seeing You," Billie Holiday's "Lover Man." The Andrews Sisters. I used to try to get Jeremy to jitterbug with me, but he was too stiff to jive.

Chase's phone rings.

"Guess your cell really is okay," I say.

He glances at the number, then shuts it off. "I think Dad needs a cooling-off period."

"He's really mad, isn't he?"

Chase shrugs. "He'll get over it. He has to control everything. Guess it's part of the package when you have a cop for a father." He passes a semi, and I can see a little boy on the seat next to the driver.

"At least you have a father." I say this in my head, but it comes out in words too. My mind drifts back to my imaginary father. Every time things got tough with Rita, I'd imagine leaving with my dad. We'd take Jeremy and go live somewhere far away.

"Where is your dad, Hope?" Chase asks. "Unless you don't want to talk about him."

I never talk about him. There's not much to talk about. "He died when I was three. Sometimes I think I remember him, his face, and his eyes. He was tall and thin. I can almost picture him wearing a red baseball cap. But I might have imagined the memory. I do that sometimes."

"How did he die?" Chase has slowed so much that the semi passes us back.

"He was run over. He drove a truck for a living, and it was a truck that ran him over." I have a picture of this in my mind, but I know I've imagined that one.

"You think Jeremy remembers him?"

"Maybe. But he wasn't Jeremy's father. We didn't have the same dad. Rita used to tell Jeremy that he didn't have a father. I guess it was true, in a way. We sure never saw him. But Jeremy believed her literally. He was so excited the first time somebody at church told him God was his father. He came right home and asked Rita where she and God met and fell in love."

"That could sure screw up a kid," Chase observes.

"Maybe. Jeremy would disagree, though." For some reason, I think of that night when Jer and I sat in that old car and Jer's song, or God's song, filled the air.

We ride in an easy quiet until we're at my house. I thank him for the ride, then run up the sidewalk, wondering why I told him so much about me.

The front door swings open and Rita steps out in her white slip, a beer in one hand. She's the only person I know who wears slips, although I've never seen her wear them under anything.

"Where in red-hot blazes have you been?"

I glance back, willing Chase to be gone. The car pulls away from the curb and drives off.

"Was that Chase Wells? Matt's boy?" She downs the rest of her beer, shaking the can to be sure she hasn't missed a drop.

"Don't start, Rita." I shove past her into the house.

She trails in after me. "Mmm . . . mmm. He's a lot better-looking than his old man, that's for sure. What were you doing with him?"

"Nothing. He just gave me a ride home." I kick off my shoes. "We didn't do anything."

"Well, you can take it from your mama—you'd better do a little something with him if you want to keep him coming around."

Only Rita would be upset because I hadn't done anything.

I try to get to my room, but she's not finished with me. She lights a cigarette and takes a deep drag. "I've been trying to reach you all day."

I pull out my cell and see that it's turned off. "Sorry, Rita. You have to turn off cell phones in the courthouse. I guess I forgot to turn it back on."

"I guess I forgot to turn it back on," she repeats, mocking me in the whine of a six-year-old. Her words slur into each other. "Don't you lie to me!"

I have to be careful around Rita when she's like this. I need to get away from her. "All right." I try to walk around her to get to my room, but she blocks me with her cigarette hand.

"Did I say you could leave?" she cries.

I stop, turn to face her, then wait. "What, Rita?"

"The sheriff called here looking for you," she says.

"Sheriff Wells? Why?"

"Looking for his boy."

I think about Chase heading home. Maybe I should call him, warn him.

"Four times! That's how much . . . how many . . . times he called." Rita sniffs, then swipes her nose with the back of her cigarette hand. "He said you and his boy were together."

"Is that a crime now?"

"Don't get smart with me!" She takes a step forward. Automatically, I take a step back.

She comes at me, but stumbles. Ashes break from her cigarette. "I'm still your mother, you know!"

"I know," I mutter.

She squints as if trying to see through me. "What happened in court today?"

"Why?"

"Because Raymond called and said things went lousy."

A rush of guilt sweeps over me. My stomach feels like I swallowed lead. "What else did he say?"

"He said *I'm* going to have to testify because you screwed up. What did you say anyway?"

She's gotten to me. Even though she's drunk enough to pass out, Rita's still got the upper hand. And once again, I feel like everything in the world is my fault. "I'm sorry. I tried, Rita. I really tried."

"Tried? All you had to do was tell them Jeremy's insane. And you couldn't even pull that one off?"

"But he's *not* insane!" I take another step back so I can lean on the couch, brace myself against it.

"Not this again!" She slams against the end table. Something falls off, but neither of us makes a move to pick it up. "Get your head out of the clouds, girl! How do you explain that bloody bat in his closet? He was there! That McCray woman saw him running from the barn, swinging that—"

"Maybe he was scared! Did you think of that?"

"He was scared all right. Scared he'd go to jail and—"

"No! Rita, listen to me. Anybody could have used Jeremy's bat. He always left it right inside the barn door. Everybody knew that. Maybe somebody's trying to frame him."

Rita lets out an ugly "Ha!" Then she takes a long puff on her cigarette stub and grinds it out on her beer can. "Framed? Right . . . just like in the movies. So, Sherlock Hopeless, whodunit? Who's framing your poor, innocent brother?"

"I don't know. Anybody on his baseball team could have done it. Any one of them could have taken Jeremy's bat. Or somebody from the stable? One of the boarders, maybe."

Rita's shaking her head, but I don't care. I've gone over this a million times. Nobody will listen to me. So even a falling-down-drunk Rita is better than nothing. "What about Coach's wife? Mrs. Johnson might have—"

"Are we talking about bedfast, cancer-stricken Caroline Johnson?" Rita asks.

"Maybe she's not as sick as she pretends. Did anybody think of that? She hated her husband." Out of all the people I know who might have murdered Coach Johnson, his wife is the most likely. I saw her go off on Coach one time before a game. She was scarier than Rita. "Don't they claim it's almost always the spouse who does the murder?"

These aren't new thoughts for me. For the first month after Jeremy was arrested, I went over and over all of this with Raymond because Rita refused to talk to me about it. Well, now she's too drunk to run away. She can just hear me out. "Jeremy didn't murder anybody. If you knew him at all, you'd know that. You and Raymond aren't even trying to prove somebody else could have done it!"

Rita points at me, her lips curled into a snarl. "You listen to me!" Her finger stabs the air with each word. "Thanks to you, Raymond says he has to call me to testify now. I'm going to have to clean up the mess you made and get that jury back to believing Jeremy's insanity plea."

"But he's not—!"

"Don't say it!" Rita screams. "We are not proving that boy innocent, because he isn't! You think I don't know my own son? He probably didn't know what he was doing, but he did it. And we're proving he's insane so they don't execute him for what he did. You get that through your empty head, hear? So don't be talking around town about how normal your brother is, because he isn't and he never has been!"

"You're wrong, Rita. My brother is innocent, and I'm going to prove it."

"You?" Rita laughs. "You and T.J. and that sheriff's boy, I suppose? That's what the sheriff tried to tell me. And I told him he didn't have to worry. You'd give up on your own sooner or later—sooner, most likely. I don't know why I'm wasting my breath."

I can't take any more of this. Rita knows exactly how to shut me down. I run past her to my room and slam the door. My whole life this is how it's been. I hate the arguing. It's so much easier just to let Rita have her way.

Only not this time. For Jeremy's sake, not this time.

12

I stay in my room until I hear Rita leave the house. The lingering toxic aroma of cheap perfume tells me she has a date and won't be back until morning.

Part of me wants to pray, to talk to God the way Jeremy does. Wouldn't God know who killed Coach, if he's keeping an eye on everybody? So I ask—not out loud but inside my head, the way Jer does it: *God, who did it? Who really murdered Coach Johnson?*

Nothing.

Okay. I'm not so sure how this works anymore.

For a minute, my mind is a blank. Then, slowly, I remember a cozy night years ago. Jeremy and I are sitting on his bed, and I'm reading from a kids' book of fairy tales. Only I'm too little to read the words, so I'm just telling the stories and Jeremy's filling in the parts I forget. He could talk then. We look so normal, both of us in snowflake pj's. This could be the best memory I have of childhood. Of Jeremy.

This is the Jer I want back home. I can't let them take him away. Not to prison. Not to a mental hospital. Home. Jeremy belongs at home, with me. I'm all he has. *I* have to find out who really killed Coach.

Unsure where to start, I go to my closet to search for something to write on. A shoe box tumbles from the top shelf, and sea glass rains down on my head. I sit on the floor and put back each piece—a pale green chip from an old railroad insulator, a red piece from a railroad lantern, a chunk of orange carnival glass T.J. said came from one of Lake Erie's famed shipwrecks. Each piece is smooth from over a hundred years of being knocked about in the waves.

I put the box back and keep hunting through the closet until I find a notebook without much writing in it. It was my American history notebook, and I gave up taking notes after the midterm, when all the questions came directly from the book. I still got a B-minus. I tear out my history notes, leaving paper pieces like tiny teeth on the left side of each page.

I settle onto my bed with the notebook. At the top of the first page, I write: *SUSPECTS.* The blank paper staring at me is almost enough to make me shut the notebook and throw it back into my closet. But then I see Jeremy at the defense table, wringing his hands and looking up at the ceiling as if he could read the outcome of the trial there.

A vagrant. That's my first suspect, listed on the pale blue line of notebook paper. I don't want the murderer to be anyone I know. Why couldn't some crazy homeless guy have been sleeping in the barn when Coach walked in and surprised him? Maybe the man didn't even know what he was doing until it was too late.

The police said nobody had seen an unknown person hanging around the barn, but maybe they were wrong. When I asked Raymond about the possibility of a stranger being the murderer, he told me the police had ruled it out because Jeremy's fingerprints were the only ones on the bat. Supposedly, the police canvassed the area for transients anyway and came up empty. In Grain, Ohio, a person who doesn't belong gets spotted fast and turned over for gossip before the sun sets.

I move on. I want a long list of suspects, especially since the prosecution has a short list. A list of one—my brother.

The Panthers. Any boy on the team could have murdered Coach. They all knew where Jeremy parked his bat. They knew where Coach would be that early on a game day, especially *that* game day. Why aren't *they* suspects? A little voice in my head answers: *Because they weren't spotted running from the scene of the crime with the murder weapon.* I ignore the voice and write down as many names as I can remember:

> Austin—first baseman, a freshman
> Tyler—catcher, new to the team, nice to Jeremy
> Greg—second base, good hitter, quiet
> Kid on 3rd who yells at umpires—has a temper
> David and Manny—outfielders

I can't come up with the rest of the team, and I want to know their last names, especially the third baseman with a temper. What I need is a team roster. I know that Coach used to post a game roster on the park bulletin board on game day, but I think he passed them out to the team too.

I search for an old team roster in Jer's room but come up

empty. Frustrated, I drop to the floor and lean against Jeremy's bed. Leaving space in my notebook for other players' names, I move on with my suspect list:

Caroline Johnson. Coach's wife has to be my number one suspect. She used to teach at the high school with Coach. T.J. had her for one class and hated her, the only teacher he never got along with, as far as I know. Married people have a bottomless pit of motives to kill each other. Money, for one. No money, for another. Since they never had kids, Caroline would get everything if Coach died. I have no idea what "everything" is. I do know that the stable was really Caroline's. Coach had an office there, but he only started getting involved with the horses after she got sick.

Jealousy—that's another good marriage motive. Maybe Coach had an affair? I'm not sure I'd blame him after seeing the way she yelled at him that day at the game. Or maybe Caroline had an affair and Coach found out about it?

Or anger. I've seen her temper in action.

It was a little over a year ago, back before she got really sick. Coach called a practice before a Saturday home game. I don't remember which team we were playing. Jeremy and I were the first ones to get there. Jer was laying out bats and balls when Coach drove up. I don't think he saw us, because the minute he stepped out of his car, his wife drove up in her car. I could hear her screaming at him before she even shut off her engine.

"You think you can get away from me that easily?" she shouted.

"Caroline, please." Coach was harder to hear because he was trying to calm her down. It wasn't working.

"*I'm* the one who's sick! *Me!* I'm the one with cancer! I won't stand for it!"

Coach said something else I couldn't make out.

Then she exploded. "No! I hate this entire business! And I hate you! I'm not putting up with this. You're going to be sorry you were ever born!" Or something like that. She climbed back into her car and roared off. Coach had to jump out of the way or she'd have run him over.

Through the whole quarrel, Jeremy kept setting out the baseball equipment. I never knew if he'd heard the yelling or not.

And me? I acted like I hadn't heard a word. It's what I do—I smooth things over. I put the whole incident out of my mind . . . until now.

I never found out what Coach and his wife had been arguing about that day. But I heard what I heard, and I saw what I saw—Caroline Johnson's rage.

Maybe Caroline Johnson didn't plan to murder her husband. Maybe she just lost her temper and snapped. One lucky, or unlucky, blow.

Rita's voice in my head is laughing, mocking me.

I don't think the police ever investigated Caroline Johnson because she's supposedly an invalid, confined to her bed and all, or maybe to a wheelchair. But what if she's faking?

On the suspect page by her name, I write: Caroline . . . a fake? . . . money problems? . . . affair?

The phone rings. I figure it's T.J., apologizing for being so weird about the cookies at his house. Maybe I can ask him to fill in the names of the Panther players and tell me more

91

about Caroline Johnson as a teacher. "Hello?" I flip on the living room lamp.

A muffled voice says something I can't make out. It's not T.J.

"Excuse me? Who is this?"

I hear breathing. Definitely breathing. Somebody's there. "Hello?"

Static hits the line, then a click. And the dial tone buzzes.

I hang up. Probably a wrong number. Or a prank. When Jeremy was first arrested, we got some pretty nasty phone calls.

I try to get back into my list of suspects and motives, but it's no use. A headache is starting at the back of my neck, creeping up like electric fingers climbing the back of my skull. I close my eyes and hear branches scratching the roof.

The phone rings again. I jump, like an idiot, then pick up after the second ring. "Hello?"

No answer. I think I hear breathing again. The line is clear as ice.

"Hey, if this is some kind of sick joke, it's not funny." I hang up, hard.

The house is too dark, so I walk from room to room, turning on all the lights. I'm never scared in the house by myself. I've stayed home alone more nights than I can count. And usually, I really like it.

But tonight feels different. I wish Jeremy were here.

The phone rings again, and my heart jumps like it's been shocked with heart paddles. We don't have an answering machine, so the phone keeps ringing and ringing and ringing.

Finally, I can't stand it any longer. I grab the receiver. "What? What do you want?"

A second of silence passes, and then a voice: "I'm watching you. Leave it alone." I think that's what he—or she—says. The voice is so muffled and faint that I'm not sure of the words.

"What did you say?" I demand.

Click. And nobody's there.

13

now, I'm sure it's kids. It has to be. I was at a sleepover once, the only one I've ever been to—the girl's mother made her invite every girl in her class—and they spent most of the night dialing numbers out of the phone book and saying stuff like "I saw what you did," "I know what you're up to," and "I'm watching you."

But no matter what I tell myself, I keep imagining men in black hoodies surrounding the house, peering into the windows, hiding in the bathroom, the kitchen, the bedroom.

I'm calling T.J. I don't care if it is late.

T.J. answers on the third ring, and I tell him about the calls.

"Okay," he says, like he's the officer in charge. "Don't answer the phone. Lock the doors, and we'll be right over."

"*We?*"

"Chase and me."

"Wait . . . what's Chase doing—?"

T.J.'s already on the move. I hear something thud to the floor and imagine him dropping his shoe. "Chase forgot his wallet. He came back for it. He's right here."

"Aren't you mad at him, T.J.? You sure acted mad before."

"Nah. We're cool. Can you run over to Hope's with me?" T.J. says this last part away from the phone.

"Wait! T.J.?" I don't understand what's going on.

"I was talking to Chase," T.J. says, sounding out of breath. "We'll be right there." He hangs up.

Chase Wells is coming here? Into this house? Jogging by is one thing. Coming inside is another.

I glance at the kitchen wall clock and try to guess how long it will take them to drive over. Not that long. I race around the house, picking up after Rita—the lacy bra strung over the easy chair, an empty beer bottle on the coffee table, one black heel in the kitchen, another in the hallway, shot glasses on the counter.

Before I get a chance to change out of the skirt and blouse I wore to court, there's a knock at the door. I sniff under each armpit. Nothing bad. Then I open the door.

T.J. looks like he just woke up on the wrong side of the bed. Chase, still in jeans and a gray shirt, could step directly onto the cover of one of Rita's celebrity magazines.

"I'll have a look around," T.J. says, pushing past me. He's only been here a few times, but he acts like he owns the place, or maybe like he's got a warrant to search it.

Chase, of course, has never been here, and I wonder if he's ever seen a house like ours close-up. The confetti carpet is worn to the paper-thin padding in spots, and furniture is arranged to hide the worst rug stains, most of which were here before we were. Furniture too. Except the TV. Rita always has a great television.

Suddenly I realize Chase is waiting for me to invite him in. I step back so he can enter. He ducks, as if our doorway is too low for him. "You didn't have to come over here. I didn't know . . . I mean, I thought just T.J. would . . . ."

"T.J. said you sounded pretty strung on the phone. What did they say? Was it kids? Could you tell?"

I try to call up the voice in my head. "I don't know. It could have been anybody. Mostly, they just breathed." I try to laugh it off, but even I can hear how fake my laugh sounds.

"And you don't have caller ID?" he asks, taking a couple more steps in.

I'm embarrassed to admit that we don't. We're probably the last people in America not to have it.

I'll kill T.J. for bringing Chase here. What was he thinking?

T.J. reappears. "Clear! Nobody's hiding in the kitchen or the bathroom. I didn't hit the bedrooms, though."

"I didn't say somebody was hiding," I snap. Chase must think I'm an idiot. "I'm sorry you guys had to drive all the way over here for nothing. I really don't need a babysitter."

"Babysitter, huh?" Chase perches on the arm of the couch and crosses his long legs at the ankles. "I always wanted to be a babysitter."

"You did not," I say.

"Seriously. I did. I didn't have little brothers or sisters. I always thought it might be cool to hang out with some-body else's. But nobody ever wanted a guy babysitter where I came from."

"So what did you do instead?" T.J. asks this like he's not really mad at Chase anymore.

"What did I do? Instead of babysitting, you mean?" Chase says. "Nothing."

"What are you saying? You've never had a job? Even an after-school job?" T.J. frowns like he can't believe this.

Chase shrugs. "Sad, but true."

I'm coming down on T.J.'s side on this one. I've had so many jobs the child labor people should have arrested Rita.

Chase turns to me. "You're a workingwoman, aren't you? I've seen you at that café on Main Street, the Colonial."

"You have?" I don't get it. I'd have remembered if he'd ever been my customer. He hasn't been. Panic strikes when I imagine Rita waiting on him, hitting on him.

"Driving by," he explains. "I've seen you through that front window?"

I didn't think Chase Wells even knew who I was. I try to picture him cruising Main Street, turning his head to see me.

Behind us, paying no attention to us, T.J. plops onto the couch. A tiny puff of dust billows up.

"Haven't seen you there lately, though," Chase says. "Did you quit?"

I'm still standing just inside the door, not sure what to do with myself. "What? No. I haven't quit working at the Colonial. Bob—the owner—has been pretty cool about the trial and Jer and everything. But customers stare and whisper. Some of them ask questions about Jeremy. Rita can handle them, but I can't. So I work in back most of the time."

I can't keep standing here, arms folded across my chest, like I used to do in fifth grade to hide my "early development."

"Want something to drink?" I shoot past them to the kitchen and inhale the scent of leather and Ivory soap Chase brought in.

He follows me. "Water would be great."

"Got any Coke?" T.J. hollers in from the living room.

I open the fridge and find three brands of beer on the top shelf, but no Coke. No juice. No bottled water. No ice cubes in the freezer, just an empty plastic ice cube tray.

I run the tap water and get down two glasses. Chase pulls back a chair and sits at the kitchen table. The chair legs squeal on the linoleum. I call out to T.J. to come in for his water.

Setting down the two glasses, I spot a Snickers wrapper and Rita's overflowing ashtray on the plastic checkered table-cloth. I sweep both items off the table and dump them into the garbage. Tiny flecks of ash float up, along with the stench of stale cigarettes.

"Sorry, T.J.," I tell him as he takes a seat across from Chase. "No Coke."

"That's okay," he answers. "Hate to ask, but I'm starving."

I watched him eat two bologna sandwiches an hour ago. He eats more than anybody I've ever met, but you wouldn't know it to look at him. "Sure. Chase?" My brain cycles through the slim possibilities for food in this house.

"Maybe. If it wouldn't be too much trouble," Chase answers.

"No trouble," I lie. I ferret through the fridge, then the cupboard. *No lunch meat. Crackers? No cheese. No cookies.* "I make a killer peanut butter sandwich."

"Prove it," Chase challenges.

"Yeah," T.J. agrees.

I laugh . . . until I picture my brother sitting at this table taking a giant bite of a peanut butter sandwich. "That's the one thing I make sure we never run out of—peanut butter. Jeremy would live on the stuff if I let him."

Before I can get the bread out, Chase is up and searching through our gross fridge. He comes out with the grape jelly, Jer's favorite.

"Know your way around the kitchen, I see," T.J. observes.

"I've had lots of practice finding my way around strange kitchens. Every time Mom remarries, it's off to a new house." He finds our silverware drawer on the second try, takes out a knife, and spreads jelly after I do the peanut butter. "Is this really all your brother likes?" Chase asks. "Peanut butter sandwiches? And bologna. How about hot dogs?"

"He loves hot dogs too." In my head, I can see Jeremy at a baseball game. He's wearing a White Sox cap and biting into a ballpark frank. "We got to go to a White Sox game once. Rita was dating some guy who'd just gotten out of prison. Anyway, he took Jeremy and me to a game, and Jer ate six hot dogs and got so sick that he threw them all up . . . and all over the ex-con."

Chase laughs.

"You never told me that," T.J. says.

"I haven't thought about it in years," I say, sounding too defensive. T.J. hasn't told me much about his past either, but I don't bring that up. It's nice having the three of us get along like this. Still, it feels a little like we're balancing on a seesaw. One shift could send the whole thing crashing down.

"Dad and I love going into Cleveland for Indians games," T.J. says. "We've made it to the home opener every year for as long as I can remember."

"My dad's never taken me to a major-league game," Chase admits, picking up his sandwich and slapping on more peanut butter. "He keeps promising to, but he never does. He and Mom used to fight all the time about Dad's promises. They fought about a lot of things. I guess they fought over me a lot. Never *for* me, just over me."

I'm not sure what to say. Even though I knew his parents were divorced, I've always pictured Chase Wells as having the perfect life, in Boston or in Grain.

"Voilà!" he says, lifting his four-inch-thick peanut butter masterpiece like it's a baseball trophy.

T.J. applauds. "I want *his* sandwich."

"Don't worry. I made you two." I pull the stepping stool up to the table and sit on it. Although I made myself a sandwich too, I'm not hungry. I let it sit in front of me while Chase and T.J. eat.

T.J. wipes his mouth with the back of his hand, smudging peanut butter to his chin. Then he nods at Chase. "Go ahead and ask her."

Chase almost chokes on his sandwich.

I glance from one to the other. "What? Ask me what?"

Chase shakes his head and won't look at me.

T.J. takes over. "Chase wanted to know what's really wrong with Jeremy. I told him I didn't know anything he didn't and he should ask you."

Chase's cheeks have turned pink. "You don't need to

answer that if you don't want to. I wasn't being nosy, but I didn't understand much of the expert testimony in court. And I wondered, when you said it would be a terrible thing if they put Jeremy in a mental hospital, why you said that. Why would it be so hard on him if he has something wrong with him that they could fix, or help? You'd be able to visit him, right?" He stops. "I'm sorry. It's none of my business. I didn't mean to bother *you* with it, Hope. I just thought T.J. could help me understand."

T.J. and I never talk about Jeremy. Usually, I hate it when people ask me what's wrong with my brother. But I don't know now. I want Chase to understand, and T.J. too. I don't want to be the only one who understands Jeremy well enough to believe he didn't do what they say he did.

"Jeremy was born with a neurological disorder. Probably Asperger's syndrome, although he's had all the standard labels pasted on him at one time or another: learning disabled, ADHD, autistic. One counselor at a school in Chicago was sure Jer had epilepsy because of his tantrum fits. And, yeah, selective mutism, which is a no-brainer since we know Jeremy selected to be mute."

"So he's been tested before all this, like in a hospital?" Chase sets down his sandwich and leans in, catching every word.

"Jeremy's been tested and retested. Every time he got a new teacher, they'd call Rita in and ask her about him. Then they'd send him to the school psychologist—those people have some big problems of their own, if you ask me. Then *they'd* give up and send Jer on to some doctor, or hospital, or specialist."

"And nobody knows why he won't talk?" Chase asks, almost like he can't quite believe this.

I understand where he's coming from. "At first, Rita thought he was just being stubborn. She'd get so mad at Jeremy." I stop talking because I'm remembering times when I had to get between Rita and my brother. I remember one time when I shoved a drunk Rita out of the way so Jeremy could escape to the bathroom and lock himself in until she got over it, or fell asleep.

But if I'm honest, there are other pictures stored inside my mind too. Rita sitting on the floor with Jeremy, holding up word cards the speech therapist gave her. Rita all excited over a new "herbologist" or "naturalist" she heard about, who could cure what didn't come out of Jeremy's mouth by being more picky about what went into his mouth.

I get up and run myself a glass of water. It tastes as cloudy as it looks and smells like iron. Then I sit back down.

"I don't remember any of that stuff going on when you and Jeremy moved to Grain," T.J. says.

"By the time we moved here, Rita was so tired of the whole rigmarole that she'd started telling new schools Jeremy had been in an accident and *couldn't* talk. She just didn't want to go through all those tests again. I guess Jer's language arts teacher, Ms. Graham, tried to teach him sign language our first year here. It didn't take, though. Jeremy likes to write notes. You should see his handwriting."

"So that's it?" Chase asks. He hasn't taken another bite of his sandwich since we've been talking about Jeremy. T.J. has finished both of his. "There's really nothing else wrong with him?"

"Nope. Not with Jer," I answer. "Nothing except the fact that people have a hard time understanding unique."

"Unique." Chase mutters this, so I can't tell if it's a question or not.

I know he doesn't get what I'm saying, and I'm not sure how to say it any better. I want him—them—to *get* Jeremy. I struggle for a minute over how to explain the Jeremy I love, what makes him who he is. And then I know.

Leaving our dirty dishes, I get up from the table. "Come with me."

14

Standing outside Jeremy's bedroom, my hand wrapped around the doorknob, I know one thing. Chase and T.J. are about to get a true glimpse of Jeremy Long. What I don't know is how they'll react. Slowly, I turn the knob and open the door.

This time, it's T.J. who hangs back and Chase who goes in first. He stares up and around, in a full circle, as if awed by a starry sky. His gaze passes over the baseball bedspread I found at Goodwill in Oklahoma. My brother loves that spread. Most days since he's been gone, I've come in and smoothed out the wrinkles. The only piece of furniture in the room besides this single bed is an old dresser I painted blue to match the bedspread. Above the dresser hangs one of Jeremy's drawings—a circle divided into sixteen pie pieces, each meticulously colored in with a different color. This is Jeremy's art. My brother has made me dozens, maybe hundreds, of these pictures, each with a different color scheme, but all the exact same design. I've saved every one of them.

But Chase isn't looking at the dresser or the color wheel. He's staring at Jeremy's glass jars. Three walls are lined with shelves. The last owner or renter must have filled these shelves with books—most people would.

But not Jeremy.

"These are the jars you talked about in court," Chase whispers, as if afraid of disturbing the row after row of emptiness. His eyes widen as his gaze shifts from one wall to the next. "How many does he have?"

"I've never counted them."

"It's pretty amazing, isn't it?" He says this like he's able to admire the collection, to respect my brother. "It must have taken him a long time to do this."

"He'd have more if a box of the jars hadn't been left back in Chicago one time. Not a pleasant experience for any of us," I admit. An image flashes through my mind—Jeremy throwing glasses and plates in our new kitchen, Rita the one hiding under the table for once.

T.J. clears his throat. It startles me, and I turn to see him still standing in the doorway, his arms straight out from his sides, like he's holding on to the doorframe. He nods at the baseball curtains I got when I found the spread. "He really loves baseball, huh?"

I sit on the edge of the bed. "At least that's something you guys can understand. You've probably been baseball-crazy since you were little boys."

"Got that right," T.J. agrees. "Dad took me to my first Wooster-Grain game when I was six weeks old."

I wait for Chase to say something like that, but he doesn't. "I don't know. I like to play, but I can't say I've ever been *crazy* about baseball."

I'm surprised. He always looks so serious about it at practices, dedicated even.

"Hold on a minute," T.J. says, venturing into the room with us. "You play here in the summer, and you're on a team in Boston too, right?"

"That was Husband Number Two's idea. When I started playing, I guess I was pretty good, like it was natural for me. All of a sudden, my dad started calling me after games to see if we won and how I did. Then he began calling before games too, to give me last-minute tips and advice."

"And that was a good thing?" T.J. asks.

"Yeah. Before baseball, Dad almost never called me. And when he did, we didn't have anything to talk about. After I got into baseball, we could talk for an hour on the phone. And things weren't as awkward when I came to visit him. We had baseball, you know?"

"I know what you mean," T.J. agrees. "My dad and I can talk baseball for hours. He can talk about grass and weeds for hours too, but I don't stick around."

Chase frowns, like he's trying to understand, so I explain. "T.J.'s dad works for TruGreen lawn care."

"Ah." Chase nods. Then he takes another long look at Jeremy's jars, tracing the shelves all the way around the room. He gets it. I can see he does.

T.J.'s already back to baseball. "Your dad played ball in high school, didn't he? Did he play with Coach?"

I'm watching the lines of Chase's forehead, and I don't think he's enjoying all of T.J.'s questions. But he answers anyway. "Dad played in high school, but he lived in Wooster. So

106

he and Coach were rivals. I'm not sure either one of them ever got over it. I don't think Coach appreciated Dad's postgame advice after our Panther games."

"Still," T.J. says, "Coach was going to let *you* start against Wooster. Your dad must have been pumped to see you pitch in the biggest game of the year."

Chase doesn't look at either of us. "You could say that. He practically ordered everybody in his office to go to the game. He even bought fireworks to set off when we scored against Wooster."

I'm beginning to think it was a mistake to show them Jer's room. Somehow we've ended up talking about the day of the murder, the game that wasn't played. I think I hate baseball.

"What's this?" T.J.'s picked up something off Jeremy's dresser. He reads out loud: "Suspects. A vagrant. The Panth—"

"Give me that!" I tear across the room and grab my suspect list out of his hands. I don't remember leaving my notebook on Jer's dresser, but I must have.

"What was that?" T.J. asks, standing on his toes to try to read over my shoulder.

"None of your business." I clutch the notebook to my chest, feeling stupid, like I've been caught at something.

T.J. won't let it go. "You're trying to solve the murder. That's it, isn't it? I knew it. You've got a list of suspects and—"

I wheel on him. "Well, why wouldn't I try to figure out who the real killer is? I'm the only one who believes, who *knows*, it wasn't Jeremy. Who else is going to—?"

"It's cool, Hope," T.J. says. "I've been expecting you to do this. I think you need to try. I want to help." He glances down at his feet. "I've just been waiting for you to ask."

I narrow my eyes, studying him. I know he wants to help me. But I'm pretty sure he's believed Jeremy is guilty all along—I've never asked. Still, T.J. has always been there for me when I really needed him. I glance back at Chase. His face is a blank. I have no idea what he's thinking.

Then, as if he's planned all of this, scripted it even, T.J. crosses the room and sits next to Chase on the bed. "You can help too, Chase, if you'll do it."

Chase stiffens. "No."

"Think about it at least, man," T.J. urges. "You have an inside track to what's going on in the trial, to evidence . . . to your dad. Hope needs us."

I know T.J. is doing this for me. I can't even look at Chase. "T.J., don't."

"What?" T.J. asks.

I stare at him. "Why would *he* want to help Jeremy?"

"It's not that," Chase says. "I just . . . I mean . . . I wouldn't be any help."

"But you would!" T.J. insists.

Chase shakes his head. "My dad barely talks to me, T.J."

"I don't care," T.J. says. "Besides, you owe me, man."

Chase's forehead wrinkles. "I thought two rides from the courthouse squared us."

"Not by a long shot." T.J. waits a minute, then adds, "And you know it."

They exchange a weird look. I am definitely missing

something. There's more to this than T.J. convincing Coach to let Chase pitch. I can tell that much.

T.J. gets to his feet and turns to me. "Chase is in. Tell us what we can do."

I don't know what's going on between them, but I don't want any part of it. "T.J., drop it. Chase doesn't want to help."

"It's not that," Chase says. "I mean, I'd be glad to help, if I could. But—"

"See? He's in," T.J. insists. "Go on, Hope. What do you need?"

I glance at Chase, and I know he's not "in." He'll probably take off as soon as he can. And that's fine. But what if T.J.'s right? What if Chase knows something that could help Jer? Something he heard from his dad or got out of the trial? It's possible. So, embarrassed or not, I might as well get what I can out of him while he's here. For Jeremy's sake.

"Okay. I know you need to go," I tell him. "But if you could help me with just one thing, that's all I'll ask. I'd really like to get my hands on a roster. Do either of you have a team roster?"

"Why?" Chase frowns at me, and I wish I'd waited until he left. T.J. probably has one. "Why do you want a roster?"

"Well, maybe I don't need a roster exactly. I just need to know the names of all the players on the Panthers. And anything else about them, especially how they got along with Coach."

"For your suspect list," T.J. says. "Right. I can give you the names of everybody on the team." He reaches for my notebook, and I let him take it. He starts filling in my list of names.

Chase stands up. "You don't really need me for this."

"Sit back down, man," T.J. says, still writing. "You know more about some of these guys than I do."

"Are you serious?" Chase asks. "You live here. They go to school with you, don't they?"

"That doesn't mean they hang out with me. They don't. They hang out with you."

I get the feeling it costs T.J. something to admit this. I'm grateful.

Chase sits on the edge of the bed and rubs his hands together as if he's warming himself by a bonfire. "Give me a name. I'll tell you what I know."

Fifteen minutes later, my suspect list has doubled.

"I have to tell you, Hope," Chase says when we're finished with the Panther list, "everybody on the Panthers really liked Coach."

"So did Jeremy," I add.

"So did Jeremy," he agrees.

T.J. has been sitting cross-legged on the floor, but he gets up. "They liked him. Maybe. But maybe not."

"What do you mean, T.J.?" I ask.

When he looks at me, his face is hard, his mouth a razor-thin line. "Coach wasn't perfect."

I'm a little stunned at the change in T.J. I know he was angry about Coach making fun of his mom, but I wonder if there's something else going on. After another minute, I ask him again, "What do you mean?"

He's quiet for so long that I don't think he's going to answer me. Then he does. "It's just . . . everybody talks about

Coach Johnson like he's this saint or something. Just because people are dead doesn't mean you forget all the bad stuff they did. He wasn't perfect. That's all I'm saying. So maybe everybody *didn't* like him."

I want to ask more, but I don't. I just say, "Good point," and let it go at that.

"Okay." Chase frowns, like he doesn't understand either. "Nobody's perfect. I'm just saying that I don't think the Panthers make great suspects."

I hate to agree with him, but I do. "I had to start somewhere. But I think the best possibility is Caroline Johnson, Coach's wife."

"You underlined her," T.J. says, sitting down again. He taps the end of the pen on the list. The *click, click* reminds me of Jeremy, the way he can drive me crazy with constant clicking whenever he has a pen in his hand.

Chase turns to me. "Did you underline her name because you really think she murdered her husband?"

"Lots of wives do, you know."

"That's true," T.J. says. "Spouses are the number one suspect in any murder. One-third of female homicide victims were killed by their husbands or boyfriends. Some say fifty-three percent of murders were done by spouses, but most of them got off."

I don't know where he comes up with this stuff, but I'll take it. Over half of victims are killed by their spouses? I wonder if Raymond knows this.

"Okay," Chase says. "But could Mrs. Johnson even get to the barn? Or swing a bat?"

"Why not? Maybe she's faking it. You don't know. Has anybody even looked into her?" I know I sound defensive. But I want them to believe somebody else did it. I want Chase to believe it.

T.J. keeps clicking his pen and staring at the notebook. The *click, click, click* is the only sound in the room.

Then Chase sits up and leans in so he can see my suspect list. "You know . . . and this is pretty random . . . I've always thought there was something wrong about that woman."

"You did?" I can't believe it. "You do? Tell me. Us."

"I don't know exactly. I've only seen her a few times when Coach had us over to his house."

"He had you over to his house?" T.J. interrupts.

"Just a couple of times. Me and Austin and Greg and some others."

"Figures," T.J. mutters.

"Go on," I urge, wishing T.J. would quit interrupting.

"I can't explain it," Chase continues. "She was friendly enough and said the right things. But there was just something about her I didn't like."

"Jeremy too!" I slap my knee, then tug my skirt down. I'm not used to wearing skirts, and I sure haven't been thinking about this one. "Jer's a great judge of character. He's always stayed away from Coach's wife, and he wouldn't tell me why."

"That fits," Chase says.

"What? What fits?" I ask.

He tilts his head at me. "That's right. . . . You weren't in the courtroom for her testimony, were you?"

I shake my head. "I didn't think she testified. I thought they said she couldn't make it to court."

"That's what I thought too," T.J. agrees.

"She didn't. Not in person," Chase explains. "But Keller was allowed to read her testimony into the record."

"Is that fair?" I ask. "Keller gets to read whatever Caroline wants to say, and Raymond doesn't even get a chance to make her take it back?"

"Jeremy's lawyer asked her questions too," Chase says. "Only not very many."

"Wouldn't he have the right to subpoena her to appear in court?" T.J. asks. "I'll bet Raymond could make her testify."

"Well, he might not want to put her on the stand," Chase says.

"Why?" I demand. "What did she say?" This is the first I've heard about any of this.

"Mostly, it was how great her husband was. She gave an account of the day of the murder, how Coach left the house early, and how my dad's deputy went to the house to give her the news."

I can tell he's leaving out things. "What did she say about Jeremy?"

Chase bites his bottom lip, then comes out with it. "It was pretty bad, Hope."

"Tell me."

"She said she was afraid of him. I guess Jeremy went to the house a couple of times with Coach. I don't know what happened, but she told Coach not to let him in the house again. She made your brother sound dangerous."

"Dangerous? Jeremy?" I can't stay sitting down, so I pace Jeremy's floor. "Jeremy's right about her. I don't trust that woman." I keep thinking about what I saw that day in the ballpark when she went off on Coach.

I start to tell them more about that argument, but the phone rings. I quit pacing and stare out to the living room, where the phone is ringing and ringing.

"Aren't you going to answer it?" T.J. asks.

Ring! Ring! Ring! It sounds angry.

"Want me to get it?" T.J. makes a move toward the phone.

"Wait!" I cry over the scream of the phone. "It could be Rita." The last thing I need is Rita making a scene because I have two guys over when she's not here.

I walk to the phone, but I can't pick it up. I'm too afraid.

Footsteps come behind me. I think it's T.J. until I see Chase reach down and pick up the receiver. The silence is like a slap, scarier somehow than the ringing. Chase holds the receiver to my ear and leans in. When I don't say anything, he does: "This is the Long residence."

I recognize the quiet that floats on the other end of the line. I know the breathing.

"Is anybody there?" Chase shouts into the phone.

There's no answer. Of course.

"Listen to me, whoever this is. Stop calling here! I'm telling the sheriff, and we'll be listening and tracing your number. Do you understand me?" His voice is getting louder and louder. "You better! This ends right now. Do you hear me? Answer me!" When nobody does, Chase lets loose a string of cusswords that would make even Rita blush. Then he slams down the phone and stares at it, like it could jump back up and knock us both down.

"Way to go, Chase!" T.J. shouts, clapping. "Didn't think you had it in you."

Chase looks at me as if he forgot T.J. and I were here. "Hope, I'm sorry. I guess I lost it."

"Kind of," I agree.

"It's just . . . I hate cowards," Chase explains, staring at the phone again. "But I should have let you handle it."

"I wasn't exactly handling it," I admit.

"If you're okay, I should go," he says. I nod. He pats his pocket, probably making sure he doesn't leave his wallet again.

"I can stay if you want," T.J. says.

"I'll be okay." I wouldn't mind having T.J. stick around. But I don't want him to have to walk home. "Besides, who would call back after a phone . . . uh, conversation . . . like that one, right?"

"Yeah. Okay." T.J. squeezes my arm. "I'll take off, then. Dad's got to be home by now, wondering where I am." He glances at Chase. "He's probably called *your* dad to get the posse out looking for me." He laughs at his own joke.

"That's all we both need," Chase says, moving toward the door.

I follow them outside. Chase stops on the step. T.J.'s already halfway to the car. "Thanks, T.J.!" I call after him. Softer, I say, "You too, Chase." I feel like I need to say more. He's gotten dragged into my mess all day long. But I stare up into those green eyes, and I can't say anything.

"Jeremy's lucky to have a sister like you," he says.

As he walks off, I think that out of all the things he could have said, this is the best. It's the only thing I've ever cared about—being a good sister to Jer.

I watch them drive away under a sliver of moon. They're still in sight when my cell phone rings. Only a handful of people have my cell number, so I answer it.

"It's me." The voice belongs to T.J., but the number doesn't. "I'm on Chase's cell. Mine's dead. I just wanted to make sure we're on for driving lessons after church tomorrow." T.J. is determined to help me get my driver's license. He's been giving me lessons Sunday afternoons for about a month. I've been doing it because it helps keep my mind off Jeremy, even if it only lasts an hour.

"I don't know, T.J. Driving doesn't seem that important anymore."

"But I want to run some ideas by you. Like surveillance on Mrs. Johnson. A couple of other things too. We can talk about the case."

I can't say no. I'm too grateful that he's taking Jeremy's case seriously. It makes me feel like it's not *all* up to me. "Okay. I'm not going to church, though. Can you come by for me?"

"I'll be around about noon, okay?"

"Okay. Thanks again, T.J. See you tomorrow." Chase's car is still in view when I sign off. What did people do before cells?

I turn to go back inside. And that's when I see it. An old white pickup truck, headlights off, creeps from the shadows and inches up the street. I step back as it passes my house and keeps going. At the corner, it turns right, just like Chase did. Then it speeds off, disappearing into the darkness . . . just like Chase.

15

While I shower and get ready for bed, I try to explain away that old white pickup. The driver might have forgotten to turn on the lights. It definitely went the same direction Chase did, but there are only two choices at that corner—straight or a right turn. It might have been going anywhere.

I know I'm being paranoid because of the crank calls, but I can't shake the idea that somebody was following Chase and T.J.

What if they didn't make it home? I grab my cell and hit T.J.'s number. The call goes directly to voice mail, and I remember he said his phone was dead. So I return the call from T.J. on Chase's phone. It goes straight to voice mail too.

This isn't good. What if the pickup ran them off the road? *Think. Think!* Maybe Chase is home already, and he's turned off his ringer because he doesn't want to wake his dad. That makes sense. I could text him. As fast as I can, I type: R U OK? Not much of a message, but I send it and wait. My stomach's cramping as I hold my cell in both hands and stare at it.

Finally, I hear the double beep. **Fine. U?**

I let out a big sigh. Now I feel stupid. He probably thinks I'm flirting with him . . . and that I'm really bad at it. I text: **Good.**

I have got to stop seeing bad guys everywhere.

By the time I climb into bed, I'm tired enough for sleep to come, but it doesn't. Twice I think I hear somebody inside the house. I call out to Rita, but nobody answers, except the old house creaking, the refrigerator roaring, and the branches scratching my bedroom window.

After double-checking the front and back doors, I get back in bed and burrow under the sheets. I close my eyes, but I can't stop imagining things. I picture someone sneaking in through Jeremy's window, and I can't remember if I locked that window. But I don't want to go check. Outside, there's a faint rattle of an engine creeping by, but not passing, the house. It could be the white pickup. I know it's ridiculous to think like this, but I can't help it.

For the first time in ages, I actually wish Rita would come home.

The second I wake up, I have the feeling someone is watching me. I stumble out of bed. My window faces west, but I can tell the sun is up.

I yawn, stretch, and check the clock. It's late, and I've already missed Chase running by. I wish he wouldn't run the same time on weekends that he does weekdays.

Thinking about Chase changes my mood. It shouldn't, not with Jeremy still in jail. But as I gaze out the window at the deserted shack across the street, images of Chase from last night flash through my mind: Chase on the edge of the couch, legs outstretched; Chase in my kitchen, spreading grape jelly and laughing about something; Chase in the middle of Jeremy's room, staring wide-eyed at Jer's jar collection. But his expression isn't just gawking. There's awe on his face. He's truly amazed.

I walk over to my closet and open the door. The wood is splintered, the latch never worked, and the closet isn't deep enough for most hangers. Jeans, khakis, and shorts are folded on the top shelf, along with other junk. A few shirts and T-shirts hang on kid hangers. I haven't been shopping since before Jeremy was arrested. If he were here, we'd be going to church, and I'd wear either the khaki pants or a long, funky, crocheted black skirt that's not at all churchy.

But I'm not going. I've only gone to church once since Jeremy was arrested. It felt like everyone was staring at me, even if they weren't. I do miss it, though, especially the songs. Jeremy says God sings everywhere, but it's easier to hear in church.

I settle on denim capris I've only worn once and a sleeveless white shirt with big buttons and just a tiny spot that I didn't see until I got it home from Goodwill.

About five in the morning, I heard Rita come in. You'd have had to be dead not to hear her. She was Happy-Singing-Drunk Rita. She pounded on my bedroom door until I got up to unhook her necklace for her. She was Rita in White—white feather collar rimming a white cardigan, the tiny buttons straining to hold her in. Rita the Chatterer: "Hope,

119

Hope, Hope," she said, taking my face in her hands. "You're a pretty girl. Did you know that? Don't ever let anybody say you're not, hear? My girl. My own little girl."

I'm hoping she sleeps until noon. I grab my bag and ease out of my room.

"Where do you think you're going?" Rita's standing in the middle of the hallway. Her slip is on inside out, and her bleached hair looks like something made a nest out of it. When she eyes me up and down, her mascara-clumped lashes make tiny window shades for her bloodshot eyes. "Is it Sunday?"

I nod, hoping she'll think I'm off to church.

Rita groans, turns her back on me, and staggers to her bedroom.

Just when I think I'll make a clean getaway, she glances over her shoulder. "Hey. What was that old truck doing last night?"

My blood stops running through my veins and turns to ice. "What truck, Rita?"

"A white pickup parked across the street. Somebody around here buy that old thing? I don't want carbon monoxide polluting our air." She coughs, like it's the truck and not the thousands of cigarettes she's smoked. "Some pervert was sitting in there too, watching me come home."

"Who?" I demand. "What did he look like?"

Rita frowns. "How should I know? I'm the one who asked you, remember?"

It had to be the same truck I saw follow Chase's car.

"What's the matter with you?" Rita scratches her belly, and her slip makes a *zip, zip* sound.

120

"Rita, I saw that truck"—I almost say "following Chase and T.J."—"last night, in front of our house."

"Probably just some loser with no life watching people who have lives." She yawns.

"And somebody kept calling here and then hanging up."

Rita lets out a dry laugh. "Let me get this straight. You think somebody's out to get us, right? That it? Somebody who murdered Coach and is so scared Detective Hopeless will uncover the truth that they're . . . what? Parking across the street? Calling and hanging up?"

When she says it like that, it does sound pretty dumb.

She yawns again, so big that her face is nothing but an open mouth. Then she shuffles back to her bedroom.

I grab a cup of instant coffee and go outside to wait for T.J. I don't want to think about the pickup or the phone calls. It's August hot, and there's no shade on the front step. I squint across the street at the empty lot, where they tore down a condemned house, leaving rubble and trash. Shards of glass catch the morning light and toss it into the air in glittering patterns of delicate color. It makes me think of Jeremy and the way he finds beauty everywhere—twigs floating in mud puddles, snowflake mountains on windowsills, crow's-feet wrinkles at the eyes of old men, pudgy toes on babies, and dandelions, frail and feathered and ready to be blown bald.

Far off, I hear a couple of lost geese honking. Closer in, a woodpecker competes with the cry of a mourning dove. I want them to smother the breathing on the other end of the phone, to cover up the chug of the white pickup truck, and to drown out Rita's voice in my head.

A horn honks. I stand up, expecting to see T.J.'s dad's '81 Chevy, but it's the Stratus Chase drives. He gets out of the car and stands beside it. "T.J. couldn't make it."

I take a couple of steps toward him. "Why didn't he call me?"

"He said your cell was off, and he was afraid to wake Rita. So he called me."

Once again, Chase is dragged into the mixed-up life of Hope Long. I'm totally embarrassed—again—but I have to admit I don't mind seeing Chase.

"T.J. shouldn't have called you. I'm sorry, Chase. Thanks for letting me know, though."

Chase meets me the rest of the way up the sidewalk. I don't think I realized how tall he is, more than a head taller than me. I'm used to looking down at T.J., not up like this. "He had to help his dad finish some big lawn job in Ashland, I guess."

"Well, thanks again." I'm not sure whether to go back in or wait until he leaves.

"Anyway," Chase says, "he felt pretty bad about you missing your driving lesson and all. So I thought maybe I could stand in for him?"

"Wait. Did T.J. put you up to this?"

Chase grins, showing straight white teeth. "No. But I got the feeling he thinks you can use all the lessons you can get. I figure this will square me with T.J. for good."

"You must have owed him big-time." I wait for Chase to fill in the blanks.

"Okay," he says at last. "But don't tell T.J. I told you. In the Lodi game last year, he didn't just talk Coach into letting me pitch. He pretended he hurt his arm so Coach would have to put me in."

"Why would he do that? I didn't think you guys were that tight. It doesn't even sound like something he'd do."

Chase seems to be studying our cracked sidewalk. Then he says, "T.J. overheard my dad and me arguing in the locker room. Dad thought I wasn't working hard enough and that was why I wasn't getting to pitch. It was a pretty big blowup. T.J. walked in on it."

Now things are starting to make more sense. T.J.'s probably never fought with his dad. He would have wanted to fix things for Chase, no matter who he was.

"It was T.J.'s idea," Chase says. "But I went along with it. I threw a horrible couple of innings, but it got my foot in the door. He's right. I do owe him."

"And teaching me to drive lets you off the hook?"

He nods again. "Not just off the hook . . . but out of the house. To be honest, I'm grateful for an excuse to get away from my dad for a while. But listen, Hope, if you don't want to, that's fine. If this is, like, your and T.J.'s thing, I don't want to get in the way of that. I make it a rule never to mess up a relationship."

For a second, I don't know what he means. Then I get it. "T.J. and me? We're friends. It's not a 'relationship.' Not like you mean anyway." I laugh a little, picturing last Sunday's driving lesson, when T.J. vowed he was quitting. "I'm a terrible driver. I wouldn't be surprised if T.J. made up the whole story about helping his dad so he didn't have to go through another driving lesson with me."

"I doubt that."

"I'm just kidding, except for the part about me being a terrible driver. I don't think I've gotten any better either." I glance at his car. It's reflecting sunlight so bright I have to squint. Did he wash it overnight? "Even if I agreed to let you waste your time trying to teach me to drive, I couldn't do that to your dad's car."

"Yeah, you could," he says, dangling the keys in front of me. "I'll have you driving by midday." His smile fades. "And there's something I want to talk to you about anyway."

He heads for the car, and I follow him. "What?"

"Later," he says. "It's about the trial."

"The trial?" I can't believe he's the one bringing up Jer's trial. Good ol' T.J. His crazy plan might be paying off already. "What about the trial?"

"Not yet," he says, motioning for me to get in the other side. "I promise. Drive first, talk later."

16

When Chase and I get to the high school, we're the only car in the parking lot. T.J. and I picked this spot because there's nothing you can hit here, except a big tree a few yards to the east, and the school, of course, but it's half a football field away. Good thing. My driving performance has never been worse. Chase makes me more nervous than T.J. does, even though he doesn't scream at me.

"Give it some more gas," Chase says, watching my feet. "Gas. That's the one on your right."

"Gotcha." I press the pedal, and the car lurches forward, so I slam on the brakes with both feet.

"You really haven't driven, like, at all, have you?" he says.

"I told you I haven't."

He laughs and makes me circle the lot until I'm dizzy. Then he has me change directions and drive in more circles "to unwind."

I'm not sure how long we do this—longer than T.J. and I

usually last—but eventually I'm not horrible. I can flick on the turn signal and make the car turn, and I can stop without dashing our heads through the windshield.

"Not bad," Chase says. "Let's take a break. Pull up under that tree on the edge of the lot."

It's the one shady spot in sight. "Are you sure? I could hit the tree, you know."

"Are you kidding? I promised I'd have you driving by midday, and I never break a promise."

I remember what he said about his dad breaking promises. Apparently, promises are big deals to him. If Rita makes a promise—to quit smoking or drinking or whatever—I don't even pay attention.

When I pull up exactly where I'm supposed to, Chase gives me a thumbs-up. Then he reaches into the backseat and brings out a cooler. "I'm hungry. How about you?"

We set up on a wool blanket by the big tree. Chase hands me a peanut butter sandwich and an ice-cold bottle of root beer. It feels like a real picnic. Jer and I used to go on picnics when we lived in Oklahoma. I can't remember why we stopped.

"I love root beer." I take a deep swig from the bottle and try to think of the last time I had one.

"Told you we were alike," he says. "I even took my shower last night instead of this morning."

I laugh. "Doesn't count. It was already morning when you left my house."

"You're right."

While we eat our sandwiches, we talk about schools, his

and mine. He asks about Jeremy, and I tell him about the time we let them keep Jer in a hospital, on a mental ward, overnight. "It took Jer a month to get over it. Rita thought it would do him some good. I knew better, but I went along." I fight off the images of my brother the day we brought him home—Jeremy without his energy, sitting in a heap wherever I parked him.

Chase talks about running, the "high" he gets running hard, alone.

Before I realize it, I've eaten my whole sandwich. "I still can't believe you made sandwiches. What if I hadn't come along for the lesson?"

"I'd have eaten both sandwiches," he answers. "I needed to stay out of the house until my dad left for work. He and I can use a little distance." He wads up his napkin and wipes his mouth.

"It's my fault, isn't it? Did your dad find out you were with T.J. and me last night?"

"Don't worry about it. It's a cop thing. He doesn't like the idea of relatives of the defense fraternizing with relatives of the prosecution."

"Fraternizing?" I can't help grinning at that one. "I'm not sure I've ever fraternized before. Is this it?"

"Apparently so. Yes."

I lean against the tree and let the bark dig into my shoulders. I don't mind.

Chase pitches his trash into the cooler and leans back next to me. The tree trunk is big enough so our arms don't touch, but I feel him there. "Okay. Let's talk," he says.

I know what he means. I've been waiting for him to tell me what he said he would, *promised* he would, about the trial. "So, tell me."

"I've been doing a lot of thinking about your brother's case," he begins. A leaf falls, spinning in front of us until it brushes the grass and tumbles to a stop. He scoots around to face me. "Okay. Hear me out on this, Hope. I think we need to keep in mind that it's not up to us, to you, to prove who really murdered Coach."

Disappointment begins as a slow burn in my chest, rising up through vessels and veins. I thought Chase understood. He doesn't. Fine. I'll do it with T.J., or I'll do it myself. I wasn't counting on *his* help anyway.

As if he's reading my mind, he holds up one finger. "Hang on. I know that's what you want, to prove somebody else murdered Coach. But it can't be easy to prove murder. I mean, even if you know who did it, it's a whole different thing proving it. I don't think even you could pull that off, Hope. But here's the good part. You don't have to. All you have to do is create reasonable doubt. And people doubt just about everything. *That's* what I've been thinking."

I want to nail the person who killed Coach and let Jeremy take the blame. But I can tell Chase has done a lot of thinking about this. And I'm not stupid. I've heard of reasonable doubt. "Go on."

"Doubt," he repeats. "That's all you need. How hard can it be to get a couple of people on that jury to doubt?"

I turn "doubt" over in my head. "Doubt. Like getting them to believe somebody else *might* have killed Coach?"

"Exactly. Or even just that Jeremy might not have. You give them a reason. Then they have *reasona*ble doubt." Chase is now kneeling in front of me, almost begging me to understand. "You can make them doubt, Hope." His eyes are intense, green as mermaid tears.

My heart quivers because I think he's right. Doubt is so much easier than proof. "Okay. I'll make them doubt." I breathe deeply, taking in clean air, sunshine . . . and hope. "I just don't know where to start, Chase."

"Hey, you two!"

Across the school lawn, I see T.J. waving his arms like he's flagging down fire trucks. Automatically, I scoot farther away from Chase. He gets off his knees and sits down. My stomach lurches, and I feel guilty, which is silly because there's nothing to feel guilty about. "Hey, T.J.!" I call.

He jogs toward us. I take the trash out of Chase's cooler and walk it over to the garbage can. Then I wait for T.J. "Sorry I forgot to turn on my cell this morning," I say when he's close enough to hear.

"Not sorry enough," he answers.

"Huh?"

"It's still off. I tried to call you again." He glances over at Chase, then back to me.

"Oops. I don't deserve the title of Cell Owner." I hand him my root beer bottle, with a couple of sips left.

He downs it. "So, how was the driving lesson? I'm guessing that's what's going on. Sully, down at the site, said he saw you two here. I figured the driving show must be happening without me." He pulls out that tin laugh again.

"Yeah. I'm giving it a try," I say, sounding really stupid.

Chase gets to his feet. "Got to say you were right about Hope's driving disability."

"Says you." I snatch the keys off the picnic blanket. "Wanna see if I've improved, T.J.?" I don't know why I'm so nervous, but all I can think is that I don't want to stand here with the two of them.

"Maybe later. I've only got"—T.J. glances at his watch—"twenty minutes before I have to get back. Dad needs to finish the job by tomorrow."

"Sure. I understand." I want to offer him a sandwich, include him in the picnic. But we're out of food.

T.J. sits on the picnic blanket as if he's put it there himself. "I've been working on the suspect list."

Chase and I join him, sitting on either side. "That's great, T.J.," I say. "We were just talking about the case. I'm really glad you're here. Chase has an excellent idea about strategy. Tell him, Chase."

T.J. frowns over at Chase.

"I'm sure you've already thought of it," Chase begins. He glances at me, then gives T.J. a shortened version of "reasonable doubt."

"You're right," T.J. says when Chase is finished. "I should've thought of that myself."

"But we still have to get clues or evidence, don't we?" I ask. "We have to have something that will make the jury doubt. Or at least make them suspect somebody else did it."

T.J. sits up, straightens his glasses, and takes over. "Means, motive, and opportunity. That's what we have to work with.

130

That's what I wanted to talk to you about." He sounds so logical. I wait for him to explain. "Stay with me. Means is the bat. That's a given. Coach was killed with Jeremy's bat. But almost anybody could have used it."

"Right!" I agree. "Everybody knew he left his bat inside the barn door when he went to the barn."

"Opportunity and motive," T.J. continues. "They're a little tougher, depending on which suspect we want the jury to doubt."

"I still vote for his wife," I say. "I know we don't have any proof or anything. But you should have heard her yelling at Coach."

Chase nods.

"Okay," T.J. continues. "But we're going to need a better motive than an overheard argument, especially since you're not even sure what the argument was about."

I try to think. "Rita told me she never thought Coach and his wife were happy together."

"Still not much to go on," Chase says.

"Yeah," T.J. admits. "But if Rita knew they weren't happy, other people probably did too. We can ask around." T.J. scribbles in his notepad, a pocket-sized black one.

I feel my blood pumping through me faster. "What about opportunity? Coach's wife was supposed to be in her house, right? That's not far from the barn."

When I glance at Chase, a stray wave of his hair blows across his forehead. He doesn't brush it back. "If you could prove that Caroline Johnson can walk, it wouldn't be a stretch to believe she could walk to the barn." Chase squints at T.J. "Have you ever seen her when you've been at the barn?"

I frown at T.J. I didn't think he ever went to the barn. He's scared of horses.

T.J. pulls a weed from the ground and begins tearing it into tiny pieces. "I don't go there anymore."

"When did you ever?" I ask. "I thought you didn't like horses."

He shrugs. "I hung out there sometimes. And I like horses, sort of."

"Yeah. Right," I say. I know he doesn't like horses. If I had to guess, I'd bet he hung out at the barn to be around Coach, not horses.

"Why are you making such a big deal out of it?" T.J. asks.

"You're right. No big deal," Chase says. "I just saw you there a few times when I was on my run, so I thought I'd ask."

"Wait. You run out there?" I've pictured Chase running through the streets of Grain every morning, not out in the country.

"Every day except game day," Chase says. "You know what Coach says—said—about saving your energy for the field."

"Too bad," T.J. says. "You might have seen the killer that day."

"Don't think I haven't thought about that," Chase says.

Me too. If I'd gone to the barn with Jer that morning, or if T.J. had wandered over there, or if Chase had run past . . . "We need to focus on what we can do *now*." I get to my feet and try to think. *Means, motive, opportunity.* "You know, anybody could have been there. The jury *should* doubt. It's crazy *not* to have reasonable doubt." Brushing grass and leaves from my pants, I stare down at T.J. and Chase. "It only took a second to kill Coach. One swing of the bat, one moment where somebody lost control. *Anybody* could have done it, don't you think?"

Neither of them says anything for a minute. T.J. won't look at me. Chase looks like he's going to throw up. I wonder if we're all picturing the same thing—that one swing of the bat. "Okay, then," I say, trying to sound more confident than I feel. "Let's show the jury. Let's make them doubt. And I think we have the best shot at getting that doubt if we go with Coach's wife. If we can prove she can walk, that she's not as sick as everybody thinks she is, that would be enough for doubt, don't you think? Raymond could get the jury to have reasonable doubt with that." I spot a gum wrapper on the other side of the tree, and I dash over to get it. Then I see a crumpled beer can, and I pick that up and throw it all into the rusty trash can. The words *reasonable doubt* swirl in my head. I really think we're onto something.

When I come back to the tree, Chase is grinning. T.J. has his nose in his notebook.

"What?" I ask.

"Does she always do that?" Chase asks T.J.

"Hmm?" T.J. doesn't look up.

"What?" I ask, confused. "Do what?"

"Hope," Chase explains, "in the middle of all this, you still pick up other people's trash. And you don't even realize you're doing it."

I glance down at my hands, but I've already thrown whatever it was away.

"It's not the first time I've seen you pick up litter," he

133

continues, still grinning. "And candy wrappers, and even cigarette butts."

"Really?" I never even thought about it. "Sorry."

He shakes his head. "Don't be."

We're staring at each other, neither of us looking away.

"Man!" T.J. springs into action. "I've got to run."

"Want me to drive you?" Chase volunteers. I feel a twinge of sadness that my driving lesson must be over.

T.J. walks backward toward the school building. "No. I'm good. Hope, you working tonight?"

"Yeah!" I shout because he's halfway to the school.

"I'll stop by the Colonial if I get done in time!" T.J. pivots and takes off running.

For some reason, Chase's keys are in my hand. "How about one more time around?"

"You're on."

I'm about to shift the car into drive when I spot something white creeping along Chestnut, the street that runs beside the high school. It's a pickup truck, and it's about a block away. "Chase! There it is!" I scream.

"There *what* is?"

Then, without thinking, I slam the car into gear and hit the gas.

17

All I can think about is catching up with that white pickup truck. The car lunges forward. The truck turns the corner.

"Hope!" Chase screams. "Brake! Hit the—!"

A branch slaps the windshield. I see the pointy green edges of leaves, the crooked knots on the branch.

Thump! Scritch! There's a whine of bark on metal. Then the car shoots across the grass and rolls to a stop.

"You want to tell me what that was about?" Chase shouts.

"I can't believe I let him get away," I mutter, as out of breath as if I chased him on foot.

"Who?" Chase demands.

"The white pickup truck." I'm a little dizzy. A wave of nausea floats through me.

"What pickup truck? Where was it?"

"Didn't you see it?" I point across the lot to the empty street. "It was right there."

"But why chase it?"

I start at the beginning and tell him about the truck following him and not turning on its lights. About Rita seeing somebody watching the house from a pickup parked on our street. "I think it's the same person who's been calling the house."

He looks away, where the truck was only minutes earlier. "There are a lot of trucks around here. Are you sure—?"

"How can I be sure? That's why I wanted to follow it." I should have known he wouldn't believe me.

"Okay. Calm down. Maybe you scared him off." He runs his fingers through his hair. "You sure scared *me*."

"I'm sorry." Then I remember the thud. The scrape. "Chase, what did I do to your car?" I pop open the door and struggle to get out of the driver's seat. At first, I don't see anything. Then I take a step back. "Oh man!" On the roof of the car is a scratch at least a foot long. "Look what I did! I'll . . . I'll get it fixed. I'll buy you a new one." *With what?* I can't believe I did this to his car, to his dad's car, the sheriff's car.

Chase walks up and puts his hand on my head. "Settle down. It's okay. Really, it is."

I throw off his hand and stand on tiptoes to inspect the scratch. It's worse than I thought. The cut is wider, a crooked silver snake across the top of this beautiful blue car. "Your dad already hates me."

"No he doesn't."

"He told you not to hang out with me. He'll probably put us both in jail."

"Hey, at least we'll go down together, right?"

Warm tears press against my throat, choking off air. I'm as close to crying as I get. "This isn't funny."

Chase's lips twist in a feeble attempt to kill his grin. "Okay. It isn't funny. But it isn't tragic either. Come on. It's just the roof. And it's just paint . . . mostly." He walks over to the car. He's so tall he can reach the roof easily. His finger runs along the scrape, as if he's petting the snake. "I can fix this."

"No you can't. Can you?" A spark of hope rises, and I snuff it out. "You're just saying that."

He leans against the car. "I mean it. I've even got the right color paint."

"How—?"

"Last summer I scratched the rear door." He moves to the passenger-side back door. "Bet you never noticed this."

I follow him, but I can't see anything from where I'm standing. "Are you telling me the truth?"

"I scraped a stop sign making a turn after a party and a six-pack. I knew my dad would kill me—I already had one DUI—so I got the right paint and fixed it before he noticed. Your scratch isn't even as deep as that one was."

My heart pounds a little softer. I'm not crazy about taking driving lessons from a guy with DUIs, but still. "You're not just saying that to make me feel better?"

"We can fix it right now, before Dad has a chance to see it, if you want to. He won't be home." Chase opens the driver's door. "Only, if it's all the same to you, I'll drive."

A few minutes later, Chase pulls the car into the garage behind his dad's house. It's a small garage, with barely enough room for one car. We get out, and I look around. Shelves are loaded with paints and stains, all neatly arranged by color and size.

"Found it!" Chase hollers from the back of the garage.

"I'm not surprised. Everything is so neat and orderly in here." There's not a single tool on the ground or slung onto a bench. Hammers hang with hammers, all according to size. Shovels and rakes line one wall.

Chase pulls out brushes and rags from a wooden worktable. It's obvious he's done this before. "Sheriff Matthew Wells is big on organization."

I watch him fill the scratch and begin the paint process, but the fumes make me cough.

"Go on in," Chase says. "The back door's unlocked."

"I'm okay," I say, but I cough between the words.

"Go. The garage is really too small for paint jobs. I'll be in pretty soon. Make yourself at home. Water and soda in the fridge, all arranged alphabetically. Just kidding. Sort of."

"You sure it's okay?" I'm wheezing a little now. A doctor once told me I might have asthma, but that was before we moved to Ohio. Still, I wouldn't mind getting out of here.

"I mean it, Hope. Go!"

I feel funny letting myself in through the back door of the sheriff's house. It's a neat brick ranch, with white shutters.

Inside, it smells like evergreen. The off-white carpet is totally clean. No newspapers or magazines strewn on this couch. Not even a jacket folded over the back of a chair. The giant brick fireplace takes up one whole wall, and there's not a speck of ash to be seen. On the entry wall is a picture of the Andover baseball team. I pick out Chase right away, the cutest guy on the team.

Crossing the kitchen to find a drink, I can't get past the refrigerator magnets. Our fridge has one magnet that holds one of Jeremy's color-wheel pictures because I put it up there myself. This fridge has magnets with ball-game schedules and chore responsibilities, plus Chase's past achievements. On one side are report cards, all of them with A's or A-pluses. On the other side, blue ribbons from baseball and track events.

Would Rita have kept things like this if I'd won first prizes and gotten all A's? I remember one time in second grade—no, third grade—when a math team I was on won a prize. Our mothers got to come to our classroom and sit in the front row. Rita came. She got there late, but she was there. I'd totally forgotten about that.

I peek outside. Chase is still hovering over the car.

I shouldn't, but I'm dying to see Chase's bedroom. What posters would he have on his walls? What books? What bed-spread? Maybe he has pictures of Boston girls on his dresser.

I wander down the hall and see three doors feeding into the hallway. I pass one room, the bathroom. The next room has white walls and a big bed in the center. There's nothing on either dresser, and the shades are pulled down. This has to be Sheriff Wells's room.

I tiptoe into the only other room in sight and know instantly that it belongs to Chase. It's almost as tidy as his dad's room—bed made, clothes picked up, shades drawn even, but at half-mast, not all the way. On the nightstand is a framed picture of a beautiful woman with blond hair and

Chase's eyes, green as emeralds. His mother. Except for some loose change, the photograph is the only thing on the little table.

I glance around the room, taking in an autographed baseball in a plastic holder on his dresser, a phone charger, and a paperback book I can't make out. There aren't any posters on his walls, but there are photographs of the Cleveland Indians and a team picture of the Red Sox.

I should leave. On the way out of Chase's room, I take one more peek into his dad's. The only halfway messy thing is the built-in desk. File folders line the back of the desktop, and even those stand at attention, like books on a library shelf.

I wonder if Jeremy's case file is in there. I check the window that faces the garage and see Chase with some kind of blow-dryer thing still hard at work on the car.

I have to see Jeremy's file, if there is one. I go back to the line of folders that stretches from one edge of the pine desk to the other. I don't have time to go through all of them.

I'm willing to bet that these files are arranged alphabetically. I thumb through, and I'm right. But there's no "L." No "Jeremy Long."

Then I get another idea. The victim.

It only takes a second to find the file labeled "Johnson." Quickly, I pull out the folder and open it. There are piles of court documents, copies of arrest and search warrants, forms and petitions.

And then I see the photos, lots more crime scene photos than I saw at Raymond's house, maybe four or five times more. I wonder if Raymond has more pictures than the ones I saw.

The photo on top is the same one I saw at Raymond's—Coach Johnson, bloody and curled into a ball on the floor of the stable. Or maybe it's not exactly the same photo. I go to the next photo in the file, and it's also like the one I saw at Raymond's, only different too. More complete somehow. But I can't put my finger on it. In a dozen photos, Coach is lying in the exact same spot. Junk from his pockets mixes with the straw and sawdust—cell phone, a receipt or something wedged under one shoulder, a ticket or stub.

A door slams.

I shut the folder and cram it back with the others, hoping I have it in the right place. "I'm coming, Chase! Right out!"

I tear out of the bedroom, straightening my shirt and trying to look normal. "Sorry, I—"

I stop. It's not Chase standing there, frowning at me, looking like he'd shoot me if he had a gun handy. It's Sheriff Matthew Wells. "What do you think you're doing here?"

18

Sheriff Wells is even bigger in his own house. "I said, what are you doing here?"

I open my mouth, but only a squeak comes out. All I can think of is what Chase said about the famous Wells temper. I try again. "I . . . The back door was open."

"So you just came on in?" He takes a step toward me. "What were you looking for? Answer me!"

"Hope?" Chase appears from the kitchen. His gaze darts from me to his dad. "Dad? What are you doing home already?"

"All right, what's going on here?" Sheriff Wells turns on his son. "You tell me right now what you two are doing snooping around—!"

"Snooping around?" Chase glances over at me. I shrug. Then he smiles at his dad. "Come on, Dad. Snooping around? We were just getting something to drink." As if to prove it, he walks to the fridge and gets two bottles of spring water. Then he comes over to me and hands me one.

"This is where you come to get water?" his dad asks.

"I'm sorry." Chase frowns. "I didn't know I wasn't supposed to bring friends over to the house."

"*Friends?*" He shoots me a look that clearly states I'm no friend of his.

"Dad, please?"

I recognize something in Chase's eyes as he talks to his dad. It's the way he tries to please him, not just make peace with him like I do Rita. Chase still wants to please his father, and that makes me sad. I gave up trying to please Rita a long time ago. Maybe I'm not sure if I'm sorry for Chase still hanging on, or sorry for me having let go.

What I do know is that I don't want to make things worse for Chase. "Sheriff Wells," I begin, "this isn't Chase's fault. It's all me." Chase starts to object, but I keep going. "I wanted to find you."

"You wanted to find *me?*" He's not buying this. Not yet anyway.

I nod. "I guess I should have called, but I wasn't thinking straight." He's staring holes through me, but I press on. "Somebody's been stalking me, and I—"

"Stalking you?" Now he looks like he can't decide whether to laugh me out of the house or force me out at gunpoint.

"I know it sounds crazy," I admit. He nods in agreement. "But it's true. Somebody's been following me, watching me. And there have been phone calls too."

"Phone calls?"

"Yeah. Heavy breathing. Hang-ups. That kind of thing."

Sheriff Wells glares at his son. "What do you know about this?"

Before he can answer, I jump in. "I've told Chase most of

it. I think he got tired of me and went out to the garage for something. That's when you came in."

"What does your mother say about all this?" asks the sheriff, some of the fire drained from his eyes.

"I haven't told her everything, but she's seen the pickup."

"The pickup?"

"A white pickup truck. Rita saw it parked on our street, and I've seen it a couple of times. It's pretty scary. And I think that's why it shows up everywhere. Somebody's trying to scare me."

"Why would anybody try to scare you?" Sheriff Wells asks, like I'm lying.

I shrug. "Maybe because I'm the only one who knows my brother didn't murder Coach Johnson. The only one besides the murderer anyway."

The fire shoots back into his eyes. "Are you insane?"

"No, sir," I answer. He scares me to death, but I won't let him see it.

Sheriff Wells squints at Chase. "Did *you* see this mysterious white pickup?"

"Not exactly," Chase admits. "But I believe Hope."

His dad reaches behind his neck and twists his head, exactly the way Chase does sometimes. "Do you have any idea how many white pickups there are in this town?"

"No, sir," I answer.

"Or kids who make crank calls?"

"Dad," Chase reasons, "could you just look into it, please? Maybe one of the patrol cars could drive by Hope's house at night."

"That's a great idea," I chime in.

"You think so, do you?" Sheriff Wells says, glaring at me.

"Absolutely. And I appreciate it. Thanks." I turn to Chase. "It was a long walk over here. Would you mind giving me a ride to work?"

"Not a problem," Chase says, following me out.

I smile back at Sheriff Wells. "I'll be looking for that patrol car tonight. Thanks again."

Once we're outside, Chase whispers, "You were great in there!" He cranes his neck around so he's staring into my face. "I never saw *anyone* stand up to my dad the way you did."

"I did, didn't I?" I'm every bit as amazed as he is. I don't stand up to people.

"I wish I had it on film. Did you see his face when you told him you'd look for that patrol car tonight? You, Hope Long, are one brave lady."

We walk the rest of the way to the car without speaking. My head is filled with what Chase said. *You, Hope Long, are one brave lady.* I have never been brave, not in my entire life. Only right now, for this one instant, as the car backs out of the driveway and onto the street, I feel brave. With Chase beside me, I feel so brave that I think I could reach up and stop Rita's hand from touching Jeremy's cheek.

Chase drops me off at the Colonial, and I head back to report in to Bob. The booths along one wall are full. So are two of the eight tables. I ignore the stares as I traipse through.

Bob's pouring coffee behind the counter. Three of the four gray vinyl stools are taken.

"Hey, Hope!" he calls. "Thanks for coming in." Bob

Adams looks like a happy-go-lucky butcher instead of a restaurant owner. I can't remember if I've ever seen him without his full-length white apron. Under the apron are jeans that are too big or too small—I can never decide which. So much of the material is taken up by the front of him that the back of him gets shortchanged. When he bends over to get clean glasses, the unlucky customer behind him sees a lot more than he bargained for.

"Looks like you got some sun, Hope," Bob observes.

Maybe I did. Or maybe my face is red from embarrassment. I hate people gawking at me.

"I need you at the tables this afternoon, I'm afraid," Bob says. "Sorry. I thought Rita was coming in."

"That's okay." We're lucky to have this job. I know he would let me hide in the kitchen if he could. Rita calls in sick all the time, or just doesn't come in, and still Bob doesn't fire her.

I put on an apron and backtrack to table four. Two little boys are shooting straw papers at each other while their mothers whisper to a woman behind them. I clear my throat, and the chubby mom with short brown hair wheels around.

"Oh, I'm sorry." Her face gives it away that the whispers were about me. "Um . . . we'll just have fries. *French* fries."

"*French* fries? Not Spanish fries?" I ask, going for humor because humor translates into tips, nine times out of ten. "Or English fries?"

"No. Just French fries," she answers, without cracking a smile.

Behind me, a chair squeaks, followed by footsteps. I turn

to see a well-dressed woman in her forties. I recognize her from church, but I can't think of her name. I brace myself for whatever she's going to say.

She leans forward and gives me a hug. "How are you holding up, Hope?"

It's about the last question I expected. "Hanging in there, I guess."

"Well, good for you," she says. "I want you to know that we're praying for you and for your brother. For your mother too. Tell Jeremy we miss him, will you? Give him our love?"

"I will," I manage.

"Tell him God hasn't forgotten him," she says. "But I'm sure Jeremy knows that if anybody does."

"Thank you." I want her to hug me again. I'd hug her back this time.

Things get crazy busy for a couple of hours. After supper, the restaurant finally calms down. About an hour later, it empties out totally, and I can retreat to the kitchen. I would rather wash a thousand dishes than talk to one more human.

As if sensing what I feel, Bob walks to the front door and turns over the CLOSED sign. Then he joins me at the sink. "Tough, isn't it?" he says.

"Yep." I hand him the dish towel, and he starts drying glasses I've washed and set to air-dry.

"How's your mother doing with everything?" Bob asks this like he's twelve and has a crush on the homecoming queen.

"Rita? She's just Rita, I guess."

Bob has a dishwasher, but he doesn't like to run the extra load at night. So when there's time, we do the leftover dishes by hand. I switch to the scrub brush and start in on the plates. "Bob, how well did you know Coach Johnson?"

"John? Pretty well when we were in school. We weren't close or anything. And we didn't get any closer over the years, I guess. I'm not sure why."

"Did you go to school with him and my mother?"

"Sure did. Your mom was really something." The angles of his face soften when he says this.

"Did Mr. Johnson think Rita was really something?" I dump in more green liquid soap and run the hot water.

"We all did. John was no exception. Heck, even Matt had an eye for your mother."

"Matt? Sheriff Wells? And Rita?" I can't picture it, not now, not then. I shut off the water before the suds overflow.

"Uh-huh. She had those Wooster boys going too." Bob takes a plate from me, holding it in one hand with the edge of the towel and wiping swift circles with the other end. "You should have seen her, Hope. She was a looker, I'll tell you. And the only girl in that whole school who knew how to flirt, I suspect."

I'd love to ask him more about Rita and Sheriff, or Rita and Coach, but I don't because I'm pretty sure Bob had a crush on Rita in school. I believe he still does. I can tell by the way he always asks about her and the look in his eyes when he says her name.

We're quiet for a few plates. Then he says, "I'm pretty nervous about testifying in court." He takes another plate to dry. "You know that lawyer's calling me as a character witness, don't you?"

"Yeah. Thanks, Bob. You'll do great." But I have to admit that I just don't get Raymond's trial strategy. First, he tries to prove Jer's crazy. Then he calls witnesses to show what a good character my brother is? Raymond says he wants the jurors to like and trust Jeremy, but he still has to get in enough stories so the jury can call Jeremy insane if they need to. I guess it's all part of that "kitchen sink" defense, as in throwing in everything but the kitchen sink. I don't think I'd make a very good lawyer.

I'm not sure what I would be good at. It's not that I've never wanted to be anything. Maybe I've thought about being too many things. I wanted to be a dancer once, but you can't make a living at it. Well, at least I'm pretty sure *I* couldn't make it pay. When I was little, I wanted to be a teacher, but that was just because I liked my first-grade teacher so much. I like art. My sea glass creations are pretty good, and I'm not that bad at drawing. But the things I try to draw never look as good on paper as they do in my head. I think I'd like photography.

Bob and I start in on pots and pans.

"I hear Rita has to testify too," Bob says, pulling my thoughts back to dishwater. I hand him the broiler pan.

I start to explain about how it's my fault Rita has to take the stand, but there's a loud knock at the main door.

Bob ignores it. We closed at eight-thirty instead of nine, but Bob's used to closing when he feels like it. The knock gets louder. "They'll give up pretty soon," he says.

But they don't. They switch to the window and tap, banging with something metal, probably car keys.

"Go away!" Bob shouts. "Dang fools are going to scratch

my window." I've seen Bob's temper blow a couple of times. Once, he threw a customer out—and I mean threw him. I don't want to see that temper now.

The scratch-tapping continues.

"I'm warning you!" Bob hollers through clenched teeth. "Stop doing that right now!"

But apparently, the wannabe customer has never seen Angry Bob. Bob flings the towel down, unties his apron, and throws it to the floor. "That's it! I warned him!" He strides to the door in four giant steps.

I peek around the corner and see Bob grab the doorknob and yank the door open.

A young guy in a white shirt and black pants almost falls on his face. He scrambles to keep hold of the camera he's tucked under one arm. "I thought you were open until nine," he says. "Is that girl still here, the Long girl?"

Bob pokes the guy in the chest and keeps his finger there, drawn like a gun. "There's a CLOSED sign on that door. Can you read, Mr. Ace Reporter?"

"Easy, fella," says the reporter. "I just want to ask her some—"

"What's your name?" Bob demands.

"Why?"

"Because I'm going to sue you, your publisher, and the pony you rode in on. Now get out of here!" He shoves the man backward and slams the door so hard the glass rattles.

19

When I leave the restaurant a little before nine, I head north to walk home. A car starts up, and I turn to see Chase's Stratus parked under the streetlight a few feet away. Surprised, I wave and wait for the car to pull up alongside the curb. Tiny bugs swirl in the headlight beams.

"Not stalking you, I promise," Chase says out his window. "I drove by a couple of times and saw you in there. Thought you ought to have a ride home."

Nobody's dragged Chase here. Not this time. He's here because he wants to be. I feel my grin stretch too wide. My teeth aren't perfectly straight and white like his. "Thanks." I jog around the front of the car and happen to glance up. The sky has cleared, and the stars are so bright I can't look away.

Chase sticks his head out the window. "You okay?"

I move around to the door and get in. "Sorry. It's the stars. They're amazing tonight."

"I didn't notice." He puts the car in gear.

"You didn't notice? How could you not notice?" A picture flashes to my mind—Jeremy and me lying on our backs, trying to count the stars. "Jer and I used to spend hours picking out constellations."

"You can do that?"

"Yeah. . . . Can't you?"

He shakes his head. "We live too close to the city in Boston. I've seen a lot of stars here in the summers—don't get me wrong. I just can't pick out the shapes everybody talks about."

Nobody should go through life without knowing how to find the Bears—the Big and Little Dippers. Or Leo the Lion? Or Draco the Dragon! I snap my seat belt. "Drive," I command.

"Where to?"

"To the greatest show on earth." I direct Chase to Jeremy's and my secret stargazing spot, an Amish pasture on the edge of Grain, where lights are not allowed unless they come from the sky.

When we get there, I spread out the picnic blanket and lie down on my back. Chase sits next to me. It was so hot in the Colonial that my shirt clung to me like plastic wrap. Now a breeze rustles the grass and fans us. Bullfrogs croak from a creek I can't see but know is there, even in August droughts. A chorus of crickets gets louder, then softer, then louder, like someone's messing with the volume control. Somewhere far away, a horse whinnies, and another one answers. "Jeremy loves it here."

"I can see why," Chase says, his head tilted up to take in the sky. "The greatest show on earth."

I inhale clover and damp grass. The sky is cloudless, and the moon barely the tip of a fingernail, so the stars pop in the sky, crystals on black velvet. "Isn't it the most beautiful thing you've ever seen?"

Chase eases himself onto his back and gazes up. "It is."

"Look!" I point toward a row of trees, where lightning bugs flash on and off. "They're signaling, looking for mates."

"Seriously?"

"It's the boy who flashes first. If the girl likes him, she flashes back." I glance at his face, rich in shadows. He's grinning up at me. "What are you smiling about?" I can just imagine what I look like after a hard shift and dish duty at the Colonial.

"I don't know. I guess . . . I wish I'd gotten to know you when I first started coming to Grain. You and Jeremy. And T.J. Maybe I wouldn't have been so lonely."

"Right. You made more friends in Grain in three minutes than I have in three years."

"And all they talk about is each other, or themselves."

"Don't you and your dad talk?"

"Dad? Dad's not much of a talker. The first summer I was here, he hardly said two words to me. I'd gotten into some trouble at home, in Boston, mostly vandalism, petty stuff. Mom thought Dad could straighten me out, I guess. But he was so used to living by himself he had no idea what to say to another person in his house, especially a kid."

"And then you got baseball," I say, remembering what he told T.J. and me.

"And then we got baseball."

153

We're lying on our backs and staring up at a sky full of stars that seem close enough to touch. "Jeremy told me that a long time ago people believed stars were holes into heaven, peeks behind a black curtain."

"Peeks into heaven," Chase muses. "I like that. Jeremy told you that?"

"Wrote it," I explain. But I can tell Chase still doesn't understand. "You're wondering how the same guy who writes amazing notes and knows what people used to believe about stars can fail half of his school classes and freak out if somebody tries to take one of his empty jars from him."

Chase shrugs, but I know I'm right about what he's thinking. "It's okay," I tell him. "Jer's impossible to figure out. 'A contradiction in human terms.' That's how the Asperger's specialist described kids like Jeremy."

We're silent as the stars for a couple of minutes. Then Chase asks, "Where will you go from here, Hope?" It makes me think he's been lying here thinking about me. I'm not used to that. "Where will you go to college? What do you want to study?"

I love that Chase assumes I'm going to college. Rita assumes I'm not. But I am. I will. "Maybe photography?"

"Cool. I'd like to see some of your pictures sometime."

"I don't have a camera," I admit. "I've bought a few of those throwaways, but I don't usually get the pictures developed." That's the trick of those instant cameras. Cheap camera, expensive developing.

We talk a little about photography and college. Chase knows a lot about lighting and shutter speeds. His mother's first husband after Sheriff Wells was a Walmart photographer who took pictures of families and portraits of kids.

"What about you?" I ask, suddenly aware that our shoulders are touching. I try to focus. "Where will you go to school? I'll bet you could be anything you want." I try to imagine what that would feel like.

"Princeton. Barry pulled quite a few strings to get me in. That's where he went. I think Barry gives the school so much money they'd let his cat in if he asked."

I have no trouble picturing Chase at an Ivy League school. "What will you study?"

"No idea."

"You could always paint cars and repair scratches for a living. Maybe you could own your own car-repair garage and call it Chase Cars, or Car Chase, or—"

"Very funny." Before I see what's coming, he's rolled over and pinned me to the ground. "Why don't you laugh about it?" Without letting go of my wrists, he manages to tickle me.

I squirm and try to kick free, but he's too strong. I can't budge. Laughing, I shout, "I give! I take it back!"

For a second, Chase stops, but he doesn't get off. Our bodies are millimeters apart, his thighs trapping mine. His face, brushed with moon shadows, is suspended above mine.

Then he eases off me and stares up at the stars. I hear his breathing, heavy and strained, and my own heart beating to his rhythm.

After a minute I point to the sky. "You can see Draco the Dragon right there. I don't think I've ever seen the whole constellation so clearly—all four stars of its head and that long tail."

"Where?" Chase tilts his head closer to mine. "I can never see these things."

Hoping against hope that my hand isn't shaking and my deodorant still works, I lift my arm and point. "See the Big Dipper there? Start at the tip and follow it over to—"

He clasps my wrist and holds it for a second, then slides his fingers down the length of my arm. Currents race through every inch of skin and bone. In one movement, he rolls onto his side. I feel his leg next to mine, pressing. His other hand reaches across so that he's above me, his head touching mine. Our breath is one. His chest rises with mine. Slowly, so that I can see every move, he lowers his face. . . .

And he kisses me.

I don't close my eyes. I always thought I would, if anybody ever kissed me. But I don't. Why would I want to miss even a second of this? With my eyes open, I can see Chase's skin, a shock of his hair that falls over my forehead. I can see stars above us, shining outside like I'm shining inside.

When he stops, when *we* stop, I whisper, "I'm not sure what to say now." I can't get over the tiny shivers in my arms and the way my heart shudders. "What do people say after they kiss?"

"Haven't you kissed anyone before, Hope?" Chase winds a strand of my straight, straight hair and turns it into a blond curl around his index finger.

"Not like that."

He grins. "You could have fooled me."

"I wouldn't want to."

"You wouldn't, would you?" He touches his forehead to mine for an instant, then pulls back. "You know, every other girl I've been with pretends to be more experienced than she really is. Don't ask me why."

"I won't. But I can't imagine why anybody would pretend that."

"That's because you don't pretend. You're real, Hope. Maybe the most real person I've ever known."

I laugh a little, embarrassed. "You need to get to know my brother."

"Tell me more about him."

I gaze up at the stars, and I think of all the times Jeremy and I have stared at the sky. "Nobody sees things like Jeremy," I begin. "I'll bet he sees more sunrises than most people. But you'd think he'd never seen one before, if you sat with him during a sunrise."

Chase laughs, but I can tell he's not making fun, so I laugh a little too. "Jeremy says that every morning God says to the universe, 'Do it again!'"

Chase is quiet for a spell. He stares at the sky. "There! I can see Draco the Dragon."

"See? It was there all the time. You just never looked."

He turns his gaze on me. "Like you."

"Me?"

"I didn't want to get involved in all this. Believe me. You have no idea. T.J. asked for that ride at the courthouse. Then, before I knew what hit me, there *you* were." He kisses me softly on my forehead. "I better take you home, Hope."

The ride to my house is too short. I'm thinking that tonight might have been the best night I've ever had. Only I feel guilty thinking that because Jeremy is locked up in a cell, where not even the moon can find him. "Will you be in court tomorrow?" I ask when we turn onto my street.

"Sure," he answers, pulling over. "I'm your ride."

"Good. And I want to start finding out everything we can about Caroline Johnson. We have to come up with something, some kind of evidence to give the jury reasonable doubt. So maybe we—"

"Hope?" Chase has stopped in front of my house. He's staring up the sidewalk.

I turn to see T.J. sitting on my front step. "What's he doing there?" I mutter.

"I'm not sure, but I don't think he knows you guys are just friends. You better go."

I'm already halfway out of the car. I can't imagine why T.J. would be here at this hour.

Chase drives off. I turn to wave. He waves back. Then I walk up the sidewalk to my friend. "Hey, T.J."

"Hey." He waits until I sit on the step next to him. He takes off his glasses, then puts them on again. "I stopped by the Colonial to see if you needed a ride. You'd already left."

"Thanks. Yeah. Bob closed early. Chase was driving by."

T.J. glances at his watch, although I doubt he can see the time. It's pretty dark on our street.

I know he's wondering where we've been. "I ended up showing him where Jer and I go sometimes. Did you know he'd never seen Draco before? I don't think I could stand living in a city again." I'm talking too much. Too fast. "So, what's up?"

He shrugs. He still hasn't looked at me. "I don't know. I had an idea, about figuring out motive and opportunity, maybe proving . . . well, at least raising reasonable doubt, about the murder."

"Great! Go on. I want to hear it."

He fidgets for his notebook and takes it out. "I got the idea from a Raymond Chandler story we read in English. I want to build a model of the crime scene, exactly to scale. You know? It might help us visualize where Coach was, where the murderer was, if somebody could have sneaked up on him, or if it had to be somebody he trusted, like his wife. I'd build a model of the barn and put in stalls and everything."

The hairs on the back of my neck are standing up.

"What?" T.J. puts his notebook back into his pocket. "You think it's a dumb idea."

"No! T.J., it's a great idea! A fantastic idea."

"Yeah?"

"Only why do it with a model? Let's re-create the crime scene, but for real." I stand up, so psyched my knees are quivering. "T.J., let's go to the barn. Right now. I want to see the crime scene."

20

I take T.J.'s elbow to pull him up, but he stays planted on the step. "You want to go to the barn? Now?" he asks.

"Now's the perfect time!" I insist. "Nobody will be there. We can look around."

"For what?"

I'm starting to get irritated. "Clues, evidence, whatever."

"Hope, it's been months. They don't even keep horses there now. We're not going to discover anything the police didn't already find and take away."

Of course he's right. But something inside me is telling me that I have to go there. "Please, T.J.? I need more before I can bring Raymond in on all this. There's got to be something everybody's missing. Not a clue, maybe. But something." I make myself picture the crime scene photos I saw at Raymond's and at the sheriff's house—Coach curled on the ground, shadowed in blood. But it doesn't feel real, more like something I saw in a bad movie. "I have to see the real scene of the crime, and I need you to take me there."

T.J. stares up at me, hard. "*Me*, not Chase?"

"You." The truth is, Chase would probably say no. And even if he agreed to go, there's his dad to think about. "Just you."

A minute later we're jostling in T.J.'s dad's old Chevy on our way to the barn, my mind bouncing worse than the Chevy's worn tires. "Wouldn't it be great if we caught Mrs. Johnson running around out there when nobody's looking? We should have a camera. 'Cause if she really is faking, don't you think that would be enough for people to believe she *might* have gone to the barn that day? That she might have gotten angry enough at her husband to kill him, even if she hadn't planned on it?"

"Maybe." T.J. doesn't sound convinced.

"What do you mean *maybe*? I told you how she blew up at the park that day. She's got a temper. I'll swear to that. If she'd had a gun that morning, I think she might have used it."

"I'm not saying she doesn't have a temper. I had her in class, remember? She could be scary."

"So?" I know T.J. well enough to sense he's still holding back on making Caroline Johnson our prime suspect. I know he thinks Jer did it.

He shrugs. "I don't know. Her fingerprints weren't on the bat, for one thing. Just Jeremy's."

"So . . ." I'm thinking out loud now. "Maybe she wore gloves." Soon as I say it, something clicks in my brain. "That's it! She wore gloves."

"Okay."

"Why hasn't anybody talked about that? Maybe there

weren't any fingerprints except Jeremy's because the killer wore gloves."

"It's possible," T.J. admits. "But aren't we going for spur-of-the-moment? Like she lost her temper and struck him? So she wouldn't have had her gloves with her."

"What about Jeremy's batting gloves? Why couldn't she have grabbed those when she grabbed the bat?"

T.J. looks confused. "Did Jeremy have his gloves at the barn?"

"I don't know. Maybe."

"Jeremy carried that bat everywhere," T.J. says, glancing in the rearview, "but I don't remember him wearing his gloves that much."

Once again, I feel this slim hope slipping away from me. "Okay. So I can't swear he had the batting gloves at the barn, but I haven't seen them around the house either. And I don't remember the police taking them."

"You could be right, Hope. But we can't sound like we're guessing. Keep it simple. Logical. Otherwise, you won't even get past Jeremy's lawyer. Like you said, he's the first one we have to convince." He takes a deep breath and lets it out. "Okay. How about this? Caroline Johnson may have murdered her husband. She's not as sick as she lets on. She has a bad temper. She would have used Jeremy's bat. She would have worn gloves—we don't say which gloves because we don't have to. That should be enough to plant doubt in the jury's mind." He turns to me. "So maybe we don't need to see the crime scene?"

I don't answer.

"Hope, do you have to put yourself through this?"

Do I? Do I really want to see where Coach was murdered? I know how my mind works. My brain will soak in dozens of images I'll never be able to erase. Part of me wants to tell T.J. to turn around. What could we get out of the crime scene so long after the crime anyway?

But another part of me knows I have to go there. Nothing will make sense until I do. "I have to see it for myself, T.J."

He shakes his head and keeps driving. We stop before we reach the barn. He pulls the car off the gravel road, but keeps the engine running. We're about half a mile from the barn and house. "This isn't a good idea, Hope. It's too dangerous."

"Nobody's there, remember?"

"What about Caroline Johnson? If you're right and she did murder her husband, she's not going to want us snooping around."

"She's not going to know. But you don't have to come. I mean it." I unbuckle my seat belt. I don't need a partner. I don't need anybody. It's Jeremy and me, the way it's always been, and that's fine with me. "Thanks for driving me out here. I'll just walk home when I'm done."

I get out of the car and start walking toward the barn.

Behind me, I hear the engine shut off and a car door open and close. Then T.J. calls up, "Will you wait until I get the flashlights?"

Purple clouds race across the sky now, making shadows dance on the path. We walk past an Amish pasture, where hay is stacked in crisscrossed bundles, lined in straight rows like nature's soldiers ready to attack. The only sound is the *crunch, crunch* of gravel under our feet.

When the path dips, we run straight into a cloud of tiny bugs. As if they've been waiting all night for us, they swarm, landing on our heads, arms, and legs. I swat wildly at them, smashing a few on my arms, brushing them off my face.

T.J. grabs my hand and takes off. "Run!"

I run. I'm an arm's length behind him, trying to catch up. His grip is tight. The bug cloud thins and finally drifts away behind us.

We slow down. I take my hand back and stop to catch my breath. My side aches.

"Are you okay?" T.J. asks, circling back for me.

"What *was* that back there?" My voice comes in spurts.

"Bugs. I've seen them like that a couple of times out here in the mornings. Once I saw Chase running like he was on fire, with a cloud of those things after him. There's a bog down that hill, where the bugs hang out. They're the same kind of bugs that helped the Cleveland Indians beat the Yankees in a play-off game a few years ago. It was all over the news."

"They're wicked."

He brushes my hair with his hand. I don't want to think that he's brushing out bugs. If I were going to give up this crime scene trip and go home to bed, this would be the moment to do it.

We start walking again. "So why *do* you come by the barn?" I don't think he ever answered that. "Or why did you?"

"I wanted to get used to horses. I don't like being afraid of

164

things." He pauses a minute. "And I guess I used to like to talk to Coach."

It's what I thought. "Chase mentioned something about you and Coach having problems, something about your mom and the cookies?"

"It wasn't a big deal," he says, but it comes out too quickly. "It was mostly the guys. But Coach shouldn't have laughed. They took their cue from him. Anyway, it's over. Forget it."

We're at the last stand of sheltering trees. The barn is out in the open about a hundred feet away, with the house another hundred feet beyond that.

"Let's do it," I whisper.

We run, crouched like we're dodging bullets. When we reach the entrance to the barn, we both just stand there, looking in.

T.J. breaks the spell. "Last chance to turn back."

I stare into the barn, toward the stalls, the place where they found Coach's body. There's no crime scene tape anywhere, no chalk-line drawing of the body. "I'm sorry, T.J. You don't have to come in. Really. But I do. I have to try to understand. I have to do that much for Jeremy."

"All right. But we better get going before the sun comes up. There's a light on in the Johnson house. For all we know, that woman could be calling the police right now."

I glance behind us toward the house. He's right. I see the light through the window. But I can't worry about that now. I take a few steps into the barn. My eyes adjust to the dark, and I point to a spot just inside the door where a stall forms a right angle with the wall. "That's where Jeremy put his bat when he came to the barn. If he'd brought his gloves, he would have dropped those there too."

"Keep going."

I stare at the exact spot where Jeremy would have left his bat. "He parked his bat there because it scared the horses. Then he'd get down to business and haul manure or groom the horses. He loved it here." I'm picturing everything in my mind as I talk. "He even loved cleaning out the stalls. Coach taught him how to brush the horses, and Jer was really good with them." I smile over at T.J. and can tell he's listening. "Coach paid him a salary. Jeremy was so proud of that, even though Rita got all the checks."

I take a few steps deeper inside the barn and inhale the scents of sawdust, manure, and horse. The smells are strong, even after so much time, but mold and must are mixed in with them. "Did you know Coach taught Jeremy how to ride?"

T.J. nods.

"He learned fast too." I can almost see Jeremy riding Sugar, Mrs. McCray's old pinto, bareback. Jeremy's mouth is open, probably catching all kinds of bugs. His green backpack of empty jars bounces on his back. It was a miracle none of his jars ever broke that way.

I feel myself getting choked up. I have to stop it. This isn't why I came here.

We move toward the last stall, the one Coach was found lying outside of. The whole barn feels eerie, as if ghost horses have taken the place of the former boarders.

"Whose horse was in that stall the morning . . . ?" T.J.'s voice fades.

"Lancer, Mrs. McCray's show horse. She boarded two horses here—Sugar, the old pinto Jeremy rode, and Lancer, a bay gelding she rode for dressage."

We're standing in front of the stall. For all I know, my feet are in the exact place where Coach was lying. I should have come sooner, when things were fresh, when I might have seen something. I turn on my flashlight and shine it on the floor.

"What are you looking for, Hope?"

I point the beam of light on the sawdust. There are feces now—mice, rats. I can almost hear the squeals of frightened horses, the thump of the bat, Coach's cry.

"Hope, are you okay?" T.J. grabs me by the shoulders. "You look like you're going to faint."

"I'm okay," I whisper. I try to focus on Jeremy again. "Jeremy would have been so excited—that's why he got up early that morning. He put on his Panther uniform, like he did every game day, and wore it to the barn, even though he knew he'd be mucking out stalls. He'd have his backpack of jars too."

"You need to hurry, Hope." T.J. glances over his shoulder.

"I know. But I have to think it through, the whole thing. Because I can feel it. I'm missing something." I turn back and stare at the sawdust beneath my feet. I can see the shadow of blood there, but I know it's in my head. "Jeremy would have looked around for Coach. They said he rode Sugar that morning. Maybe when he didn't see Coach, he decided to go for a ride." I look over at T.J. "That makes sense, doesn't it?"

He shifts his weight from one foot to the other.

I keep going. "Normally, Jer would never ride before he

finished chores. I guess he might have wanted to ride so bad that he went ahead. Coach wouldn't have minded." This part of my story is shaky, and I know it. Why would he ride that morning, on a game day? Why would he ride without doing his chores? "Maybe Coach told Jeremy to go riding, and he'd clean the stalls himself."

"Okay. Move on, Hope," T.J. urges.

"And that's when Caroline saw her opening," I continue, visualizing her hobbling to the stable. "Opportunity. Means. She sees Jeremy take off on Sugar, and that is her cue. So she comes to the barn, brings her own gloves or puts on Jeremy's, picks up the bat, and—"

"Can we go now, Hope? Please?"

But the images are running through my mind. "She hits him. She hits him with the bat. His knees buckle, and he goes down."

"Stop it, Hope."

But I can't stop. Because I can see it. I can see Coach. The blood. Stuff flying from his pockets. The life going out of him.

"Please—!" T.J. begs, shaking me by the shoulders. I barely feel it.

"She drops the bat. Maybe she's horrified at what she did. One instant. That's all it took. And everything changed. She gets back to her house and climbs in bed, pulling the covers over her head, and shutting her eyes to block out what she's done. Jeremy finishes his ride and returns to the barn. He looks for Coach, because he doesn't speak so he can't call for him. When he sees his boss, his coach, his friend, lying in a pool of blood, Jeremy runs to him. He cradles him and rocks him. But Jeremy knows he's dead. Maybe he knows he'll be blamed. Maybe not. Maybe he's so shocked he picks up the bat and holds on to it until he gets home. Or maybe he sees the killer and, scared to death, runs for home. But that's when he bumps into Sarah McCray." I can picture all of these things as if they're in my memory instead of my imagination.

Only why now? This is the question that pounds in my head. "Why would Caroline Johnson choose that morning to kill her husband? What happened? Did she find out something about him? Did they argue? What about? If we knew that—"

T.J. takes hold of my hand. "Hope," he whispers, "you have to stop this." He leads me away, up the stallway. I let him. But I can't get the crime scene photos out of my head.

I spin around to face him. "What did Coach have on him?"

He frowns. "I—I don't know."

"But you heard some of the testimony. Things fell out of his pockets. What? What was lying on the ground beside him? Surely they showed that stuff in court. It's evidence, right?"

He scratches his head. "A cell phone, I think. Keys maybe? A stub of something, like a ticket maybe?"

"A ticket to what?"

"How should I know? What are you getting at, Hope?"

"I don't know, not yet. Just tell me. What else?"

"Gum? Or gum wrappers? What does it matter?"

I can't answer that, but I know it matters. I just know it. I want Raymond's picture side by side with the ones I saw at Sheriff Wells's. Something was in one of those photos that wasn't in the other ones. But what? What was it and where did it go?

"Come on," T.J. says. "We're getting out of here."

"Not until I find what I'm looking for."

"What are you looking for?"

"I don't know. But I'm not leaving here until I find it." Near the door, where T.J. has practically dragged me, there's a little room with a glass window. I was in there once when I was looking for Jeremy. "That's Coach's office, isn't it?"

"I hope you're not thinking what I think you're thinking."

"T.J., we have to search that office."

21

"I can't believe we're doing this," T.J. mutters for the thirteenth time as he watches me try to work the lock to Coach's office. "We are so getting out of here after this."

"Fine. I want to leave as much as you do."

"I doubt it."

I don't have a bobby pin or a credit card, like people use to open locks in movies, but I have a horseshoe nail I found on the stable floor. It's flat and thin enough to poke into the lock and twist. Finally, the lock clicks. "I did it!" The knob turns, and I'm in.

"Great," T.J. says. "Now what?"

"Now we search."

"Search for what?"

"Clues," I answer, stepping inside. "A divorce letter or a journal would be great. Maybe some hate notes from his wife. I don't know." The police must have searched Coach's office, but it doesn't look ransacked. I'm guessing Sheriff Wells didn't waste his time looking into anything or anybody, except Jeremy. The only two pieces of furniture in the room, besides several chairs, are a big desk and a tall metal filing cabinet. "You take the files, and I'll take the desk. Deal?"

"Are you sure we shouldn't be wearing gloves?" T.J. asks, stepping over a pile of trash on the floor. "What about our fingerprints?"

"Nobody cares about our fingerprints. They're done with this office."

T.J. mumbles something, but I can't make it out.

Coach's desk looks like it hasn't been touched in months. Even the papers on it are dusty. Mouse droppings form a trail across the glass-slab surface of the desk. There's a framed photograph of Coach and his wife on their wedding day. I pick it up and dust it off. "They don't look that happy to me," I observe. "And it's their wedding day."

"I'll bet she was hard to live with," T.J. mutters.

"How come?"

"You didn't have her for English. Trust me. She was hard to take for fifty minutes a day. I can't imagine having her twenty-four/seven."

I shine the light on the faces in the wedding picture. Their expressions are relaxed rather than excited. "Comfortable. That's what I'd call them. Not in love, but comfortable."

I set down the photograph. Just above the desk are two pieces of paper pinned to the wall. Color wheels. Right away, I know they're Jeremy's. I would have sworn on a stack of Bibles that nobody except Rita and me ever got one of Jer's drawings. He must have liked Coach a lot. This extra loss for

Jeremy makes my throat burn—as if my brother hadn't already lost enough.

The file cabinet rattles. "Man, look at this!" T.J. calls.

"What?" I start to go over and see.

"This whole drawer is filled with baseball trophies."

I return to the desk. In the middle drawer, I find a photograph of Jeremy sitting on Sugar and another one of Jer grinning in his Panther uniform. It might have been taken the first day Coach let him suit up. Coach must have taken it himself. Looking at it makes me sad. I put it back.

"Find something?" T.J. asks.

"Nothing."

Under the photos, there's a pile of long, skinny strips of paper, like you'd use to write a grocery list. I pick them up and see they're all printed with numbers from one to ten, with a blank after each number. I know they're team rosters because Jeremy brought some home. I hold one of the rosters and imagine how excited Jer would have been to see his name written on there. Guys and their sports.

I open the bigger drawer on the right. There's only one thing in it, a framed letter. I take it out and shine the flashlight on it. "T.J., you've got to see this." It's typed on New York Yankees stationery, and it's addressed to John S. Johnson. "Is this what I think it is?"

T.J.'s already reading over my shoulder. "Wow! That's the real deal, Hope. They were asking him to play for the Yankees. Coach never said a word about this, not to me anyway— not that that's saying much. He might have told Chase and the others."

"I can't believe he didn't talk about it all the time." I put the letter back and close the drawer.

"Some of the guys used to ask him about when he played ball, but he'd say, 'The past is in the past. And any man who has to live in his isn't doing what he ought to in the present.'" He does a lousy imitation of Coach's voice.

"I don't know," I say, thinking out loud. "It might be kind of nice to have a past you'd want to live in again."

In the bottom desk drawer, I find a stack of old high school yearbooks. I bring them out and stick the flashlight between my teeth so I can thumb through. I flip pages and pages of kids who look too old to be in high school.

I'm leafing through the last yearbook when I see a picture of Rita in a cheerleading uniform. She's trim, at least thirty pounds thinner than now, with the same giant boobs. No wonder every guy in the tricounty area had a thing for her. There's some writing on the bottom of the picture. I take the flashlight and get a better look. It says: "To my Jay Jay—Hugs and kisses . . . and so much more! Love, Rita."

I close the book and put it back where I found it. Rita was a tease. A flirt—that's what Bob said. She probably wrote that in every panting guy's yearbook.

I know we have to leave. T.J.'s on the last drawer of the file cabinet. But I haven't checked the piles on top of the desk. I shine the flashlight around. Coach had sticky notes to remind him to do everything: "Turn off lights." "Buy feed." "Call Max." But none of the notes sound threatening or suspicious.

There's a small pile of rosters to one side of the desk. I

shine the flashlight in that direction. These rosters are filled in, held together by a rubber band. I fan through them. They're dated, and they seem to be in order too. The top one is for June eleventh, the day Coach was murdered. My stomach knots, and I take a few short breaths. It almost feels like I shouldn't be holding this—was it one of the last things Coach touched?—but I can't help myself.

I move the light down the row of names. They're all familiar now, part of my suspect list. Only the top name is crossed out. I hold the roster closer, shining my flashlight directly on it. "Chase Wells" is crossed out, and "T. J. Bowers" is penned in. I check the date again. It's definitely the right day, the right game, Wooster versus Grain at home.

"T.J.?"

"Hmmm?"

"Didn't you say Chase was going to be the starting pitcher for that Wooster game?"

"Yeah. Why?"

"Look at this." I show him the roster with his name written in as starter. "What does it mean?"

"I don't know. Maybe Coach came to his senses?" He laughs a little, but it's a fake laugh. "It's weird, though. I wonder when he did it." He stares at the roster, at his scribbled name, as if it's a code he's trying to decipher. "I admit I was pretty surprised when Coach said he was going to start Chase. He's good—I don't mean that. He may even be a better pitcher than I am. But he can't bat worth a hoot. Dad said he thought Chase's dad had something to do with Chase getting to start that game."

"Really? I thought Sheriff Wells and Coach didn't like each other." I remember what Chase said about Coach not appreciating the sheriff's after-game criticism.

"You got that right. Manny—you know him, center fielder for the Panthers—he said he heard Coach and the sheriff really getting into it after practice. Maybe Sheriff Wells won the argument, but Coach changed his mind later? Who knows?" He turns away. "It doesn't matter anymore anyway. Can we get out of here now?"

"Not yet, T.J." I start to take the roster with me so I can show Chase. But I change my mind. What good would it do for him to know that Coach didn't choose him after all? It sure wouldn't help for Chase's dad to know. At least now his dad gets to think Chase was going to pitch.

"Hope, maybe there's something here." T.J. is still at the files.

I tuck the roster at the bottom of the stack. Then I join T.J. at the file cabinet. "What did you find?"

"Loan applications. Some went through. Some got denied. There are a bunch of unpaid medical bills here too. Maybe Coach really did have money troubles."

"Maybe his wife did."

I stare at the papers in T.J.'s hands. He pulls out another file full of forms.

"T.J., we have to take these with us. I want Raymond to see them."

"You can't just take them," T.J. protests. "That's theft. Besides, they can't be evidence unless the police find them. Tell Raymond they're here and let him worry about it." He shines his flashlight on his watch. "*Now* can we go?"

"All right. Just let me finish with the desk. One drawer left."

"Hope," he whines.

I pull at the tiny drawer on the left side of the desk, but it's stuck.

"Hope?"

"One minute." I yank hard, and it comes out. The whole drawer is filled with canceled checks. I look through them. Everything seems pretty normal—electric, gas, groceries, feed store—until I see four checks, dated December, January, February, and March, each for a thousand dollars . . . and all made out to Rita Long.

22

"T.J., why would Coach Johnson pay out that kind of money to Rita?" We're walking away from the barn so fast that I'm straining to catch my breath. Our footsteps and my heavy breathing sound out of place in the stillness around us.

T.J. sticks out his arm like a school-patrol fifth grader and stops me cold. "Wait," he whispers, looking both ways before letting us cross the open barnyard. "Okay. Now!"

We tiptoe-trot, zigzagging like we're dodging gunfire again. When we slow down, camouflaged by the tree-branch shadows, I ask him again. "Tell me! Why would Coach give Rita so much money?"

"I don't know, Hope. You said Jeremy was a great stable hand."

"Not *that* great! Nobody's that great." A dozen possible reasons for those checks fly through my head, none of them good. Was Rita having an affair with Coach Johnson? Her Jay Jay? She'd been staying out all night. Even the night before Coach's murder, Rita hadn't come home until after dawn.

T.J. takes my hand: "Don't turn around, but we're being watched."

Immediately, I imagine that white pickup truck. I glance over my shoulder, expecting to see it, but I don't see anything.

"I said, don't look." His grip tightens. It hurts a little, but I'm too scared to care.

"Is it the stalker?" I whisper, making my eyes focus straight ahead.

"It's Caroline Johnson," he whispers back. "We should have gotten out of there before she spotted us."

I whirl around before he can stop me. In a lighted window of the old farmhouse, I make out the shadow of a woman in a dress, or maybe a nightgown. "She's standing up! T.J., did you see—?"

He yanks me back around, jerks me up beside him, and keeps me there, one arm around my waist. He's about ten times stronger than he looks. "Don't let her see your face."

I fall into step and do what T.J. says, but I know it's too late. She's seen us, and she's seen us seeing her. She knows that we know. Everybody else believes poor Mrs. Johnson is bedridden, that she needs help getting in and out of her wheelchair. But we've seen her. "She can walk. Coach's wife could have walked to the barn, T.J. She could have murdered her husband."

"Yeah, but who's going to believe we saw her?" he says, speeding up. His dad's car is in sight now. "And who are we going to tell?"

"We can tell Chase. And he can tell his dad."

"I can see that," T.J. says, his voice filled with a sarcasm I didn't know he had. "'Dad, when Hope and T.J. were breaking

179

into Coach's office after ransacking the crime scene, they happened to see Caroline Johnson standing on her own two feet. So that proves she murdered her husband, right?' I'm sure the sheriff will run straight over and arrest her—after patting *us* on the back for breaking and entering."

I hate sarcasm. But I have to agree we'd be in a lot more trouble than Caroline Johnson if we told what we saw. And she knows it.

We reach the car and get in fast. T.J. starts the engine, then turns to me. "We'll figure something out." He backs up and wheels the car around without turning on the headlights. "Hope, what if Caroline knew about the money Coach was giving Rita?"

My brain hasn't even gotten that far. "Do you think she did? Of course she did. She had to know, didn't she? I mean, with him not making all that much money, and her not making any, and a thousand dollars going out each month? You can't hide a thing like that. She would have known."

"Uh-huh. And that would give her motive. I don't know if she knew about her husband and Rita, or the money, but it's got to be good enough for reasonable doubt." The car hits a rut, and I remember to fasten my seat belt. T.J. still hasn't turned on his headlights. I know he's trying to get out without anybody seeing us.

"Plus," I say, gripping the dash, "we've got those rejected loans. They give her a motive for killing her husband—money."

"And the canceled checks," T.J. adds. "All great stuff for giving her motive."

"Motive, which is something Jeremy never had. Raymond has to get Caroline back on the stand and ask her about the money. Just asking her about it should give the jury reasonable doubt."

T.J. is quiet for a minute. Then he glances over at me. "Only . . . only that means everybody will know about the money he paid to Rita. They'll say things about Coach and Rita, whether they're true or not, Hope."

"Do you think I care if the world discovers Rita and Coach were having an affair, or worse? The only thing I care about is getting my brother out of jail."

T.J. still hasn't turned on the headlights. He quits talking and keeps taking peeks in the rearview mirror. I turn around and stare out the back window. Far behind us, about the length of a football field, I see two headlights, white eyes watching us through the darkness.

"T.J.!" Panic rises like bile in my throat.

"I know." He touches my knee, then puts his hand back on the steering wheel. I don't understand how he's staying on this road without headlights. He must really be familiar with this part of Grain. The road winds one way, then the other, with no warning. He takes a turn, and for an instant there are no lights behind us. Then they pop up again. "Who'd be following us this time of night? If Mrs. Johnson called the police, they'd just arrest us and get it over with."

"It's the white pickup truck," I mutter. When he frowns at me, I explain as fast as I can.

"Why didn't you tell me somebody was following you?"

Because I told Chase. "I should have. What can we do now?"

181

He rolls down his window. A rush of humid air floods the car, bringing in clover and dust and a faint scent of skunk. "I'm pretty sure there's a path up on the left," he shouts above the wind. "I think we can lose him if I can find— There it is!"

He brakes, and we swerve left. Weeds slap the sides of the car. There's a blur of fence, barbed wire. The car skids at a ditch and stops.

I look behind us in time to see a pickup speed by our turnoff. "He's gone. You did it! You lost him."

T.J. leans his forehead on the steering wheel. "I think I'm turning in my license." He looks over at me. "Was it the pickup?"

"You didn't see it?" My heart is clawing to get out of my chest. "It was definitely a pickup. I couldn't tell the color, but it had to be the same one. Why would anybody do that?"

In almost a whisper, he says what I've already figured out. "Because somebody doesn't want us investigating Coach's murder."

Rita's car is gone when T.J. pulls up in front of my house. He insists on walking me to the door and checking inside before he leaves. We're both so tired we can barely stand up. "See you in court," he says, glancing at his watch. "In a couple of hours." He starts down the sidewalk but turns back, hands in his pockets. "My dad needs the car again today. I asked Chase to give us a ride to court."

"Okay." I try to pretend like it doesn't matter one way or the other. Then I race inside, and the first thing I do is text Chase. I can't text everything I want to, but I get in the general outline of the night, knowing he won't get the message for a couple of hours anyway.

Two minutes later, my cell rings. "Chase?"

"Hope, what did you do? Tell me I didn't read your text right."

I tell him about the loans, the checks, seeing Coach's wife standing up, and about the white pickup truck. When I stop, he doesn't say anything. "Chase? Don't be mad. I had to do it. I needed to see the crime scene for myself."

The silence is too long. Finally, he says, "I thought . . . I was going to tell you I couldn't help you, that we shouldn't see each other anymore."

Something burns a hole in my chest. I don't want it to matter. I don't want *him* to matter.

"But I can't," he says.

"Can't see me anymore?" I ask.

"Can't stop seeing you."

Neither of us says anything, and I picture our breaths traveling from cell tower to cell tower and back.

"Start over, Hope. At the beginning. Tell me everything."

I do. I go into more detail this time.

When I'm done, he says, "Those checks? Hope, what do you think they mean?"

That's what it comes back to—the checks made out to Rita. "I don't know," I tell him. "But as soon as Rita steps in the door, you can bet I'm going to find out."

23

An hour later, Rita still hasn't come home. I pace the living room, trying to come up with an explanation for those thousand-dollar checks. If Rita did have an affair with Coach, who's she seeing now? I never ask. I never want to know.

I have to do something, so I search Jeremy's room for his batting gloves. Then I check Rita's room for her old high school yearbooks.

Zilch. Nothing.

After another restless hour, I stretch out on the couch to see if I can catch a few minutes' sleep. But when I shut my eyes, I see Caroline Johnson standing at the window, watching. Or I see Coach Johnson curled up on the barn floor.

A few minutes before six, I can't wait a second longer. I have to call Raymond and tell him about the new evidence.

The phone rings and rings until the answering machine picks up. While I'm waiting for the beep, I try to figure out how to word what I want to say.

But before I can leave my message, Raymond answers. "Hello?"

"Raymond?" The machine finishes telling me to leave a message, then squawks out a beep. "Raymond, I'm sorry if I woke you up."

"Hope?"

"Yeah. Listen, I have to tell you some stuff, but I don't want to tell you how I got the information."

"Just a minute." He sounds like he's underwater. I hear the receiver clunk. A minute later Raymond is back. "This better be good, Hope."

I fill him in as much as I can without telling him about breaking and entering the crime scene and Coach's office.

"Wait now," he says. "How did you . . . ? No. Never mind." His sigh carries over the phone wires. "What does your mother say about the checks?"

"I haven't asked her yet." I don't add that I haven't had a chance to ask because she's stayed out all night.

"Well, it might not matter."

"Are you kidding?" I shout. "Raymond, how could that not matter? Don't tell me I broke into Coach's office for nothing!"

"I didn't hear that," Raymond says, not shocked or surprised, like he's already figured out that much. "I don't know about the checks, Hope. But the other things, the loan apps and the bills, nobody's said anything about Coach's finances. Where there's debt, there's motive. How many loan refusals were there?"

"I'm not sure. Three or four, at least. T.J. could tell you."

"T.J.?"

Rats! I shouldn't have brought him into it. Such a long silence follows that I'm not sure if Raymond is still on the line. "Raymond?"

"Hmmm? Sorry. I'm thinking. . . ." More silence. "Okay. I'll level with you, Hope. Your testimony didn't help our insanity plea any."

"I'm sorry, Raymond." I get a flashback of that second in court when I realized I'd walked right into the prosecution's trap. Keller looked at me like I'd single-handedly won him his ticket to Washington, D.C., and bigger fish to fry. I can see his nose hair in his left nostril, the bead of sweat on his curled upper lip.

"It's not just your testimony," Raymond continues. "My *expert* witness didn't do much for us either. Insanity is a hard sell around here. People are too practical."

"Too insane, if you ask me."

"Could be," he admits.

"So what do we do?"

"I think I'm starting to agree with you, to tell the truth," Raymond says.

"Really?" I'm not sure what I expected. Maybe that this was going to be a much harder sell to Raymond. "That's great!"

Raymond keeps going, and I think he's talking to himself more than to me. But I don't mind. "We need to begin creating doubt, give the jury a few reasons to find Jeremy not guilty." He sighs. "Thank God for the double plea—not guilty by reason of insanity, and not guilty."

Maybe Raymond is right. Maybe that really is something

to thank God for. I haven't done much thanking lately. I have a feeling that even in jail, Jeremy isn't forgetting to thank God. I can almost hear him: God, *thanks for these bars that make cool shadows. And thanks for my roommate, Bubba, and the pretty tattoos on his arms . . . and legs, and shoulders, and head.*

"Hope, did you hear me?"

"What?"

"I said, I'm going to issue a subpoena to have Caroline Johnson testify in person. If there's an objection, the judge will have to rule. We could establish motive. And that's more than Keller has done with Jeremy. They haven't even suggested a motive."

"Yes! Raymond, would it help if you had two people who've seen Mrs. Johnson standing on her own and staring out her window?"

"Not if those circumstances would put the two people in prison for breaking and entering."

"Got it. It will be so great to watch her squirm on the witness stand, though." Sometime during our conversation, the phone cord got wrapped around my arm. I work on unwrapping it now. "Don't forget to ask her if she can get out of the wheelchair on her own. And ask about money. And the loans. And those canceled checks to Rita."

"Easy, Hope," he interrupts. "I don't even know if the court will allow this. And if they do, we could be too late. Trial is winding down, whether we want it to or not. My witness list isn't that long."

"What about Rita? What about her testimony? Are you still going to make her tell all those stories about Jeremy, the

187

ones that make him sound crazy?" I hate those stories. Rita tells them to strangers in bars and grocery stores: about the winter Jeremy wandered off without his shoes or coat and ended up with frostbite; about the time he walked up to the screen at the movie theater and punched a hole in it; or the day he grabbed a kid in his stroller and ran and ran until the police stopped him—Jeremy had seen the mother hit the little boy, slap him on the cheek.

"I'll put Rita on hold and see if we still need her," Raymond says.

"Great!" I'm glad Rita's not testifying.

"There are a lot of variables here, Hope. I might not get permission to bring in Mrs. Johnson. And if I do put her on the stand, she may not be a good witness for us."

"I know. Chase told me she's not a big fan of my brother."

"Chase? Chase Wells?"

"Y-yeah." I shouldn't have brought him into it either.

"Well, it's true. Mrs. Johnson did some damage," Raymond admits.

"Why would she say she was scared of Jeremy? People ignore my brother. They don't understand him. They're uneasy around him. But they're not afraid of him."

"Maybe she's not scared of him," Raymond says. "Maybe she just wants the jury to be scared of him."

All right, Raymond! It's the first time I've felt that Raymond believes Jer might be innocent. "You have to get the jury to see through that woman," I tell him. I think about her dark figure watching T.J. and me leave the barn. "Um . . . you know those two people who saw her standing at her window?"

"I do. I know one of them rather well." Raymond's voice has a little smile to it.

"Well, they saw her tonight. . . . And I'm pretty sure she saw them too."

"Hope!"

"Plus, if Mrs. Johnson owns a white pickup truck, or knows somebody who has one, it would explain a lot of things."

"Do I want to know about this pickup truck?" Raymond asks.

Whether he wants to know or not, I tell him. And I tell him about the phone calls.

"I don't like this," Raymond says. I've been so afraid he wouldn't believe me. Instead, I'm pretty sure he sounds . . . worried. "Have you told anybody about this?"

"I told Sheriff Wells, and he said he'd drive by the house at night, even though I know he didn't take me seriously."

"You need to call him, or dial 911, if anything like that happens again. I mean it, Hope. Or call me."

I like having Raymond worry about me. A giant yawn comes up from nowhere, making me exhale into the phone.

"See if you can get some sleep," Raymond says. "I need to get going on that petition to the court."

"Good luck, Raymond." I yawn again.

Before I can hang up, Raymond shouts, "Hope! You be careful, okay?"

In spite of everything, I feel myself smile. "Thanks, Raymond."

24

"The defense would like to call Andrew Petersen."

"Andrew Petersen!"

Chase, T.J., and I are in the back row of the courtroom. Raymond said it's ok for me to be here now that I've testified, as long as the prosecutor doesn't object, which he hasn't yet, and which is why I'm lying low. On the drive over here, I sat in the front with Chase, leaving nowhere for T.J. except the backseat. Since T.J. didn't say more than two words to either one of us the whole drive, I figure he doesn't like riding in the backseat by himself. But I don't have the energy to make sure everybody's happy. I have to focus on the trial.

The problem is, I don't understand how trials work because I slept through most of eighth-grade civics and government classes. Leaning toward Chase, I whisper, "Who's Petersen and why is Raymond making him testify?"

"Petersen testified for the prosecution and claimed he saw Jeremy twice that morning—once galloping through the fields on that spotted horse."

"Sugar."

"Right," T.J. throws in. "I was here for that part of the prosecution's case too."

I watch Petersen stroll across the courtroom. He's tall, balding, and maybe fifty or sixty years old, wearing glasses and a black suit with a red tie. "So why would Raymond want him testifying again?"

T.J. and Chase exchange weird looks. Then Chase whispers, "Petersen claims he saw Jeremy carrying a bat and running away from the barn."

I look over at Jeremy. He's sitting up straight, his gaze on the judge.

I make myself listen to every word of the testimony as Raymond leads Mr. Petersen through the events of his morning, including what he ate for breakfast—instant oatmeal, wheat toast with fake butter, OJ, and coffee. He tells us where he found his morning paper—in the bushes—how loud the neighbors' dogs are, and when he saw Jeremy. He's a horrible storyteller, wasting time trying to recall details nobody on earth could care about.

"I've called that newspaper office to complain," he drones, "seven times. Or was it eight? I remember the sixth time clearly because it was after the Fourth of July and those kids down the street were still shooting off their firecrackers. Then I found my newspaper on the roof, saw it right up there when—"

Finally, Raymond retakes control and interrupts the winding, windy trail of Mr. Petersen's thoughts. "Mr. Petersen, how do you know Jeremy Long, the defendant?"

"Everybody knows the Batter," he answers. That's the horrible name the *Cleveland Plain Dealer* gave to Coach Johnson's murderer. CNN picked it up.

Raymond moves closer to the jury. "I meant *before* everybody became familiar with the defendant. When did you first come to know Jeremy?"

Petersen's face wrinkles, and he looks like he's pouting or about to cry. "I don't understand."

"Let me clarify," Raymond says, smiling. But I'm thinking Raymond may be a better lawyer than he looks. "When did you and the defendant first meet?"

Petersen frowns. "I . . . I never met him."

"No?" Raymond looks surprised. "But you'd seen him around? You knew what he looked like? Before the murder?"

"No," Mr. Petersen admits.

Raymond looks puzzled and turns to the jury for his next question. "Then how did you know that the boy you saw running with a bat was Jeremy Long?"

"I didn't. Not at first, leastwise."

"So what you saw was *a* boy running with a bat and *a* boy riding a horse?" Raymond keeps going, leading Petersen on a trail that ends up with the man admitting he didn't know who Jeremy was until the newspapers told him. And he hadn't been wearing his glasses.

When Petersen is so confused he'd have trouble identifying himself, Raymond moves in for the kill. "So, you didn't really know who the boy was running. And you didn't report this alarming incident because, although you believed the bat was bloody after the papers reported it, at the time you assumed it was a muddy bat. Have I got that right?"

"Yeah. I guess," Mr. Petersen admits.

Raymond smiles up at the judge. "Then, Your Honor, I have no more questions for this witness."

Mr. Petersen hurries out of the witness box and out of the courtroom. The whole question-and-answer routine took a lot longer than things take on TV court shows. Twice it looked like Juror Number Seven fell asleep.

But not Jeremy. I could tell my brother was tuned in, listening to the testimony, absorbing it. If Jeremy is focused on something, he's smart, really smart. It's just when he loses interest that he drifts into his own, much more fascinating world.

The judge announces a short recess, and when we get back, Raymond calls Bob Adams to the stand. Bob is a few rows up from us, but he glances back as he steps over people to get out of his row. I smile at him, relaxing a little because I know Bob likes Jeremy. That's why Raymond wanted him to testify about Jeremy's character. When we first moved to Grain, Bob hired Rita on the spot. When I began standing in for Rita, mostly because she wanted to sleep in or just didn't feel like working, Bob wasn't crazy about the idea. But when he saw how hard I worked—a lot harder than Rita—he came around. He came around with Jeremy too.

Bob swears on the Bible to tell the truth, then makes his way to the witness box, where he balances himself on the edge of the wooden seat, like he may need to get away quick. I might not have recognized Bob outside of the restaurant if I'd seen him dressed like this—gray suit, blue tie, leather shoes, and no apron. I try to remember if I've ever seen Bob outside of the Colonial Café, and I don't think I have. He clears his throat. His hair is slicked back, and he looks as nervous and out of place as a cat in a courtroom full of rocking chairs.

Raymond has Bob identify himself, and then he starts asking Bob about Jeremy.

"I've always thought Jeremy was a great kid," Bob answers. "A little different maybe, squirrelly, you know, what with not talking and all. But nice. Real nice."

Bob gives examples of nice, like when Jeremy would come by the Colonial and jump right in to help wash dishes for no reason and no money. Or the time Jeremy picked black-eyed Susans and put a glass full of flowers on every table in the Colonial.

I'm thinking Bob's done a good job talking about my brother. Jeremy comes off as different, just in case we still need the insane version of the plea, but nice and regular too.

Raymond announces that he's finished with the witness, and Bob starts to get up to leave.

"I have a few questions for the witness," Prosecutor Keller says from behind his table. He stands and buttons the middle button of his light gray suit.

The judge nods, and Bob sits back down.

Keller is all smiles, which makes me nervous. "Mr. Adams, wasn't there a time when Jeremy caused some disturbance in your restaurant?"

"That . . . that was nothing," Bob answers, but he shifts his sizable weight in the witness seat and loosens his tie. I know what's coming, and I'm sure Bob does too.

I glance at Jeremy, and he's staring at Bob like he'd trade places with him if he could, just so Bob wouldn't have to be on that witness stand any longer.

"You say it was nothing? Really?" Keller turns his wrinkled-up, surprised look on the jury. I've come to hate that look. "Didn't someone call the police? Didn't Sheriff Wells have to restore order?"

I glare at the sheriff. I know he had to be the one who told Keller about this.

"It all got blown out of proportion," Bob answers.

It really did. It shouldn't have been such a big deal, and it wasn't Jeremy's fault anyway. He lost his temper, but only because some jerk at school told him that Rita served horse and dog meat at the café. Jer loves animals, so he got upset.

"Mr. Adams," Keller insists, "I remind you that you're under oath. Please tell the court what transpired about a year ago on August second, when Sheriff Wells was called to your establishment."

Bob glances over at Jeremy, then back to Keller. "Well, Jeremy came storming into the restaurant at lunchtime. It was a Saturday, and we were busy. He ran from one table to the next, over to the booths, and down the short-order counter, peering at every plate."

"Go ahead, please," Keller urges.

"If a customer had a hamburger, say, well, Jeremy grabbed the plate and tossed the whole thing into the garbage. It all happened so fast. I guess some kids in one of the booths tried to hang on to their plates, and Jeremy got a little carried away. But it was them kids at his school that done it. They messed with Jeremy's head, telling him his mother was serving horse-meat and dogs."

A ripple of restrained laughter flicks across the courtroom. I can't believe anybody thinks this is funny.

"Mr. Adams, tell us about the plates," Keller urges.

Bob stares at his pudgy hands. "He broke most of them," he mutters.

"Speak up, please," Keller says, "so the jury can hear you."

"He broke them!" Bob shouts, staring Keller straight in the eyes. "Jeremy broke them plates and a dozen others, okay? But that busybody Mrs. Rouse had no call to phone the sheriff. We didn't need the police. We could have handled it."

"It's a shame you couldn't have been in the barn to handle things the day of the murder," Keller says.

Raymond stands up and pounds the table. "Your Honor! I object!"

But the judge is already on it. "Mr. Keller, save your comments for your closing. I'm watching you."

"Sorry, Your Honor," he says, clearly not one bit sorry. He turns to Bob and smiles. "Mr. Adams, Bob, you like Jeremy Long, the defendant, do you not?"

Bob looks at Jeremy again. "I like Jeremy fine," he says, still obviously upset at Keller.

"Would it be fair to say that you like Jeremy's mother too?" Keller presses.

My stomach twists. I'm not sure why, but I know something bad is coming.

"What are you saying?" Bob demands.

"Just that I believe you like Jeremy and his mother."

Raymond stands up, but only halfway, like he's not quite sure of this one. "Your Honor, I object to this line of questioning."

"Goes to motive for testifying, Your Honor," Keller explains.

"Overruled. Answer the question, Mr. Adams."

"Fine. I like Rita and Jeremy. So what?"

"Could we say that, at least in the case of the defendant's mother, Rita Long, you more than like her?" He sounds like a second grader teasing a kid with a crush.

"Your Honor!" Raymond complains, starting to stand again.

The judge raises her hand to stop him. "Move along, Mr. Keller."

This is what I'm thinking—move along.

"Isn't it true that you and Mrs. Long are lovers? That you—"

"I object!" Raymond screams. I have never seen him this angry.

I object too. But I have to admit that I'm not surprised. I knew Rita was seeing somebody. I should have guessed it was Bob, if I guessed about it at all. I knew Bob liked her. I've just never seen the "like" coming back from Rita's side.

"Mr. Keller, that's enough." This is as firm as I've heard the judge, and it makes me like her even more.

"All right," Keller says. "Just one more question, Mr. Adams, and then I can let you go. Where were you the night before Coach Johnson was murdered?"

"Home." Bob stares at his hands again, and I get a sick feeling about where this is going. Rita and I are the only alibi

Jeremy has, and I was asleep until the sheriff woke me up pounding on the door.

"You were 'home alone,' as they say?" Keller asks.

I want to smack that grin off his face.

"No," Bob answers, barely above a whisper.

Keller acts amazed. "Really? Who was with—?"

Bob doesn't wait for the question. "Rita! Okay? Rita Long was with me."

"Ah," Keller says, as if everything is finally all cleared up. "I see. Um . . . excuse me for asking, but all night?"

"Yes. I went into work at six-fifteen, like I do every morning."

"And Jeremy's mother was still there?"

Bob nods.

"For the record, Mr. Adams, will you please answer the question aloud?" the judge asks.

"Sorry, Your Honor. Yes. Rita was there when I left at six-fifteen."

The spectators break into murmurs, and the judge bangs her gavel and asks for order.

I don't know what to think or how to feel. I try to figure out how bad this is for Jeremy, but I can't. So Rita slept with Bob? So she wasn't home to make sure Jeremy was in his bedroom all night. That one would have been pretty hard to prove anyway—what with the bloody bat and Jeremy's bloody uniform. And it's not like Rita would have checked in on Jer even if she had been home all night.

Chase looks over at me, like he wants to see how I'm taking it.

There's a tap-clapping noise at the front of the courtroom. I can't see where it's coming from, but I have a good idea. A chair squeaks and somebody slaps a table. Every other noise stops. The slap sounds again and again.

"Mr. Munroe, can you please control your client?" asks the judge.

I lean to the left until I can see between two reporters' heads and get a view of my brother. Jeremy is swaying back and forth. His hands fly above his head like frightened birds.

"Mr. Long," says the judge, "you must settle down, or I'll need to have you removed from court. Do you understand?"

Jeremy's hands twist in the air, clenching and unclenching as he moves faster and faster. Raymond puts a hand on his shoulder, and Jeremy shakes it off like Raymond's hand is made of fire.

From where I sit, in the back, my brother's face is split in shadows. He is Jekyll and Hyde, light and darkness.

I don't want the jury to see him like this.

I don't want Chase and T.J. to see him like this.

I don't want *me* to see him like this. And in that fraction of a second, I wonder. *Did he do it?*

25

I make Chase drive me straight home after court. It's probably the quietest car ride any three teens have ever taken. I'm saving every word I have for Rita. I can't believe she didn't tell Raymond, or me, about her affair with Bob. What did she have to worry about, her reputation?

Chase pulls the car next to the curb in front of my house, and I see the light of the television glowing from the living room. "Want me to come in with you?" he offers.

"Yeah," T.J. says. "*I* could come in with you."

"No. Thanks. This is between Rita and me."

When I walk in, I see Rita in her white slip, kicking back on the couch. Her feet, crossed at the ankles, are propped up on the coffee table. It's four-thirty in the afternoon, but she's got a beer in one hand and two empties on the table.

"Hey!" she calls, all cheery. "You ought to watch this. Dr. Phil's about to let this loser have it right between the eyes." Her speech is slurred already, making me wonder what she had before the beers.

I charge the TV, shut it off, and stand in front of the screen.

"Hey!" she whines. "I was watching that." Under her makeup, Rita is a child, with pouty lips and fuzzy slippers.

"Why didn't you tell me you were sleeping with Bob?"

"What?"

"Bob! You know, as in our boss, Bob?"

She frowns and sets down the beer. No coaster. I've told her to use coasters. Our table looks like a bad version of the solar system, with the planets out of whack. "How did you—?"

"He testified in court, Rita."

"About us?" Her forehead wrinkles form a V as she tries to grasp this. "Why would Bob—?"

"Because things come out when you're on the witness stand, Rita. The truth comes out. I don't care what you do with your life. Not anymore. Not for a long time. But it made it look like you and Bob were lying to protect Jeremy—and all you ended up doing was making Jeremy look more guilty!"

"Hold on a minute." She's coming out of her drunken state. Angry Rita is hardening in front of me. "What's one thing got to do with the other? And what's any of it got to do with you?"

"Jeremy is my brother!" I shout. "I know he couldn't have murdered Coach Johnson, and I'm trying to prove it, but you—!"

"Don't tell me you haven't given up on that yet." She falls back onto the couch and turns on the TV with the remote.

I slam the TV off again. "Rita! Don't you care what happens to Jeremy?"

She sits up straight. "Of course I care! He may be a legal

adult, but he's still my boy. I borne him. And I don't want him to go to prison. I want him safe, in a mental home, where people can look after him and he won't get into no more trouble. That's what I want!"

I feel like throwing the TV at her. How can she be so cold?

Rita shoots me a look I've seen a million times. Lips pressed together and shifted sideways, her head tilted, eyes full of disgust. If I had just one picture of my mother in my head, this would be the expression on her face, a look that says, "I'm sick to death of you. You're too stupid to talk to. Get out of my way."

"We're done here, Hopeless." She takes a gulp of beer and drains the can. "Get me another one of these from the fridge."

Here's where I would give in, do what she says so that things wouldn't get uglier, so that nobody would get hurt. Here's where I always make peace by giving up, by giving in.

Only not this time. "Rita." My voice is calm. I see her flinch at the sound of it, surprised maybe? "Why was Coach Johnson paying you off?"

Her body stiffens, and she scoots to the edge of the cushion. At last, I have her attention. "I don't know what you're talking about."

"Really? You and *Jay Jay*? Are you saying he wasn't writing you checks?"

She tucks her feet under her and smooths her slip over her flabby thighs. "I had him pay me Jeremy's salary for working in the barn. So what? Jeremy wouldn't know what to do with a check."

"A check for a thousand dollars? Every month?"

"Where did you—?"

"Were you and Coach, 'Jay Jay,' having an affair, Rita?"

"Shut up!" Rita screams. "This is none of your business!"

"Was it *your* business? Was Coach paying you to keep quiet?"

"You little—!" The words squeeze through her teeth, greased by spit.

"Was he afraid his wife would find out? You were blackmailing him, weren't you!"

"You don't know what you're talking about!" she screams.

I have never seen Rita so angry, and that's saying something. But I'm not backing down. This is too important. "Is that why you're so eager to send Jeremy away to a mental hospital?"

Quick as a flash, Rita picks up the remote and flings it at me. I dodge, but it catches my cheekbone before crashing into the TV. The remote breaks into pieces. Batteries fly. The screen looks chipped. She gasps. "Hope, are you all right? Are you hurt?"

"You're pathetic, Rita!" I feel something trickling down my cheek. I touch it, and my finger comes away red. I don't care. I can't feel anything. My body's shaking. "You'd send your own son away to keep your ugly little secrets from getting out! You'd help them convict Jeremy of murder just so you wouldn't have to be tried for blackmail?"

Rita stands up, and I think she's going to fly across the coffee table and tackle me. But I don't move. I don't care.

Instead, she shakes her finger at me. "I would send my own son away so he wouldn't kill anybody ever again!"

"He didn't kill anybody!"

Her eyes narrow, and I know I'm about to get the worst of this argument, the worst of everything. "Hope, he did it. I know without a doubt that your brother murdered Jay Jay."

I want to yell again. I want her to throw something else at me. I don't want this.

She continues, her voice calm, "I saw him washing that bat of his in the bathroom sink the morning of the murder."

Her words take the rest of the fire out of me, out of both of us. I want to call her a liar, but I'm doused, drowning in her words.

Rita is quiet now. The whole house has turned silent. "I saw him, Hope. I came home that morning and tried to go back to sleep. I thought you and Jeremy must be in bed still. But I couldn't sleep, so I got up and went to the bathroom. I opened the door, and there he was. He was trying to wash blood off his bat."

"What did you do?"

"I looked at him. He stared back at me with his wide, panicked eyes, like he was begging me for something I couldn't give him. I closed the door."

"You—?"

"I know. I should have asked him right then and there what he done. But I figured he'd clubbed some animal—not a dog or a cat, but a squirrel or a gopher. And I didn't want to deal with it." She stares past me, at the blank TV screen. "I didn't think he'd . . . he'd . . . used that bat on a . . . a person."

I've been backing away from her, stumbling toward the door. Images of the crime scene flash through my head. They bring pain, as if they're mounted on arrows. Coach, bloody, curled on the stable floor. Jeremy curled in the corner of his bedroom.

My back slams into the door. I reach behind me, frantically feeling for the doorknob. I have to get out of here.

Rita is shouting at me, but I can't hear her. A buzzing in my head drowns her out.

I'm outside. I take off running. One foot, the other foot. I used to read a book to Jeremy when we were little. Dr. Seuss. *One foot. Two feet.* I can't remember how it goes. *Left foot? Right foot?*

I keep running. I want the pain in my chest to hurt more. To explode.

My run ends in front of an old church that's been turned into an antiques store. If it were still a church, could I pray? Would it help? A dozen signs are posted on the big front door: DON'T TOUCH ANYTHING! IF YOU BREAK IT, YOU BUY IT. NO CHECKS, NO CHARGE. CASH ONLY. NO RUNNING. NO EATING.

I shove the door and go in. I've been here before. Every inch of this place holds a table, or chair, or dresser, or picture frame, or statue, or trinket. The smell of dust and must mixes with lemon and varnish.

"May I help you?"

May she? May anybody?

God? I ask in my heart. *May you help me?* Is it a question? A plea? An antique prayer?

I shake my head, then walk to a wooden banister and climb the stairs to the loft. It's been transformed from a choir loft to period rooms. Dresses from the 1920s hang on a rack in front of the open room. Inside, there are helmets and uniforms from every war. Did their original owners kill people? Did they have sisters at home who would have died for them? Who believed they were heroes, no matter what they'd done?

I sit on an army trunk tucked in front of a Japanese silk-screen room divider that splits the space in half, the West and the Orient. A bayonet hangs on the wall to the left, rifles and pistols in a glass case against the opposite wall.

I want out. Out of my own century and into this one, the past. I don't want the present, and I don't want the future. "I can't do this." I say it out loud, even though there's nobody to hear except God and me. I can't prove Jeremy didn't kill Coach Johnson. All I've done is wreck his chances for being found insane.

Rita was helping Jeremy more than I was.

26

"Hope? Hope!"

The shout jars me back to the present. I get up from the army trunk, walk to the balcony railing, and peer down. I know it's Chase even before I see him. I turn away and slink back to the war room. I don't want to see him. I don't want to see anybody.

But Chase must have spotted me. "Hope?" I hear his footsteps on the stairs. He barges into the past, my room, shattering the quiet here.

"Go away."

"Hope, listen. . . ."

I shake my head.

"What did you do to your face?" He touches my cheek.

It doesn't hurt. I can't feel it. Maybe I'll never feel anything again. I brush away his finger.

He sits down beside me on the trunk. "Talk to me."

"Go home, Chase. Leave me alone." I stare at the floor,

the wooden slats that let light peek through from below. Choirs used to sing here.

"What happened?"

I shake my head. "It's over. I'm done."

"You don't mean that. What about Jeremy? He needs you. And now you've got Caroline Johnson coming to court and reasonable doubt and—"

"Wait. How did you know I was here?"

"Rita," he answers.

"Rita?"

"She called me, Hope. How else did you think I knew to come looking for you? She's worried about you. She was afraid you might do something stupid."

This isn't making sense. "Wait. Rita called you?"

He smiles and nods. "Surprised me too. I don't think I was her first choice. But she *is* worried about you. So am I. You can't give up. I think things are looking better for Jeremy than they ever have."

"No. They're not." I shake my head and lower my voice. "Rita saw Jeremy that morning. Chase, he was trying to wash his bat." I can see it in my head—Jeremy trying to get the bat into the sink, water and blood splashing, and that look, the wide-eyed look of being caught in the act. "Why would he do that if he hadn't . . . ?" But I can't finish.

"First of all, whatever Rita saw, Jeremy washing the bat, might never come out in court."

"If Rita has to testify, Keller will get it out of her." My hand hurts, and I raise it to see why. My fingernails have left deep marks on my palm from the fist I must have been making.

"Rita might surprise you. She kept it from you this long. My money's on her keeping what she saw out of court."

Chase is right. Rita's stronger than I am, a better match for the prosecutor. "Still . . . it doesn't change what she saw." I make the fist again. I want it to hurt.

"What did she see?" Chase asks. "Jeremy cleaning his bat? So what? Who knows why he was doing it? Even you don't know how his mind works all the time. Maybe he loved his bat so much that he couldn't stand to have it dirty. Or maybe he was trying to cover up for somebody, to protect somebody."

"Like who? Caroline Johnson? They didn't even like each other."

Chase shrugs. "Okay. So maybe he wasn't trying to cover up for anybody. Maybe he just couldn't stand having Coach's blood on his bat."

That rings true to me. "Jeremy hates the sight of blood. Once when I got a nosebleed, I grabbed the nearest thing, a dish towel, to stop it. Jeremy made me throw it away, outside of our apartment."

"See?" Chase says, like I've proved him right. "Maybe that was why he tried to wash the bat. Or not. We don't know, Hope, and we probably never will know. But it doesn't prove anything. That's all I'm saying. What Rita told you hasn't changed anything. We've still got reasonable doubt. Jeremy still doesn't have a motive for killing Coach, and Caroline Johnson still does. After Bob's testimony, the jury could even believe that *he* had a motive."

"Bob? Why would he have a motive to kill Coach?" I can't imagine Bob hurting anybody, not really.

"Who knows?" Chase takes off one running shoe and dumps out a tiny pebble. He's not wearing socks, and his shoes aren't tied. "But if your mother was having some kind of love triangle thing going with Coach and Bob, that would give Bob a motive. I'm not saying he did it, just that he has a motive."

"And Jeremy doesn't." Relief, mixed with guilt, rushes over me. It's hot, blazing hot, up in this loft. "Jeremy doesn't have a motive."

"And," Chase continues, the lines of his face deep and intense, as if he's willing me to believe, "juries don't like to convict without a motive, no matter what the law says about not needing to prove one. My dad's always told me that people on a jury have to understand why someone would kill. That's just human nature, and jurors are human."

I close my eyes. A picture comes to my mind of Jeremy about eight months ago, standing on top of a hill, ready to ride his sled. He's the perfect image of innocence. It's nighttime, and the stars are out in full force. I remember thinking that he looked close enough to heaven to touch it. And I thought about the song I'd heard in the car that day, a decade ago, the God song Jeremy "copied." I'd give almost anything to hear that song now.

"Jeremy couldn't have done it," I say quietly. I feel grief, a deep sorrow at having even for a minute believed that my brother could have committed murder. "I was ready to quit on him," I admit, too ashamed to look at Chase.

He wipes away whatever is on my cheek—blood, tears. "I doubt it."

I frown up at him.

He shakes his head. "Not a chance. The Hope I know would never quit on Jeremy. I've seen the way you love your brother."

"But—"

He puts his finger to my lips to stop words from coming out. Then he draws his fingertip across my bottom lip.

I still feel his touch on my mouth, even after his finger is gone. Slowly, he leans in and presses his lips to mine, moving softly across the spot where his finger was. The heaviness in my body lifts until I feel like I'm floating. Around us, army uniforms, guns, and helmets watch as decades melt into each other, bringing us into the timeless group of lovers.

"You up there! What's going on?" Mrs. Gance, the owner, shouts, and stomps one foot, like we're mice to be scared back into the walls.

Chase and I break apart. He walks to the railing and calls down, "Sorry, ma'am! We were kissing."

"Chase!" I whisper, but it makes me grin.

"In my store?" Mrs. Gance sounds horrified. "Well, you two can just skedaddle, you hear me? No kissing in my store!"

"Sorry," Chase says, running back to me and grabbing my hand to pull me up. "We must have missed that sign on the way in."

We thunder down the stairs and out the door. The sun is setting, and a flock of geese aim for it, honking. We stand on the sidewalk, facing each other. I'm pretty sure Chase is about to kiss me again. And if he doesn't make the move, I will. We kiss again. I've closed my eyes without thinking about it, and I don't want them closed, so I open them.

T.J. is standing there. "What is this, some kind of joke?"

I shove Chase away, so hard he nearly bumps into T.J. "T.J.? Wh-what are you doing here?"

"Rita called me. She said you were going to do something crazy." He glares at Chase, his brown eyes tiny dots filled with hate. "I guess she was right." He turns his hate on me. "I just don't understand why she had to bother me with it."

"Let's go sit somewhere and talk, okay? I was upset . . . about the case, and Jeremy, and something Rita said that—"

"I don't care." T.J. shakes his head.

"Come on, T.J.," Chase says, his voice calm. "We need to talk about this."

"Talk? *I'm* the one who made you help out Hope in the first place. You didn't even want to." He stabs the air at both of us. "I sure didn't mean this! But I should have known. You are such a phony! You're no better than all the rest of them. Your dad. Coach. Coach's wife. And now Hope? Everybody treats you—and guys like you—like you're kings. So what am I? Some cockroach? Just because I don't have your money? Because I'm not *cool*?"

"T.J., what do you—?" Chase tries.

"I'll bet you and Coach got a lot of laughs out of me and my family, didn't you?"

"If this is about the cookies," Chase begins, "I said I was sorry. I don't know what else I can say. And as for Hope and me, I'm sorry you—"

"Right!" T.J. is screaming now. Two boys on bikes cross to the other side of the street, staring at us. "You're sorry. So that fixes everything, then, doesn't it? Do whatever you want, then say you're sorry? Well, it doesn't work that way! Some things you can't take back! They're done. Over. But they're not, not really. And you can't take them back!"

I glance at Chase, who looks stunned to silence.

"T.J., calm down," I plead. "I'm sorry you're hurt, but you're scaring me. Can't we talk?" I move toward him, but he steps backward.

"No! We *can't* talk. Don't expect me to do handstands for you anymore either. I'm done! I'm done with the whole trial. And I hope your brother—!" He stops, choking on his own words. Then he turns and runs away, dashing into the street without looking.

"T.J.!" I scream.

A car slams its brakes and swerves to miss him. T.J. barely glances at it. The driver honks his horn, then takes off, tires squealing.

I watch my friend disappear behind a row of houses.

27

I keep staring long after T.J.'s out of sight. "Chase, we have to go after him."

"That's not a good idea, Hope." He takes my hand. "Not now anyway. Give him time." He starts walking toward my street, and I let myself be drawn along with him.

"Why did he act like that?" I've never seen T.J. so upset, even when guys at school teased him or messed up his locker.

"I told you he didn't think of you as just a friend," Chase says softly.

"But it's more than that. Do you think he's really finished helping Jeremy?" I glance up at Chase, and he shrugs. "What did he mean about not being able to take things back?"

Chase doesn't answer for a minute. Then, without looking at me, without slowing down, he asks, "Hope, how well do you know T.J.?"

"How well do I know him?" The question takes me by surprise. "T.J. was my first friend when we moved here. After the popular kids realized I wasn't one of them, I didn't have anybody at school. I don't think I'd even noticed T.J.—and we had three classes together—until he brought in sea glass for a science project. I love sea glass. I used to make necklaces and earrings out of it. He walked me home that day, to see the glass I'd brought with me from Chicago. After that, he'd bring me a few pieces, and we'd hang out together. We went on walks, or we went cricking—you know, trolling creeks for fossils or cool rocks. It was nice to have somebody to talk to at school. I've eaten every lunch in the cafeteria with T.J. for the last three years."

"But how well do you really know him, Hope? And think about it before you answer."

"Why are you asking me this?" My stomach is twisting. I don't want to answer Chase's question. How well *do* I know T.J.? We don't talk the way Chase and I do. After three years, I still don't know how he really feels about being labeled one of the weird kids at school. He never tells me anything personal—like about the team making fun of his mom, about Coach joining in. He never said a word about going to the barn, not even when he knew I was trying to get a timeline fix on how Coach spent mornings at the stable.

On the other hand, how open have I been with T.J.? I never talk to him about Jeremy or Rita or what it's like for me not having a dad, moving all the time. "What are you getting at, Chase?"

"I'm not getting at anything. It's just . . . Well, if you need another suspect for reasonable doubt, I nominate that guy."

"You can't be serious!"

Chase's phone rings, cutting me off. He checks the number, then swears under his breath. "I have to answer this." He turns away slightly, and into the phone says, "Hey, Dad." He glances over at me. "Yes, she is." He holds the phone away from his ear while his dad screams at him. When the yelling lets up, Chase puts the phone to his ear and says, "Okay. I'll be right home."

He hangs up and stares into space a second, and then smiles over at me, like he's apologizing. "Sorry I have to go like this, Hope. My dad is on the edge. I don't want to push him over."

He takes the time to walk me home first. When we're a block away, he asks, "You okay?"

"I'm pretty confused . . . but I'm not going to do anything stupid, if that's what you mean." I squeeze his hand, loving the feel of his fingers wrapped around my palm. "Thanks for finding me, Chase."

"My pleasure." He stops in front of my house. "And don't worry about T.J. He's a big boy. He can take care of himself. You've got enough on your mind with Jeremy. He's the one who needs you now. And he's lucky to have you." He leans down and kisses me goodbye. "Call me if you need me."

A glow from inside the house spills over the lawn. It flashes on and off as the TV images change. I guess we didn't break the television. There's no sign of Rita, but her car is here. The last thing I want to do is talk to her.

So I do something I haven't done in way too long. I dig out the lawn mower. It starts on the first try, although I don't know how much gas I've got.

Mowing our lawn is tough going because of the weeds. But once I make a clean swipe the length of the front yard, it feels great looking back and seeing what I've done. Maybe that's why I like mowing. That, plus the fact that it gives me time to think. Mostly, my thoughts keep bouncing back to the way my hand felt in Chase's, the way his finger felt on my lip, the way his lips felt on mine. I can almost feel him here with me as I walk back and forth across the grass, bringing order to the chaos of our lawn.

Then, just like that, my mind flashes back to T.J. outside the antiques store. His hair is wild, his eyes too deep into his skull, like somebody pitched them there too hard. I don't want this image of T.J. in my head. I try to picture him in his Panther jersey at a ball game. I can see Jer in his uniform and T.J. in his, but I don't have a single memory of Jeremy and T.J. together. Why is that? T.J.'s never been mean or rude to Jer, like some of the guys were. But he and Jeremy have never been friends either. I accepted that. Maybe I shouldn't have.

My mind spirals down to Jeremy, and a whole tangled ball of nerve endings shoots through my brain. *Jeremy.* I miss him. I miss walking into his room and plopping onto his bed so I could tell him everything about my day at school while he placed one of his jars on a shelf. I miss "talking" with Jeremy. He'd write his calligraphy almost as fast as I could talk. Sometimes we'd sit outside, each of us with a notebook, and we'd write miniletters to each other, exchanging them, then writing again. My handwriting always looked like somebody was elbowing me, but Jeremy's was perfect, each letter a piece of art.

I haven't seen a note from Jeremy in weeks. They let me visit him in jail twice, with a plate of glass between us and two phones, which didn't help much because Jeremy wouldn't pick his up. I tried writing notes and holding them to the glass window: "Jer, pick up the phone!" "Are you OK?" "Write me!" Jeremy smiled at me and touched the glass with both hands. But he wouldn't write.

By the time I finish mowing, it's pretty dark, but I go ahead and weed anyway. My eyes are used to the dark. I've caught Rita peeking out from the living room window a couple of times and from the back door once. I act like I don't see her.

I'm almost finished outside when the front door opens and Rita steps out. She's wearing too-tight blue jeans and a peasant blouse tugged down over both shoulders.

She stops when she gets to me. I'm kneeling by the sidewalk, and I brace myself for Rita's attack. But she gazes around the yard and says, "It looks real nice, don't it, Hope? Real, real nice."

I stare after her, still waiting for the punch line. It doesn't come.

When I go inside, my arms and shoulders cry out for a long, hot bubble bath. I start the water, then remember to close the shades and curtains. I'm struggling with the living room curtains when I catch sight of something white across the street. It's the pickup truck.

How long has it been there? Was someone watching me while I mowed? I shiver, thinking about it, picturing it. What if they were waiting for Rita to leave?

Fast as I can, I lock the doors. Then I edge toward the window and peer out.

Nothing moves.

No cars drive by.

If the pickup is still there, I can't see it. But I didn't imagine that truck.

I hear the bathtub water running and dash in to shut it off before it overflows.

911. I need to dial 911. I race through the living room looking for my cell. I don't know what I did with it. I don't have time to look.

Heart pounding, I run to the house phone. I reach for it, and the phone rings. I jump back.

Ring! Ring! Ring!

I watch as my arm stretches down and my fingers wrap around the receiver. I lift it to my ear, but I don't speak. I don't breathe.

Someone's there. There's a rustling noise. I think I hear an engine, a car. Then he—or she—says, "I'm watching you." The voice is calm, firm, as sexless as it is faceless.

"Who are—?"

"Quit poking around where you don't belong. Leave . . . it . . . alone." The line goes dead.

I stand there, receiver to my ear, until it buzzes. I drop the phone back onto the holder.

Almost instantly, it rings again. I stare at it.

Ring, ring, ring. It won't quit.

I jerk the phone off its hook. "Stop it! Stop calling here! You leave *me* alone!"

"Hope? What's wrong? Did they call again?"

It's Chase. I burst into tears.

"Hope, is Rita there with you?"

I shake my head. "No."

"Hang on. I'll be right over." There's a click, then nothing but the scream of the dial tone.

28

I curl up on the couch, pulling the afghan blanket around me. And I wait. Pipes creak. The fridge roars. Branches scratch the roof. Each noise is louder than the one before.

Outside, I hear a car drive up. A car door slam. Footsteps running up the walk. A knock. A banging at the door. It gets louder and louder.

"Hope! It's me! Open up!"

I fling the blanket to the floor and rush to the door. The lock won't turn. My hands are shaking. Finally, I yank the door open and throw myself into Chase's arms.

Without a word, he picks me up and carries me to the couch. He has to go back to the door and lock it.

"Chase?" I call.

"I'm here." He kneels beside the couch and wraps me in the blanket. "You're shivering." He rubs the blanket, warming my arms and legs. "Tell me what happened."

"The truck was outside." I start to sit up. "It might still be there!"

He eases me back down. "It's okay. I didn't see it out there. Go on."

"The phone . . . rang. They said to stop poking around, or something like that." I can't finish because that scratchy, breathless voice is in my head, telling me to let it go or leave it alone.

Chase sits on the couch and holds my head in his lap. He strokes my hair, and I wonder if this is what children feel like when their parents take care of them when they're sick or frightened. I think it might be.

"Hope?" His voice is as soothing as his fingers on my hairline. "Talk to me. Tell me again what the caller said."

I tell him. It's easier now. I'm safe.

When I finish, Chase lets out a breath, like he's been holding it during my account. "Did the person on the phone sound like a man?"

"Yes. At least, I think so. I guess it could have been a woman. It didn't even sound human. But I thought it was a man."

"It's got to be the same person who's stalking you," Chase says, "the guy in that pickup. I wish I'd seen him."

"You believe me, don't you?"

"Of course I believe you," he answers quickly. "I'd just like to be able to tell my dad that I saw it too, with my own eyes."

"I knew he didn't believe me."

"I'm not sure he would have believed me either, to tell the truth. I doubt if he even sent that patrol car over here to watch out for you."

A shiver passes through me, shaking my whole body.

"You need something hot to drink." He stands up, gently

settling my head on the arm of the couch. "Do you have any tea without caffeine?"

"I don't know." Since the trial, I haven't gone to the grocery store regularly. I haven't felt much like eating. My clothes are baggy, and I haven't even cared. I start to get up to search the cupboards for tea bags.

Chase eases me back onto the couch and tucks the blanket around me. "Stay where you are, and that's an order."

I listen to cupboards open and close while my mind tries to fight off the images racing through my head—blood, bats, a dark figure behind the wheel of a white pickup. The pictures won't stop until Chase comes back into the room.

"Here. Hot chocolate." He sets a steaming mug on the coffee table, but not before finding a coaster.

"We have hot chocolate?" I inhale the warmth. I'm so cold, even though I know it's hot outside.

"But no marshmallows." He helps roll me to a sitting-up position. I'm still wrapped in the blanket, swaddled. I wriggle my hands out and reach for the cup, but a stabbing pain knifes the top of my head and forces me to sit back.

"What's the matter?" Chase asks.

"It's okay. I think I'm getting a migraine." This time, I'm pretty sure it's coming. I haven't had a real one in a couple of months, but this sure feels like the beginning of the bad.

"Can you take anything for it? Can I get you something?"

I try to smile at him. "You didn't see any aspirin in the cupboard, did you?"

"I've got aspirin. Wait here." He races out of the house and is back in seconds. "Dad always keeps some in the glove compartment." He opens the little plastic bottle and taps two pills into my palm. Then he caps the bottle and shoves it into his pocket.

I know these won't do any good, but they can't hurt. Chase brings me a glass of water from the kitchen and watches me swallow the pills. Then he hands me the mug of hot chocolate and sits beside me.

I take a sip of the chocolate because he went to all that trouble, but if this is a real migraine, I shouldn't put anything into my stomach because it will come right back up sooner or later. Still, it feels great to hold heat in my clammy hands. "Nobody has ever taken care of me like this." Steam from the cup floats away with my breath.

"Seriously?"

"Seriously."

He puts his arm around me. "Then that's a shame because you deserve to be taken care of."

We sit like this, and Chase talks to me about his dad, his mom, and his life in Boston. I listen, tuned in to the sound of his voice more than the words. I have to close my eyes because the light digs into my skull like an invisible hatchet. My hair follicles prickle. The roots are needles sticking into my scalp. And yet, I have never felt more at home in my own home than I do right now.

When I wake up, I'm on the couch, the blanket tucked around me and a pillow under my head. There's a note on the pillow. I have to squint to read it. My eyes are still blurry from the headache.

Had to leave. Sorry. Call me if you need me.

I need him. But I don't call. Instead, I go back to sleep and dream of him.

I don't know how much time has passed when I wake up to the door slamming. I sit up so fast that my head takes a minute to catch up with the rest of me.

Rita bursts through the room, a cloud of smoke floating in with her. "What are you doing up? Did you sleep out here?"

"Rita, somebody was outside." Light filters in. It's morning.

"What?" She drops some things in the kitchen and drifts back into the room.

I shed the blanket. "And I got another one of those phone calls. Only this time—"

"Just hang up. I told you that's how you handle prank calls. Hang up hard." She yawns. "I'm going to bed. Are you going to court today?"

It's no use talking to her. She doesn't believe me. But Chase does. And that's all I need now. "Yeah, Rita. I'm going to court."

Raymond has good news when Chase and I get to the court-house. He's been granted his subpoena for Caroline Johnson to appear before the court—just like T.J. said would happen. I wish T.J. could hear it too. I text him the news. He doesn't text me back.

It will take a couple of days to make it happen, but Caroline

Johnson will have to sit in the same seat I did and answer Raymond's questions, whether she wants to or not.

In the meantime, Raymond puts everybody who ever liked my brother on the stand to testify as character witnesses. As I listen to their accounts of Jeremy, I hope Jer is taking in all the kind words people are saying about him, from the woman at the IGA and the post office person to the first teacher Jeremy had here.

Chase and I sit through every testimony for the next three days. I can't stop looking for T.J., expecting him to walk through the courtroom doors and take his seat with us. But he doesn't show. It's like he's disappeared, like he was never there in the first place.

We still sit toward the back, surrounded by reporters. People greet Chase as if they've known him all their lives, but only a few speak to me.

On the day I'm sure Caroline Johnson will show up, she doesn't, and Raymond has to call more character witnesses. He even recalls Sarah McCray, the woman who found Coach dead. Chase and I watch her take the stand, and I feel a dull thud on the side of my head. I close my eyes and touch the spot, hoping the migraine isn't coming back.

"You okay?" Chase whispers.

"I think I'm getting a headache."

He digs into his backpack. The security people searched it by hand before letting us come in. Chase brings out his little bottle of aspirin. "I brought it just in case," he says. He shakes out two pills and hands them to me. "Here. Can you take them without water?"

I never have, but I toss them into my mouth and swallow. They scratch going down.

Raymond has Mrs. McCray identify herself again. After thanking her for returning to court, he begins the real questions. "Mrs. McCray, do you like Jeremy Long, the defendant?"

Mrs. McCray smiles at Jer. I watch my brother's feet kick the floor, faster and faster. He doesn't look at Mrs. McCray. "I've always liked Jeremy very much. He is such a polite, sweet boy."

"And you let him ride your horse, Sugar, isn't that right?" Raymond asks.

"I did."

"You must have trusted Jeremy to allow him to handle your horse," Raymond observes, facing the jury.

"That's right. I don't let just anybody ride my horses. A few of the children in town like to visit the horses and would like to ride mine. But horses are sensitive creatures. I can't just let anybody ride."

"And yet, you allowed Jeremy Long to ride your horse?" Raymond continues.

"Yes. I knew John would teach Jeremy what he needed to do to get along with my Sugar."

"John, as in John Johnson, correct?"

"Yes."

I look over at Jeremy. From where I'm sitting, it doesn't look like he's paying much attention to the testimony. He's swaying, and his fingers are playing something on the table. He could just be listening to his own music inside his head . . . or he could be starting to get upset about something.

I see the judge glance his way, but Jer doesn't see it. Neither does Raymond.

"Mrs. McCray," Raymond says, "I'm sorry to make you think back to the day of the murder, but I do have a question I need to ask." She nods and grips the chair with both hands. "When you first saw the body and realized John Johnson had been killed, murdered, even after Jeremy had bumped into you with that bat, was your first thought that Jeremy killed Mr. Johnson?"

"No! Not at all."

"Were you frightened? Didn't you fear that Jeremy might come back with his bat and go after you next?" Raymond asks.

"Certainly not! That sweet boy? How could I have had such thoughts?"

I feel like running up to the witness stand and hugging Mrs. McCray. I crane my neck to get a better look at Jeremy. I want to know if he heard her. But I see right away that he didn't. Jeremy's arms are raised, and he's swaying. He's closed his eyes. It's too bright in here for him, at least when he's like this—more agitated than usual. There are too many sounds—buzzing in the walls, screeches from chairs, murmurs from the gallery, where people are starting to watch Jeremy instead of Mrs. McCray.

He's getting worse. His hands twist. With his eyes shut, I know he's imagining an empty jar in his fingers, one hand screwing the lid on tight. It's been too long for him, too long without his jars. They calm him.

228

"Mr. Munroe, will you please restrain your client?" the judge asks.

Raymond turns around. His eyes double in size when he sees Jeremy jerking back and forth, arms raised, his fingers working an imaginary jar. The motion looks weirder if you don't know that's what he's doing, pretending he has his jar.

Raymond rushes to Jeremy and whispers fast to him. He touches my brother's arm, but Jeremy jerks away. He makes a tiny squeal, the sound of an animal caught in a trap.

"Mr. Munroe," the judge says, "if you can't get your client under control, I'll have to ask that he be removed from the proceedings."

Raymond can't help my brother.

I turn to Chase. "Give me the aspirin."

"It's too soon, Hope."

"Give it to me!" I'm loud enough that people around us turn to stare.

Chase gets the bottle out of his pack. "You shouldn't—"

I yank the bottle out of his grip. "Open your hand."

"What?"

"Just do it!"

He opens his hand, and I dump the entire bottle into his palm. Several pills fall to the floor.

Jeremy's noise gets louder. He doesn't speak, but there's nothing wrong with his vocal cords.

"Mr. Munroe?" the judge demands.

I'm on my feet, bottle in hand, sliding through the rows of spectators, not stopping until I reach the defense table.

People are talking now, and the judge bangs her gavel to stop them. Or me. "Order in the court! Mr. Munroe, do you want to tell the court what's going on at your table?"

I know any other judge in the world might have thrown me and Jeremy and even Raymond out by now. So I turn to her, picturing that Grateful Dead T-shirt under her robe. "Your Honor, I'm his . . . his helper?"

"His helper?" she repeats.

I elbow Raymond until he gets it. "Um . . . my assistant. In a manner of speaking."

"Uh-huh." The judge's eyebrows arch up to her forehead.

I reach across the table to give Jeremy the bottle. I don't know if he realizes I'm here.

"Just a minute," the judge warns. "May I ask what it is you're trying to pass to the defendant?"

"I object, Your Honor!" Keller stands up as if he's been asleep and has to make up for lost time.

"To what?" the judge asks.

It takes him a second to answer. "To the disruption to the proceedings, Your Honor. This is totally out of order."

"I'll take care of my own court, thank you, Mr. Keller. You may sit down." She turns to me. "Will the attorney for the defense's *assistant* please approach the bench, with whatever that is you're trying to hand over to the defendant?"

I glance at Jeremy. He's looking at me now. He sees the bottle. His eyes are wide open. He reaches for it.

"Ms. Long?" the judge calls.

"Yes, ma'am. Your Honor." I head for the bench. Behind me, Jeremy starts up with the animal noise. It's louder now, filled with pain. I run the rest of the way to the judge and hand her the bottle. "Please," I beg. "He needs to hold this bottle." I can imagine what's running through her mind. *Is he addicted to aspirin?*

Jeremy whimpers. Then from deep in his throat comes a scream. Not a regular, mouth-open scream, but a throat scream, filled with guts and stomach and insides. The whole court-room goes silent, making the growl sound louder.

"Your Honor, I object," Keller says, sounding a little bit scared, I think.

"To an empty aspirin bottle, Mr. Keller? I don't remember anything on the books about that one." The judge shoves the bottle back into my hand and waves me off. "Go, girl!"

I run back to the table and put the bottle into Jeremy's hand. His eyes flick open, and the sound cuts off as clean as if somebody shut off the sound track. I hand him the cap to the bottle. He stares from the bottle to the cap. He breathes more easily as he clutches the bottle to his chest.

"It's plastic, Jer," I explain. "I don't know how long they'll let you keep it. But if they give it back to me, I'll put it on the shelf with the rest of them. I'll try to bring you another one too. I'm sorry I didn't bring you one before."

I breathe in the scent of my brother. He smells like mint toothpaste or mouthwash, and sweat. He's back. The real Jeremy is back. The good Dr. Jekyll.

I risk glancing at the jury as I turn to go. They're all wide awake now. What are they thinking? What are they saying about Jeremy?

I take my seat next to Chase, but my gaze is fixed on my

brother. He sweeps the bottle in the air above him, and with his other hand holding the cap, he brings them together and caps the bottle, as if capturing a rainbow no one else can see. The act itself transforms my brother's face into something angelic. I want the jurors to see this change, this face. But I don't think they're watching. They're listening to the testimony that's started up again.

I listen too. But I keep one eye on Jeremy.

I glance at the jurors, and I catch Juror Number Three looking at me. I smile, then nod at Jeremy. She doesn't look at my brother, but she gives me a tiny smile—I'm almost sure of it.

The instant court is adjourned, I'm out of my seat and heading for my brother. Nobody stops me until I'm almost there. One of the officers of the court puts out his arm. "I'm sorry, miss. I can't let you get closer. They're taking him back now."

I shout over the guard's arm. "Jeremy! I know you didn't do it. Everybody can see that. You could never kill anybody. *I* could, if I got mad enough long enough." I can imagine an instant of hate exploding out of my hands in a black smoke of anger. "Or Rita. We've both seen that temper of hers. It's not a very big leap to imagine Rita doing it."

Jeremy stops fidgeting with the bottle and glares at me. The angelic look disappears from his face.

"But not you," I say quickly, finishing my thought. "I can picture almost anybody I know losing his temper and in a single instant doing something he'd regret. But I can't picture you doing it." I lean in and lower my voice. "And I know you're not crazy. I'd sooner believe the whole world is crazy than believe you were crazy for one minute."

"We have to go." The guard steps away from me and takes one of Jeremy's arms, with a second guard holding Jer's other arm. He goes with them without a struggle, his back straight, his chin held high, like he's been invited to visit royalty.

29

After court, Chase drops me off in front of my house. As soon as he drives away, I feel someone watching me. My skin tingles, and for a second I can't move from the sidewalk. I glance around for the pickup truck I know I'll see, but it's starting to get dark, and I can't make out forms across the street.

Then I see him. T.J. He's standing in the neighbor's yard, leaning against a tree, staring at me.

"T.J., you scared me half to death!" I start toward him, but I'm struck with a mixture of sadness, loss, and something else . . . fear. I stop a few feet away from him. "I've missed you."

He doesn't say anything. He just keeps staring, his mouth hard, his eyes invisible behind those glasses.

"I look for you every day in court," I say, my voice sounding thin and false, even though I'm telling the truth. "I can't believe you stopped coming."

"I've been there." He doesn't budge. I don't think his lips

moved. If I didn't know better, I'd think somebody else had spoken, not T.J.

"I didn't see you."

"I saw you. You and Chase."

"But how—?"

"From the gallery." His voice isn't angry or hurt, but something worse. It's cold as death.

I don't know what to say to him. "Well, I wish you'd come sit with us."

I think he laughs, but his face doesn't change expression. The word *us* hangs in the air. "We've been friends a long time, T.J."

He takes a step toward me. It's all I can do not to run away. "Have we?"

I watch him walk off. And this time, nothing in me wants to run after him.

Finally, it's the day we've been waiting for—Caroline Johnson is called to the witness stand. Reporters are on the edge of their chairs. Nobody on the jury looks the least bit sleepy.

The double doors open, and as if she's been waiting her whole life for this grand entrance, Caroline Johnson is wheeled into the courtroom. It's a thousand degrees in this room, but she's wearing a tailored business suit, solid navy or maybe black, and she has a plaid blanket folded over her lap, topped off by a box of tissues.

Seeing her makes me think of T.J. He was trying so hard to help me find something against this woman. The morning after we searched the crime scene, T.J. texted me that he wished he could get a look at Mrs. Johnson's shoes. He'd seen some TV show where they proved a guy was lying about being stuck in a wheelchair because the bottoms of his shoes were all scuffed up. I try to get a glimpse of Mrs. Johnson's shoes as she's wheeled in, but her feet rest on little footrests.

I want to wipe out my last conversations with T.J. I want to forget the way I felt the last time I saw him. I just want to hold on to how much he tried to help me, how much he's always tried to help me.

Instead of making Caroline Johnson walk to the witness chair, which I totally believe she could do, they have a ramp in place so she can be wheeled right up and into the box. Raymond smiles at her, and she sort of smiles back, but it looks more like a wince. I can't help analyzing every move-ment, wondering if she's for real. On the one hand, she's taken the time to paint her fingernails and put on lipstick. On the other hand, if she is faking, then she should get an Acad-emy Award because even I'm starting to feel a little sorry for her.

I try to bring back the image of Caroline Johnson scream-ing at her husband in the ball field parking lot. How does *that* Caroline fit with the withered woman in front of me? I want the jury to see *that* Caroline Johnson, not this one.

RAYMOND: First of all, Mrs. Johnson, I'd like to express how sorry I am for your loss.

MRS. J.: Thank you. (*She pops a tissue out of the box and dabs one eye.*)

RAYMOND: And I'd like to say how grateful we are that you've made this effort to appear before the court. If there's anything you need, please let us know.

Mrs. J.: Thank you. I'm all right. (*She takes a whiff of her asthma inhaler before going on.*) I want to do all I can to make sure justice is served. That's what John would have wanted.

I whisper to Chase, "Right. And it only took a court order to get her here."

Raymond: Mrs. Johnson, did you and your husband ever argue?

Mrs. J.: What couple do you know who don't argue once in a while? We were married for fifteen years.

Raymond: I suppose you're right about that. And they say that the number one reason for arguments in marriage is money. Did you and your husband argue about money?

Mrs. J.: After I got sick, I left the finances up to John.

Raymond: At this time, I'd like to offer as exhibit G an acknowledged copy of a letter from First National Bank, denying Mr. and Mrs. Johnson's loan application three months prior to the murder. (*Turning to the witness*) Mrs. Johnson, is this your signature on the application?

Mrs. J.: Yes.

Raymond: Would it be fair to say that your illness and the decline of your stable business, which Mr. Johnson tried to maintain, put a strain on your finances?

Mrs. J.: I suppose.

Raymond: And isn't it true that you—or your husband— made several applications for loans, and that you were turned down by at least three banks?

KELLER: Your Honor, I object to this whole line of questioning.

JUDGE: Overruled. The witness is directed to answer the question.

MRS. J.: We tried to get a loan, yes.

RAYMOND: Thank you. Now, Mrs. Johnson, can you explain why, especially in light of your financial constraints, your husband would pay out one thousand dollars a month to Rita Long?

MRS. J.: That's absurd!

KELLER: Your Honor! Objection! Facts not in evidence and prejudicial. I ask that the question be stricken from the record.

JUDGE: Sustained. The jury is instructed to disregard counsel's question.

RAYMOND: Mrs. Johnson, are you familiar with Rita Long, the defendant's mother?

MRS. J.: I know who she is. She and John went to high school together for a couple of years. Neither of us had anything to do with her after she moved back to town.

RAYMOND: So you're saying that you knew nothing of a relationship between them?

KELLER: Your Honor! I object!

JUDGE: Sustained. Move along, Mr. Munroe.

RAYMOND: Mrs. Johnson, did your husband have a life insurance policy on you?

MRS. J.: He had a small policy with his teachers insurance plan, I believe, although I can't see what—

RAYMOND: Thank you. And do you have a life insurance policy on your husband?

MRS. J.: I . . . I suppose. John took care of those things.

RAYMOND: Perhaps this will refresh your memory. (*He hands her a document, explains that it's exhibit K, and opens to the last page.*) That is your signature, is it not?

MRS. J.: Yes.

RAYMOND: Would you please read the death benefit on John Johnson's life insurance policy, the amount that goes to you, his spouse, in the event of his death?

MRS. J.: Five . . . five hundred thousand dollars.

It's all I can do to keep from shouting, "Go, Raymond!" I admit I wasn't crazy about Raymond bringing up Rita like that, but it's clear that I have seriously underestimated Raymond Munroe, Attorney for the Defense. He leads Caroline Johnson through a series of questions and answers about her husband and Jeremy. Even she has to admit how much they liked each other. I whisper to Chase, "I'm so glad Raymond got her on the stand. Everybody has to see that she did it, or at least that she could have done it."

Chase isn't bubbling over like I am. "Don't be too sure. Keller will get another crack at her when Raymond's done."

This is something I hadn't thought about, and it doesn't seem fair. Keller already had his turn when she was *his* witness, even though she only testified on paper. Raymond finishes his questions, and I still think he nailed it. But Chase is right. Keller stands up the second Raymond announces that he's out of questions.

KELLER: Mrs. Johnson, on behalf of the court, I'd like to apologize for putting you through this today. You've been most gracious to come to court and help us finish up the trial.

May I get you anything? I'm sure the judge would consider a short recess.

MRS. J.: No. Thank you. I'm here to help.

KELLER: I'd like to revisit your husband's relationship with the defendant. Can you describe it for us?

MRS. J.: Of course. John felt sorry for the boy. Well, I suppose one has to, doesn't one?

KELLER: So he spent time with the defendant and gave him a job?

MRS. J.: John was always generous to a fault. He taught the boy how to care for horses and taught him to ride, not that John had that kind of time. After the cancer made me an invalid, John had to do his own job and mine. He took over the stable. He let Jeremy muck the stalls, and he undoubtedly paid the boy much more than the task merited.

KELLER: And what about Jeremy and the Panthers, your husband's baseball team?

MRS. J.: Again, John's heart was too big for his own good. Jeremy couldn't play on the team, of course, so John let him carry the clipboard and equipment bag. John even gave him a uniform.

KELLER: Forgive me for making you relive this one more time, but I need to talk about Jeremy's bat. Do you know where the defendant got his bat?

MRS. J.: From my husband. John bought it for the boy. And it wasn't cheap. All the other boys wanted aluminum bats. But John said Jeremy wanted a *real* bat, a wooden one. I never liked seeing Jeremy with that bat of his. I knew it was trouble from the minute I—

240

RAYMOND: Objection!

JUDGE: Sustained. Just answer the questions, Mrs. Johnson. Proceed.

KELLER: Did you ever see the defendant with his bat?

MRS. J.: All the time! He carried that bat with him everywhere. He scared a couple of our broodmares with it. John wheeled me to the barn from time to time so I could be around the horses. That was before this last bout with the cancer.

KELLER: And you saw Jeremy in the barn? With a bat?

MRS. J.: Yes. I'm the one who insisted he leave the bat at the entrance the minute he stepped inside the barn.

She breaks up, and Keller hands her one of her tissues. I think her crocodile tears are a crock. I stare at the jury and hope they got the part about her knowing exactly where the bat was kept.

KELLER: After you stopped going to the barn, did you see the defendant again?

MRS. J.: John brought him by the house, but . . .

KELLER: Please go on, Mrs. Johnson.

MRS. J.: But that boy always made me nervous. Anxious.

KELLER: Anxious? How so?

MRS. J.: He brought that bat into our house, for one thing.

KELLER: Tell the court about the last time you allowed the defendant into your home.

MRS. J.: Jeremy had supposedly gotten a splinter in his finger from one of the spades or pitchforks in the barn. John brought him to the house so he could get a pair of tweezers. He needed more light to see the splinter, so they used the bathroom. On the way out, they stopped by the bedroom so John could check on me and explain. I tried to put the boy at ease and asked him questions about the horses, yes-or-no questions. But he got more and more agitated. He started swinging that bat. He swung it around and around, harder and faster, until I was frightened. He ended up breaking my bureau mirror, my grandmother's mirror. John said it was an accident, but I don't know.

KELLER: What do you mean?

MRS. J.: I thought then—in fact, I was sure—that Jeremy had swung his bat into my mirror on purpose. He knew what he was doing, all right.

After Keller sits down, Raymond stands up and tries to get in some last words about how much Jeremy and Coach liked each other. But it doesn't help. He can't erase Caroline Johnson's words. They're stuck in our heads, and nothing is going to drive them out: *He knew what he was doing, all right.*

I'm so angry when court adjourns that my stomach aches and my whole head feels like it's on fire. "That woman is evil!" I tell Chase as we watch his dad and a deputy wheel her out of the courtroom. "She made my brother sound like a bat-waving, mirror-breaking, weapon-swinging maniac."

"I know."

"And I guarantee she knew about those checks to Rita and maybe what Coach was paying Rita for."

"You don't know what those checks were for, Hope."

"*She* knew. I know she did. Give me ten minutes alone in

that house, and I'll bet I could find more canceled checks and who knows what all." We're at Chase's car in the parking lot, and I wait for him to unlock the doors. Across the street, in front of the courthouse, an ambulance drives up. Sheriff Wells pushes Mrs. Johnson's wheelchair into the back of the ambulance. "Chase, what's that about?"

"Didn't you hear them when they were wheeling her out? Dad and Keller are taking her to the doctor to have her checked out after the 'ordeal.' It's all for show, if you ask me."

"Wait a minute." I hadn't heard one word of that conversation. I'd been too wound up to hear anything. "Are you telling me she's going to the doctor, and your dad *and* the prosecutor are taking her?"

"That's what they said." He climbs behind the wheel and unlocks my door. "Why?"

I slide into the seat next to him. "Don't you see what that means? Chase, not only will she be out of the house now, but your dad will be out of the way too!"

Chase rests his forehead on the steering wheel. "Hope, no. Please?"

I buckle up. "We have to do it, Chase. It's our last chance to prove that Caroline Johnson is a dirty rotten liar."

30

Twenty minutes later Chase pulls up at Caroline Johnson's house. We don't have time to park far away like T.J. and I did when we searched the barn and Coach's office, so Chase cruises behind the house and parks around back.

As we make our way to the front porch, I'm still fuming. "Jeremy never liked that woman. And he's an excellent judge of character."

"So you've said. On numerous occasions." Chase tries the front doorknob. "Locked. I think we should leave, Hope."

"So *you've* said on numerous occasions."

He doesn't smile.

"Please, Chase? Maybe there's a key hidden around here." I check under a pot sitting on the front porch, under the planters along the sidewalks, and all around the porch swing. Chase doesn't help. He's definitely getting restless. I don't know how much longer I can keep him here.

"Let's try the other door," I suggest. I jog to the back of the house. The screen door is locked too. Chase comes up behind me. I rattle the screen. "Can't we yank it open? Or cut the screen?"

"Not unless you want to end up in jail." He steps in front of me and takes his car keys out of his pocket. "Here. It's just a fall latch."

I watch while he jimmies the latch and pulls open the door in one smooth move. "Where did you learn to do that?"

His mouth twists like somebody snapped a rubber band over his lips. Then he says, "I told you I ran with the wrong crowd in Boston. Enough said?" He says this like he's mad at me.

"Enough said." I shove in front of him and try the doorknob. It turns. I push the door until I can squeeze through. A strong odor hangs in the air—a mix of bacon grease, burned cookies, and sickness. Or maybe death. I don't move from the doorway.

"Are you sure you want to go through with this?" Chase asks, making it clear he doesn't.

I turn and face him. It's dark inside the house. Outside, the sun has stopped shining for the day. "I have to, for Jeremy. But you don't. You could wait in the car."

He sighs. "Do you even know what you're looking for?"

"One of those checks to Rita maybe? A divorce paper? Or a journal, where Coach's wife tells how she did it? Or a copy of a contract she gave to a contract killer?" I smile up at him, willing him to smile back.

He doesn't. But with one finger, he pushes back a strand of my hair that's sprung loose. "Well, we better hurry. They could bring her home any minute."

I squeeze his arm and hope that he can read how grateful I am that he's staying with me.

I'm afraid to turn on lights. Chase opens the back door wider so the remaining light of dusk sneaks in with us. I've never been inside this house before. The floor creaks with every step. The air is too moist, like in our house.

After a second, my eyes adjust to the shades of gray, and details sharpen, coming into focus as if I'm turning the lens of an expensive camera. I try to take it in: white lace on end tables that flank a light green sofa, doilies under lamps and vases, lacy curtains. The whole house is frilly. You'd think two old women lived here. On the walls and on the hall table are pictures of Caroline with her horses. Over the couch hangs a giant painting of a little girl holding the reins of a pony in one hand and a blue ribbon in the other. The kid has to be Caroline.

I bump into a table and hear something wobble. There are breakables all over this place. No wonder they never had kids. Children wouldn't last two minutes in this house. "Chase?" I whisper. My heart thumps because I can't see him.

"In the kitchen," he calls out in a normal voice. Why not? If anybody's here, they've already heard us.

I stumble over a recliner with the footrest still up, then make it to the kitchen. "Find anything?"

"I don't know. But I don't think she's bedfast like she claims. She'd have to get around pretty well to keep some of this stuff on top shelves."

"She probably has a housekeeper."

"True. How about you? Anything?"

"Way too many pictures of Caroline." I open a cupboard

246

by the fridge. I try to imagine how the murder might have taken place. "She pretends she can't get out of that wheelchair, but she can. So maybe she got up early that morning. She could have had a blowout argument with her husband— about money, or about those checks to Rita, or a million other things married people argue over. She makes her way to the barn. Jeremy's bat was there, so she grabbed it." I'm picturing the whole thing: Caroline in a cotton nightgown, pink flowers and white lace. She's screaming at her husband. She sees the bat, lunges for it, and—

"Hope, we have to finish up and get out of here."

Chase is right. I need evidence. "I'll take the den we passed when we came in. You take the bedroom. Check the bottoms of her shoes!" I cross back through the living room to the den, or study.

Before I reach the desk, Chase cries, "They're back!"

I hear gravel crunch in the driveway. The sound of a car engine is drowned out by brakes. The engine cuts off.

"Great," Chase mutters.

Please! I'm not sure if it's a prayer or a wish. I grab Chase's hand and pull him to the back door.

"What are you doing?" He tries to tug his hand away, but I hold on.

"Quiet!" I stumble and bump into the couch. It hurts my hip, but I keep going until we're outside. I shut the door, then the screen. Reaching up, I straighten a lock of Chase's hair, then smooth my own. "Let me do the talking."

"Why? Hope, what—?"

I shush him and wait.

A car door slams. And another.

Part of me wants to run and hide. But Chase's car sits six feet away in plain sight. I hear their footsteps on the front porch. A blend of voices. The front door being unlocked. Opened. They're inside.

I haven't let go of Chase's hand. With another wordless prayer, the kind I may have inherited from Jeremy, I reach up and knock on the screen door, hard.

"Hope?" Chase whispers.

I ignore him and keep banging on the door, my heart thudding against my chest with every knock. "Hello? Anybody home?" I open the screen and bang even harder on the door, shouting, "Yoo-hoo! Mrs. Johnson?"

I hear footsteps storm through the house toward us. The back door opens, and Sheriff Wells frowns down at us. "What in blue Hades are you two doing here?"

Chase opens his mouth to speak, but I beat him to it. "Sheriff Wells? I was starting to think nobody was home."

He ignores me. "Answer me, Chase! What are you doing here?"

"Don't be mad, Dad. We just—"

"We just wanted to ask Mrs. Johnson a couple of questions." Somehow, my voice is strong, friendly even.

"You what?" Sheriff Wells shouts. He glances back over his shoulder, then lowers his voice. "I can't believe you're this stupid."

Chase flinches.

"We didn't mean to cause anybody trouble," I say reasonably. "It's just that Mrs. Johnson said some things in court today that hurt Jeremy, and I thought if I could just talk to her for a minute—"

Sheriff Wells glares at me. "You want to ask her questions? Hasn't your family done enough?"

"Dad!" Chase steps in front of me, like he thinks his dad might come after me. I wouldn't be surprised. He looks mad enough to spit nails.

The sheriff takes a deep breath, sucking in anger through his teeth. "Look, miss, I have nothing against you. But you better leave this poor woman alone."

"Poor woman?" I'd like to tell him what I really think about this *poor woman.*

He turns to me, and if looks could kill, the sheriff would be on trial for murder. "I just came from the doctor with her. Mrs. Johnson isn't expected to live out the year. So you can tell your brother's lawyer that she won't be around long enough to collect that insurance money, much less spend it."

In spite of everything, and even though I don't want to, I feel sad for her. I wonder how long she's known.

The sheriff straight-arms Chase in the shoulder, knocking him back a step. Then he turns to me. His bushy eyebrows meet above his nose, and his upper lip curls to show teeth. "You kids leave it alone, you hear? *Leave it alone!*"

"We hear, Dad," Chase says. He takes my hand and tugs me toward the car.

I let him. I let him because suddenly cold fear is slicing through me like sharp knives.

We drive a long way in silence, leaving the barn and the Johnson house behind us. A couple of times, I glance over at Chase, but it's like he doesn't even know I'm in the car with him. That's how far away he seems. His forehead is wrinkled, and every now and then he rolls his lips over his teeth and makes a weird noise, almost like he's fighting himself. I'd give a lot to know what's going on inside his head, but I'm afraid to ask.

Finally, Chase speaks without looking at me. "My dad's right, you know."

"Right about what?"

"She didn't do it."

"Mrs. Johnson? Of course she did it! We just didn't have time to—"

But he's shaking his head and won't let me finish. "To what? Find some kind of smoking gun? The police already have the weapon. And that woman, no matter how nasty she is to your brother, didn't kill anybody. She's dying, Hope. You heard what they said."

"Maybe she's *not* dying. Maybe she paid the doctor to—"

"Don't even go there. This isn't some big conspiracy, with the doctors and my dad and Mrs. Johnson all in on it together."

"I didn't say it was. But she's the one with a motive—the only one with a motive."

"The only one? How about Rita? Or Bob? Or T.J.?"

I don't know why he's so angry. "I can't believe any of them would have killed Coach and let Jeremy be blamed for it."

"Fine. If you can't believe it, then I guess it isn't true." His sarcasm stings. "So get Jeremy's attorney to use Mrs. Johnson for reasonable doubt, but I'm telling you nobody's going to believe she did it for the insurance money. Why would she?

You heard my dad. She won't be around to spend any of it. And all you're doing is ruining the little time she has left. But don't listen to me. You won't listen to anybody anyway."

My throat burns. I don't know what I did to make him so angry, why he's changed on me all of a sudden. "Why are you doing this?" My voice sounds like I've swallowed sand.

"Enough is enough, Hope. Dad's right. We've done enough."

"*I* haven't done enough until I get Jeremy out of prison!"

"Don't shout at me."

I hadn't realized I was shouting. I take a deep breath. I hate this. We've been so close, so together in everything. "Chase, what is it? Is it your dad? Are you afraid of what he'll do when you both get home?"

"Yeah, I am." He glares over at me, and for a second he doesn't look like Chase. His green eyes are black. He has his father's mouth. "He's really mad, Hope. And maybe he's got good reason. I don't know what he'll do this time. Just be glad you don't have to go home to him."

"Right. Because I have it so much better going home to Rita."

"You don't understand how good you've got it having a mother who doesn't care, instead of too many parents who care too much."

That hurts. I know Rita doesn't care, but it stings to hear Chase say it. I sting back. "Fine. I didn't realize you were so scared of Sheriff Daddy. Just take me home."

"That's what I'm doing."

We don't speak until he pulls up in front of my house.

I pop the seat belt before he comes to a stop. I'm so mad that I'm fighting tears. "Thanks for the ride," I mutter.

"Don't mention it."

"I won't. Don't worry." I slam the door and stomp up the sidewalk.

Then I wheel around. "I was doing all right taking care of Jeremy on my own. I don't need you, or T.J., or anybody else to help me now! It's always been just me and Jeremy. I should have known better than to—" A lump fills my throat and blocks the words. So I turn and run into the house, slamming the door behind me.

Once inside, I can't stop shaking. I collapse to the floor and cover my head with my hands, letting my hair make a tent around my face, shutting me off from everything and everyone.

31

A noise makes me look up. A sob, or a sniffle. Rita's sprawled on the floor, leaning against the couch. In her lap is a shoe box, and in front of her, spread out in a semicircle, are photographs. She holds one up and cocks her head to the side. I don't think she knows I'm here. At first I think she must be drunk, but I don't see a glass or a bottle.

My mother is crying. She is, in fact, sobbing.

"Rita? What happened?"

She doesn't answer.

I move in closer. She's holding a baby picture, taken at a hospital. The baby wearing a white pointy cap and wrapped in a white blanket looks like every other baby I've seen in hospital photos. Only somehow I know it's Jeremy.

I sit beside her and finger through the photos scattered on the carpet. Half a dozen look like the one she's holding, Jeremy a couple of minutes old. But there are other pictures of Jeremy—outside on a lawn somewhere, in the back of a faded car, in a building with other kids his size, no older than two. I've never seen these pictures. Where did she get them? How did she manage to hold on to them? *Why* did she?

"He's my boy," she says, not looking at me. "My own little boy."

I don't know what to say. This isn't the Rita I know. It makes me think of what Chase said about me: *The Hope I know . . .* , something about how the Hope he knew wouldn't give up on Jeremy. And the Chase I just left in the car, was he the Chase I know? The sickly Caroline Johnson on the stand, was she the same woman who screamed her hate at her husband? The T.J. who ran away without looking back, who scared me, was he the same T.J. who brought me mermaid tears and ate lunch with me at school every day?

I pick through the pictures of Jeremy. This is the Jeremy I know, sweet, innocent.

Are we different people every single moment of our lives?

"I have to testify for Jeremy," Rita says, not taking her eyes off a photo of a much younger Rita and her son.

"What? Why?"

"I'm Raymond's star witness."

"Wait. Did Raymond call and tell you he wants you to testify?"

"Yep. Saved the best till last." She leans back and takes a deep breath that turns into a cough.

I think I may hurl. Rita's going to testify? And she's the last person the jury will hear from? I don't understand why Raymond would do this, even with his stupid kitchen-sink strategy . . . unless Caroline Johnson really did that much damage.

"Rita, did you and Raymond rehearse what you're going to say?"

She wipes her eyes with the back of her hand, the same hand that's holding the photograph of Jer and her. "I got to get to Raymond's."

I call Bob and ask him to drive her. Rita isn't drunk. She hasn't been drinking. But she's shaking, shaken and stirred. I don't trust her behind the wheel of a car.

I volunteer to cover for them at the restaurant, but Bob says he doesn't need me. In twenty minutes, I have Rita dressed and ready.

"Don't you leave the house again!" she calls to me on her way to Bob's car. "Not like you ever do anything I say," she mutters. Then she's gone.

I put away the pictures of Jeremy. With Rita gone, the house turns up its noise volume—a hum from the fan becomes a roar; water leaking in the toilet, a waterfall; and the fridge groans like it's being tortured. I lock the doors and windows, trying not to think about the stalker. What if he knows I'm alone, really alone now? No Rita, no T.J., and no Chase.

Exhausted, I lie down on my squeaky mattress, and my thoughts go to Chase. I miss him already—not just his help, but him. I miss his slow smile, like he's grinning against his better judgment. And the way his voice gets deeper when he's trying to explain about his life in Boston. Raising my hand, I think about how his large fingers feel interlocked with my small ones.

What have I done?

Chase has been so good to me. Did I really accuse him of caving to his "daddy"? He didn't have to help me in the first place. But he did, even when his dad tried to keep him away from me.

I need to apologize. If I never see him again, he has to know how grateful I am for everything he's done. I don't think I could have made it this far without him.

Since the last person I called was Chase, I take out my cell and hit Send. His phone goes directly to voice mail. No way I can say what I want to say on a recorder. I hang up. In a few minutes, I try again. And again. I don't know how many times I dial Chase over the next hour. Finally, I give up and decide I can, at least, text him. He'll have to read that, and I can delete before sending if I screw it up. I punch in: I'm sorry. Hope. Then I change it to: I'm sorry! Hopeless.

I send it and wait, staring at the screen until it goes blank. I picture Chase hearing the beep. He glances at the number, sees it's me, and . . .

No answer.

I try again: Please, Chase. Can't we talk?

I send it and go back to waiting. Jeremy and I used to text each other before Jer lost his cell. Our exchanges were as fast as phone calls.

I'm not giving up. Chase said it himself. The Hope he knows is no quitter. I send another text: Meet me tonight? Now? I don't want him to come to my house, and I sure don't want to go to his. So I keep typing: At school? Driving practice? He'll know what I mean. He'll remember that day when we were so close we read each other's thoughts, when he didn't get mad at me, even after I wrecked his car.

I wait for a reply. While I'm at it, I should text T.J. too.

We were friends for a long time. I stare at the screen, trying to think of a message for him. But I can't.

My phone beeps. It's Chase. I have a message: OK.

It takes me five minutes to change into jeans and brush my hair. I'm as nervous as if it's our first date. I try to tell myself not to get my hopes up. He's agreed to talk. Nothing else.

I hurry outside and up the walk in the direction of the school. It's muggy out, and a cloud of gnats hovers around me. I shoo them away and keep going.

Behind me a car starts up. Headlights pop on and shine through me, turning my shadow into a jagged ghost.

Coincidence. But I walk a little faster.

The car creeps along behind me. I want it to speed up. I want the lights to vanish when I turn onto Walnut Street. But the headlights stay with me, like two giant flashlights keeping me in their sights. I walk faster. It's all I can do not to break into a run.

The car pulls up beside me, keeping pace with me. Then I hear a voice: "Hope?"

"Chase! How did you—?"

"Get in." He's ducking low from the driver's side so we can see each other.

I climb in, my heart still jittery, maybe more so. Then I scoot as close as I can get to him. "Chase, I'm sorry. I'm so sorry."

"I know. Me too." He reaches out an arm, and I fall into him.

I close my eyes and let myself soak up everything about

this moment, his strong arms around me, my head on his chest, rising and falling with his breath. I want to dissolve into him, to lose myself in Chase Wells.

Suddenly I pull away so I can see his face. "Were you out here the whole time?"

"Yeah. As soon as Dad finished yelling at me—which only happened because he had to go in to work—I came over here. I was pretty sure he was never going to have a patrol car on your street, so I thought I'd better keep an eye on things myself, in case that pickup came back."

"You've been guarding me? Even after I said those horrible things to you?" I snuggle closer.

"I admit I was pretty mad when I drove away, but not mad enough to leave you for the stalker." He grins down at me. I want to freeze that look, the dimples, the warmth.

"Nice to know you wouldn't throw me to the stalker in a fit of anger." I stretch up and kiss him, then pull back. "Why didn't you answer your phone?"

"You called me? Sorry. Dad played the big-bad-father card before he stormed out. I'm grounded—yeah, right—and phoneless. He made me turn in my cell. I'll get it back. Don't worry."

"Wait a minute. He took your cell?"

"Yeah. I'm surprised he didn't take the keys to the car, my driver's license, and—"

"But you're here." Something's wrong. Really wrong.

He squints at me. "Don't look so worried. I haven't been grounded since I was ten. He'll get over it."

"But how did you know to come and meet me?"

"Meet you? What do you mean?"

My mind is spinning, trying to piece together the messages. "I sent you a text. We're supposed to be meeting at the school parking lot."

"Didn't get the message, Hope. I didn't have the phone. I just saw you leave because I was guarding the—"

"But you answered. You texted me back and said okay."

Chase's face changes. Even his eyes seem to darken. He takes me by the shoulders and eases me back into the passenger seat. "Hope, that wasn't me."

Neither of us says a word until I can't stand the silence. "Chase, if you didn't send the message . . ." But I can't finish it.

So he does. "My dad did." He stares at his hands. "I was afraid of that."

"But why would he do that? Why would he tell me to meet you at the school?"

Chase still won't look at me. "I don't know."

He's hanging over the steering wheel as if his bones have dissolved from his body. He knows something. When we drove away from the Johnson place, I sensed something wasn't right with him. "Chase," I whisper, "you have to tell me what's going on."

Finally, he looks at me. "I think my dad is the stalker."

"What? That's crazy! Your dad is the sheriff! Why would he stalk me?"

Chase is shaking his head. "He's not. He didn't. Not really. Not *stalk*. I'm sure he didn't mean to hurt you, Hope. He just wanted to scare you."

"Well, he did that all right! But it doesn't make sense. Why would he—?"

"He wanted us to stop investigating. Dad's a control freak,

Hope. I knew he didn't like me blowing him off and seeing you anyway. But I didn't start figuring things out until this afternoon, after we saw him at Caroline Johnson's. I've never seen him that desperate. There was something in his eyes." He puts his hand on my head and strokes my hair. "He's not a stalker, Hope. He probably just didn't know what else to do— and I'm not defending him. Believe me, if I'd known he was the one calling you, I would have made him stop. He kept telling me to leave it alone, and—"

"That's it! *Leave it alone!*" Those words have been circling like a tornado in my brain. "Chase, that's what the stalker said on the phone, and it's what your dad said this afternoon." The pieces click together. I should have figured it out before now. "Could your dad get a pickup from that police impound?"

Chase nods. "He can drive anything on that lot, and nobody knows or cares."

I don't know whether to be relieved that the stalker is the sheriff . . . or terrified that the sheriff is the stalker. "So why did he want me to show up at the school lot tonight?"

Chase's lips tighten. He sticks the key into the ignition. "I don't know, but we're going to find out."

Chase drives through the fast-food parking lot to come in behind the school. He stops just inside the fence, too far away for us to see much. "I know he's out there, watching."

I scan the field, imagining myself walking across the parking lot, calling Chase's name, no answer but the wind, a warm August breeze. I'd get closer and closer to the tree. Maybe I'd sit there, waiting. And then what? What would he have done?

A flash of white shines from behind the big oak, the one I scraped. "Chase, there! Behind the tree."

"I see him." He swears under his breath. His eyes narrow to black slits. "I've spent half my life trying to be like him, trying to be who he wanted me to be. Perfect son. Perfect student. Perfect pitcher. Not anymore."

"Chase? What are you going to do? Chase!"

He doesn't answer me. He backs the car up, then eases it all the way around the lot until the truck is in full view. Without a glance at me, he floors the accelerator. The car squeals and shoots forward, back tires skidding, then righting to aim us directly at the pickup.

I scream. We're going to ram into that truck. "Chase!"

Inches away, he slams the brakes. I catch myself, hands braced on the dashboard. The car swerves. I feel a *thunk*. I open my eyes and see that we've bashed in the door of the white pickup truck, pinning it to the tree.

Sheriff Wells swears so loud I hear the words, the hate, through our closed windows. Chase jumps out of the car, leaving the driver's door open. He waits, legs spread, hands on hips, while his dad struggles to get out of the truck. But the driver's door is blocked by our car, and the passenger's door is smashed against the tree. He kneels at his window and lets out a string of cussing.

Midway through cursing the day Chase was born, the sheriff stops. I think he notices me in the car for the first time. His glare raises the tiny hairs at the base of my neck. Nobody has ever looked at me with so much hate before. I want to curl up in a ball on the floor of the car.

"Are you done?" Chase asks his father. He takes the ground between them in three strides until he's face to face with his dad, still trapped inside the cab. My Chase is strong and fearless, and he's not backing down a single step.

I want to be with him. He's standing up to his dad for me. I open the car door and start to get out, but my seat belt yanks me back. Fumbling with it, I manage to get free and step outside. Without glancing at the sheriff, I walk around the car to stand beside Chase. He and his dad are inches apart, locked in a stare-down.

"I asked you if you're finished." Chase's voice is hard, controlled.

"Finished?" Sheriff says, shifting his weight from one knee to the other, still caged inside the truck. His head has to bow to keep from hitting the ceiling. He rolls down the truck's window, but it won't go past halfway.

"Finished stalking Hope?" Chase says.

"I wasn't stalking anybody." Sheriff Wells turns to me. "I was just trying to get you to stop nosing around in things you had no business in. You should have left it alone. Then I wouldn't have had to—"

"Stalk me?" I finish his sentence. "How could you do that? You're supposed to be . . . I don't know . . . a protector. Not a stalker." I feel Chase's hand wrap around mine.

"You're really something, Dad," Chase says.

"You don't understand. You're just kids! You are nothing but a child, Chase!" Sheriff Wells shouts. He turns to me. "Look. I know you want to get your brother off, but you're out of your league. You're just going to make the jury send Jeremy to prison, instead of a mental hospital, where he belongs."

"You have no right to say where my brother belongs!" I shout. "You don't know Jeremy. And you don't know me."

"What were you going to do if I hadn't shown up, Dad?" Chase demands. "What would have happened tonight if Hope had come here alone, like you planned? Huh? Answer me!"

"Quit yelling!" Sheriff Wells shouts back. "Don't talk crazy. I'd never do anything to the girl. I figured she'd show and you wouldn't, and that would be the end of it. She'd think you stood her up, that you were done with her for good, which is what you should be."

"I'm done, all right," Chase says. "Only not with her. With you."

32

Rita is sound asleep when I get back home. I want to
wake her up and tell her what happened. I want her to know
that it wasn't just kids trying to scare me. It was Sheriff
Matthew Wells, someone who should be looking out for kids
like me, for kids like Jeremy.

I open her bedroom door and start to go in when I realize
I'm about to wake up my mother for a mother-daughter talk.
It's ridiculous. I can't explain why I want to talk to Rita after
so many years of not talking to her.

I shake off the notion, step back out of her room, and
close the door. I need sleep. So does she. I want her to be the
best witness for Jeremy she can be tomorrow.

In the morning, Rita tries on every outfit in her closet as if
she's going for an audition. She settles on a peach blouse and
a straight black skirt that's a little small for her, but not too
bad. This is definitely the most courtworthy outfit in her
closet. After trying her hair up, then down, she compromises,

pulling the top part back and letting the rest hang in bright yellow waves. She looks pretty good . . . until she adds giant hoop earrings I can't talk her out of wearing.

"How about you let me wear one of those necklaces you used to make?" Rita asks. "The ones with those little stones from the lake?"

I'm amazed she even knows about my mermaid tears. "Sure, Rita. Hang on." I find a necklace with a piece of sea glass a little darker than Rita's blouse, and I put it on her.

Rita fingers the necklace. "That's real nice. Real nice, Hope."

I ride with her to the courthouse. She checks herself out in the rearview mirror at least a dozen times, nearly ramming into the back of a police car at the courthouse intersection. "Good luck, Rita," I tell her as she steps out of the car.

"Don't you worry none, Hopeless. Rita has everything under control."

Chase is already there. I slide in next to him, in the seat I've sat in ever since I testified. I can't believe it could all be over today, except for the closing arguments from the lawyers. Rita takes a seat in the first row, behind the defense table. Jeremy is already restless, his hands flying over the table's imaginary keyboard. It's too early for him to be this nervous.

I watch as Jeremy takes something from his pocket. The aspirin bottle? I can't believe they let him keep it. But it's not the same bottle I gave him. It's bigger, a different shape. Somebody has given my brother an empty bottle. I'm so grateful that I thank God for every drop of kindness left in the world, this being one of those drops.

Rita swears on the Bible, her voice loud and dramatic, like

she's kicking off her audition. She takes her seat and crosses her legs.

Jerking his tie to one side, Raymond gets up from his seat behind the defense table. He walks right up to the witness box. "Good morning, Mrs. Long," Raymond says.

Rita gives him her biggest, fakest smile, but maybe the jury won't know it's fake. "Good morning, Mr. Munroe," she says.

Raymond starts out kind of slow . . . and dull and boring. He walks Rita through her life, or parts of it, growing up in Grain and then moving back here with me and Jeremy three years ago. She tells the court about her parents being dead and about how she works at the Colonial Café. To hear Rita tell this, you'd think she was one of those heroic and stoic single mothers who fight off the world in order to raise their children.

Then Raymond zeroes in on Jeremy.

RAYMOND: When did you first notice there was something, well, wrong with your son?

RITA: I knew right away. A mother knows these things. He just wasn't right, that's all.

RAYMOND: Go on.

RITA: Well, the older he got, the more *insane-like* he got. When he went to school, them teachers didn't know what to do with him. I'd get these phone calls from the principal that Jeremy wasn't paying attention. He didn't talk. He didn't get on with the other kids. Well, it hasn't been easy raising two kids anyhow, all by myself. And then I get this one, who's messed up in his head.

RAYMOND: How old was Jeremy when he quit talking?

266

RITA: Six or seven, I guess. Or maybe more like nine. I'm not
    sure. But that ought to tell you all you need to know about
    Jeremy. The boy can talk—all the doctors agree on that
    one. He just *won't* talk.

I want to stand up and scream at both of them. Raymond
and I agreed to stop making my brother out as insane and start
showing he wasn't the only one who could have killed Coach.
Raymond is supposed to be creating doubt, the reasonable
kind of doubt, like that Caroline Johnson might have done it.

Clearly, Raymond and Rita have been plotting strategy
without me. They've shut me out, just like before. And it's
not fair. Rita conspires with Bob, with Coach Johnson, with
Raymond—with everybody except me.

Furious, I whisper to Chase, "Why are they doing this?
They're trying to make Jeremy look crazy again."

He whispers back, "I think they have to, Hope. Raymond
probably didn't like Caroline Johnson's testimony. Maybe he's
afraid she made Jeremy look too guilty. I think he's just covering all his bases."

I don't want Chase to be right.

I listen to a couple more Crazy Jeremy stories that I can
tell Rita and Raymond have cooked up together. And then
Rita, sounding too confident, launches off on her own. I
cringe when I hear her start the next story, and I'm pretty sure
Raymond has no idea what's coming.

RITA: Okay. Here's another one. Jeremy has always been real
    big on God and church—not that that makes you crazy

267

necessarily, if you know what I mean. Even as a baby, he loved those hymns and them big brick churches.

RAYMOND: Uh-huh.

RITA: I've never been much of a churchgoer, so the church bus would come by for the kids on a Sunday morning. This was when we were living in Chicago, I think. Yeah, that's it. Well, anyways, Jeremy came home from one of those Sunday school meetings all excited. He still wouldn't talk, but he wrote in great big letters on his notebook paper: "How did you and God meet?" "What?" I asked him. He wrote again: "How did you and God meet and fall in love?" Well, come to find out, their lesson that day was on God the Father. Some teacher had told him God was his father. I've always told the boy he don't have no father. Well, it's easier that way for him. So that kid was all excited thinking he'd found out who his father was. God! And he wanted to know how I met his father. That boy. Another time, he—

RAYMOND: Mrs. Long, let's get back to Jeremy and the deceased. Did Jeremy like John Johnson?

RITA: He liked him fine. He loved going to ball games. He even loved shoveling sh—uh, manure out of them stalls. You'd have thought he had the most important job in the world.

RAYMOND: And you can't think of a single logical reason why Jeremy would want John Johnson dead?

RITA: Of course not.

RAYMOND: Thank you.

Rita starts to get up, but Prosecutor Keller is on his feet and heading straight for her. I shiver remembering the look on

Keller's face the second I realized he'd led me right into his trap. I pray Rita doesn't have a trap waiting for her.

KELLER: Good day, Ms. Long. I won't keep you, I promise. Just a few questions to clear up a couple of matters.

RITA: You go right ahead.

KELLER: Let me see if I have this straight. You told your son that he didn't have a father?

RITA: It was easier than going through the whole story with him, you know? He wouldn't have understood.

KELLER: But, of course, Jeremy does have a father?

RITA: Sure. I'm no Virgin Mary, if that's what you mean. But he might as well not have had one, for all the good it did him.

KELLER: I'd like to explore that a bit. Tell me about Jeremy's father, if you—

RAYMOND: I object! Jeremy's heritage is irrelevant and immaterial.

JUDGE: Mr. Keller?

KELLER: I believe I can prove it is highly relevant, Your Honor. If you'll allow me to make the connection, I'm confident the court will agree. Besides, the witness has opened the door. She brought up the subject of Jeremy's father.

RITA: I did no such thing!

JUDGE: The witness will refrain from comments unless directed to answer. Mr. Munroe, I'm afraid Mr. Keller has a point. Your witness opened the door. But, Mr. Keller, make your point quickly and move along, understood? Now, Mrs. Long, please answer the question.

RITA: What question? I can't remember the question.

KELLER: That's all right. Let me rephrase. In fact, let's back up just a bit. You said you went to high school in Grain, isn't that right?

RITA: Part of high school.

KELLER: Why did you leave?

RITA: I felt like it.

KELLER: I see. You left in the middle of your sophomore year. Is that correct?

RITA: I suppose.

KELLER: Either you did or you didn't. Which is it, Ms. Long?

RITA: Fine. I left during my sophomore year. Are you happy?

KELLER: Were you dating anyone at the time?

RITA: Do I have to answer this?

RAYMOND: I object to this line of questioning!

JUDGE: Mr. Keller, the court asked you to move along with this line of questioning. Move along. I'll overrule the objection, but the clock is ticking, Mr. Keller. Mrs. Long, answer the question.

RITA: Yeah, I was dating. So what? Maybe you didn't date in high school, but the rest of us did. And last time I looked, it wasn't a crime.

KELLER: You and John Johnson were in high school at the same time, isn't that true?

RITA: So were a lot of other people in this town.

KELLER: But John—I think you called him Jay Jay—and you, you liked each other. You dated, went steady, whatever they were calling it then?

I am in the middle of a train wreck. I'm tied to the railroad tracks, and the train is coming fast. Rita feels it too. She's acting all cocky, but I see through that act to her fear. I can count on one hand the number of times I've seen her scared, and this is one of those times. I glance over at Jeremy and see that he's full-on watching this happen. His empty bottle sits on the defense table, as if he's forgotten about it. He is watching Rita, and he's not breathing.

Something bad, very bad, is coming.

33

KELLER: Ms. Long, I'll ask you again. Were you and John Johnson in an exclusive dating relationship in high school?

RITA: Yeah. So what? That was a long time ago, in case you don't know that. I dated a lot.

KELLER: But that year, were you in an exclusive relationship with the deceased, John Johnson? Or did you sleep around?

RAYMOND: I object!

RITA: So do I!

JUDGE: Overruled. But, Mr. Keller, I'm pulling in your chain. Get to it.

KELLER: I'm sorry, Your Honor. Ms. Long, I don't know how else to ask this. And I apologize if the question embarrasses you. Were you Jay Jay's girlfriend? Did you sleep with him?

RITA: Yes. Okay. Yes, I was his girlfriend. And I did sleep with him, but I didn't sleep around. Just him. You can ask anybody.

KELLER: Thank you. I have. Let's change the subject for a minute.

RITA: Good idea.

KELLER: You ran away from Grain how long ago?

RITA: About twenty years. I couldn't take it here anymore.

KELLER: And yet, here you are. You came back. Why was that?

I'm getting a sick feeling in my stomach. I think I know where this is going. How could I have been stupid enough not to guess it before now?

Rita is rattling on, like she does when she gets nervous. Raymond has to have told her what he told me: Keep your answers short. Stay on point. Don't offer up information not asked for. But she won't stop talking, and I know where it's going to get her, to get Jeremy.

"I think my parents were too old to be parents, God rest their souls." Rita crosses herself, but she's never been Catholic. I think she does it wrong. "They're both dead now, so I suppose that's why I came back. I could still have a fresh start here. I figured I could get a job waitressing."

Keller moves in closer, the predator creeping toward his prey. "About twenty years?" He nods, as if calculating, counting on invisible fingers. He turns and looks at Jeremy. "How old is your son, Ms. Long?"

Jeremy doesn't flinch.

Keller wheels back around to Rita. "Ms. Long, how old is your son?"

Rita stares at the ceiling, then spits it out: "Almost nineteen."

Keller's lip curls up—a grin? a snarl? "Were you pregnant when you left Grain and dropped out of school?"

Rita turns to the judge. "He can't ask me that, can he?"

The judge looks like she feels sorry for Rita.

Raymond's slow on the draw, but he jumps up. "Objection!"

Keller smiles at the judge. "Goes to motive, Your Honor."

Does it? Does it go to motive?

I lean way forward so I can see Jeremy's face more clearly. He's staring at Rita. His eyes are still and deep. He knows. I can see that. Jeremy knows exactly what's coming.

"Overruled," says the judge. "Please answer the question."

"I was pregnant," Rita says softly, not looking at Keller.

"Was the child Jay Jay's?" Keller asks. "Is Jeremy the son of John Johnson?"

The courtroom goes crazy. Everybody's talking at once. The judge bangs her gavel and threatens to clear the courtroom if we don't shut up.

"Do you need me to repeat the question?" Keller shouts. "You're under oath, ma'am."

"I know that!" Rita snaps. "And I don't see what any of this has to do with anything. Yes! Jay Jay was Jeremy's father. Okay? Is that what you wanted? But Jeremy didn't know it."

I haven't taken my eyes off my brother. Rita is wrong. He did know. I can read my brother better than anyone on earth. Jeremy knew that John Johnson was his father. I don't know how or when he discovered it, but I can see the truth in his eyes. There's not a hint of surprise on his face.

Why didn't he tell me, write me a long note in his delicate calligraphy? I thought Jeremy told me everything. How could he have kept this enormous secret from me? I will myself to quit staring at my brother. When I look back to Rita, she's wringing her hands in a way I've never seen her do before. I hate her for keeping this secret, but I almost feel sorry for her too.

Keller isn't finished. "Are you positive John Johnson was Jeremy's father?"

Rita acts insulted. "I told you! I didn't sleep around in high school. I think I ought to know who the father of my baby was."

How many times have I asked her about Jer's father? I try to picture the two of them together, Rita and Jay Jay. But I can't. He was quiet, patient, good-natured. I don't think I ever saw him say more than a couple of words to Rita. She never talked about him. On the other hand, I have a dozen memories of Jeremy and Coach together. Jeremy and his father: in the barn, at the ballpark, with the horses.

I try to listen to what else Keller will make Rita say.

KELLER: Did you and Jay Jay pick up where you left off when you returned to Grain?

RITA: No!

KELLER: But he gave Jeremy a job, didn't he? And he took the boy under his wing, let him help out at ball games. Weren't the two of you having an affair?

RITA: We were not having an affair!

KELLER: But Mr. Johnson gave you money. Isn't that right?

RITA: So what? He should have been giving me child support all those years. It was the least he could do to try to make up for that.

KELLER: How much was he paying you?

RITA: Oh, he was real generous at first. Helped us with the

security deposit on that little house we rent. And he helped with rent.

KELLER: At first? You said he was generous at first? When was that?

RITA: When I first told him Jeremy was his son.

KELLER: And when was that?

RITA: Right after we moved here. So about three years ago.

KELLER: Not before then?

RITA: That's what I said. I'd started a new life for myself, and it didn't include a husband and father. I didn't need him trailing after me. No way I was going to get stuck in this town my whole life.

KELLER: But things changed when you moved back and told him Jeremy was his son? He paid you money, helped with the bills . . . at first?

RITA: Yeah. Then he stopped, refused to pay me a penny.

KELLER: When did he stop giving you money?

RITA: Last spring.

KELLER: Why did he quit paying?

RITA: He said he didn't have it. He said he had hospital bills and responsibilities. What did he think *we* were? We were his responsibilities too.

KELLER: Is that what Jeremy thought?

RITA: Jeremy? He never knew about Jay Jay or the money.

KELLER: I find that hard to believe. Didn't Jay Jay want to tell Jeremy he was his father?

RITA: Huh-uh. He was the one who didn't want Jeremy to know. I didn't care either way.

KELLER: Why? Why would John, Jay Jay, want to keep Jeremy a secret?

RITA: Because of his wife having the cancer and all. She couldn't have children, he said. He didn't want her to know that he already had one.

KELLER: But you told Jeremy anyway, didn't you?

RITA: No! I didn't tell him nothing. Jeremy didn't know.

KELLER: Ms. Long, when was the last time you saw John Johnson alive?

It seems like a full minute of silence passes. I think the courtroom is holding its breath.

KELLER: Your Honor, will you please instruct the witness to answer the question?

JUDGE: Mrs. Long, please answer the question.

RITA: I don't remember.

KELLER: I'll ask you again. If you lie, you'll be subject to a charge of perjury. Do you understand? One more time. When was the last time you saw the deceased?

RITA: That morning. The morning of the murder. I stopped by the stable.

I cannot breathe. Rita didn't say anything to me about seeing Coach then or any other time. "What time was this?" Keller presses.

"Just after seven," Rita mumbles.

"Please speak up," Keller asks, but there's no politeness in his voice. "What time was it, and how do you remember the time?"

Rita squeezes her lips together so hard it looks like she doesn't have teeth. "It was seven-oh-seven, and I know

277

because they said so on the radio right before I shut off the engine, okay? Station seventy-point-seven at seven-oh-seven. AM radio in the AM."

"Where exactly did you find Mr. Johnson that morning?" Keller asks. I get the feeling that he knows the answer to every question before Rita opens her mouth.

"I told you. In . . . the barn." Rita cocks her head at him, then looks down.

"Was Jeremy with you?" Keller asks.

"No!" Rita snaps. "I was going home from Bob's, but I decided to stop by the barn and talk to Jay Jay face to face about the money he owed me."

"So you argued?" Keller asks.

Rita squirms in her seat. "He owed me child support. I had that coming. I just wanted what was rightly mine. He had no right to stop paying. Jeremy was his son, his flesh and blood! And we needed the money. I could have asked twice what I did. But I didn't."

"I understand," Keller says, like he's suddenly on Rita's side. "You and Jeremy deserved that money, and he was cutting you off."

"Exactly!" Rita sits up straighter.

"When you told Jay Jay that you and Jeremy deserved that money, were you loud?" Keller asks.

"Yeah. You ever argue without being loud?" Rita challenges.

"Precisely where did this argument take place?" Keller asks.

"Near one of the back stalls. I had heels on, and I remember that I had to watch where I was stepping and walk way to the back because Jay Jay wouldn't come up front and talk."

"So if someone had been in the stable, for example, they would have heard you?" Keller asks.

"They'd have heard us. But nobody was there," Rita says.

"You're wrong about that." Keller turns and points at Jeremy. "Your son was there."

Rita gasps. She shakes her head. "No. That can't be. He never . . . He didn't . . ."

Raymond jumps to his feet and objects all over the place. He yells phrases like "facts out of evidence" and "move for a mistrial" and other things I can't hear because everybody is shouting. I don't have any idea how Keller knows what he does about Jeremy finding out Coach was his dad that morning, but I recognize truth when I hear it. And that's truth. Jeremy knew. He didn't know before that morning, so he must have heard Rita screaming it. That's why he doesn't want to see me, why he won't write to me. He couldn't keep that secret if he did.

The judge is angrier than I've ever seen her. She pounds her gavel and orders the courtroom cleared.

I watch Rita staring at Jeremy. Tears stream down her face. Mascara streaks her cheeks like tribal paint. Over and over again, she mutters, "I'm sorry, Jeremy. I'm so sorry. I didn't know. I just didn't know."

Chase and I are ushered out of the courtroom like everybody else. The second we're outside, I dash around the corner and hurl. I vomit again and again until nothing else is in me.

Rita, how could you?

I don't know what will happen in the courtroom, or what it will mean. But I do know this for sure. My mother has just given the jury the one thing they didn't have—motive.

279

34

Chase drives me around and tries to talk me down, but I'm too angry. It's all so unbelievable, even for Rita. "All that time," I say, to myself as much as to Chase, "she knew who Jeremy's father was, and she didn't tell him? I don't care if Coach wanted Jeremy to know or not. *Jeremy* wanted to know! Didn't that count for anything?"

"You really didn't have any idea, did you?" Chase says. Mostly, he's let me rant and has just been circling Grain while I blow off steam.

I glare at him. "Are you kidding? There's no way I would have kept it secret if I'd known."

"Maybe your mother was trying to do what she thought was best for Jeremy."

"Rita?" I let out a one-note laugh that has no laughter in it. "She did what she thought was best for Rita. It's what she always does." I think about those pictures of Jeremy in Coach's desk, Jer's special color wheels pinned up on the wall in his office. "They might have had a relationship, Chase. A shot at a father-and-son relationship, if Rita had told Jeremy the truth."

Chase sighs. "I don't know. Father-son relationships are overrated, if you ask me."

"You don't mean that. I've missed my father my whole life, and I never got to know him in the first place."

He reaches across the seat and puts his hand on the back of my neck. "Ready to go home?"

Rita is waiting for me when I walk in. "Don't start, Hope," she warns the minute I close the door.

I stare at her. Her hair is a mess. She's in that same white slip. And she's drinking, not bothering with a glass. She tilts her head back and gulps. I watch the whiskey travel down her throat, making waves in her neck.

"How could you do that to Jeremy?" My voice is quiet, but I'm screaming inside.

She shakes her head, coughs, then chokes out her answer. "I didn't do nothing to that boy."

"True enough," I admit. "You didn't tell him he had a great father, who really cared about him."

"Jay Jay didn't want the kid to know!" Rita screams.

"Since when do you care what anyone else wants?" The anger is bubbling up now. "You didn't tell Jeremy because you were afraid Coach would stop giving you money. Was he paying to keep you quiet? That's blackmail, Rita."

"That's not the way it was." She sprawls on the couch, the bottle cradled between her knees. "He didn't want his wife to find out."

"So you took advantage of that. You made him pay you to keep your mouth shut." I can see on her face that I'm right.

"You don't understand," she moans.

"And when *Jay Jay* stopped paying, why didn't you tell Jer then? He would have been so happy, Rita. Now he won't ever have that, the feeling that he has a father who loves him. You should have told him."

"Jeremy was all right. He was already spending lots of time with Jay Jay. I thought I could change Jay Jay's mind. I thought I could get him to start paying up again." She shoves her hair out of her face and takes another drink.

"That's what you were doing the day he was murdered? Trying to get more money out of him? What happened, Rita? What really happened that morning?"

"Get away from me." She says this because I've slipped in front of her, eased onto the coffee table so we're face to face.

"Tell me the truth. Did you lose your temper?" I've seen Rita lose her temper. I've felt her temper. "You did, didn't you?" I can see it in my mind—Rita exploding in front of Coach, grabbing the bat, swinging it. "You killed him. And you're letting Jeremy take the blame." Pieces fall together when I say this. "Is that why you didn't tell anybody, even Raymond, that you went to the stable that morning? That you talked to Coach? That you—?"

"Shut up! I didn't—!"

But it's making sense now. "Jeremy saw you. He saw you kill Coach. And he's trying to protect you! He's covering up for *you*! *That's* why he wouldn't see me. He knows I'd get the truth out of him."

"You're as crazy as he is." Rita shoves me, but I won't give an inch. "Why would I kill Jay Jay?"

"How should I know why you do anything? Maybe you couldn't stand Jeremy having another parent, a *good* parent, in his life. Maybe you killed him for that."

"Don't be a fool." She takes another swig, a big one this time.

"You couldn't stand for Jeremy to have a real parent, someone who was kind to him. Was it like that with *my* father, Rita? Were you glad when my father got killed too?" Those dreamlike images of my father shoot through my brain, too fast for me to tell whether they're real or imagined. "Two fathers, two sudden deaths. Quite a coincidence . . . Or was it? Was it, Rita?"

She shrugs. "You're talking crazy."

"Rita, did you kill my father too?"

Rita raises her arm and aims the back of her hand toward me. I brace myself for a slap, but I don't budge. She lowers her arm. "You don't know what you're talking about."

"I remember."

"You were three years old. You don't remember nothing."

"He was wearing a baseball cap. A red cap. And it was sunny."

That makes her look up at me. "How did you . . . ?"

"Tell me what really happened."

"He was run over by a truck. How many times do I have to tell you?"

This is what she's told me every time I've asked. But it's not good enough now. I'm standing up to her. I want answers, real answers. "Why? How did it happen? Why would he be in the street? Did he run out in front of the truck?" I pause because the image is there. My father. Me. And Rita. Rita, her arms outstretched. Then I say it, what I think I've wanted to ask her my whole life. "Did you push him?"

Again, I think she's going to hit me, but I don't care. I don't flinch, or duck, or scoot back to break the impact. "Did you kill him? Did you push my father in front of that truck because you were tired of him? Because *he* wouldn't pay you anymore? Rita! Did you kill him too?"

"You crazy little—!" Her teeth are clenched. Her eyes are watering. She stands up, weaving from side to side. Then she leans forward and gets in my face. I smell her stale breath, the liquor like vomit in her mouth. "If anybody killed your father, it was you."

I start to yell back at her, but I stop. I remember something—an image in black and white. They're never in black and white. It's blurry too. I think it must be cloudy, but then the day clears, and it's sunny. I can see a tall, thin man in a baseball cap. The red cap is the only color in the scene. I'm looking up at him, and he seems like the tallest person in the world—in my world, at least. I walk away, laughing. The ground is dry and lumpy, and it's hard to walk without tripping. The picture is joined by other images, one after the other, fast, like animation, a jagged film. A shaggy puppy dances around my feet, then dashes ahead of me. I laugh and run after it. There's a curb, and I spread my arms to step down from the grass to the pavement. Cars are parked there, but I follow the puppy and go between them. Someone's yelling at

284

me from behind. It's a game, so I keep going, chasing Puppy. I hear footsteps behind me and more shouts from Daddy, who lets me call him Daddy and wants Jeremy to do the same. I hear thunder from the street and screeching that makes me stop so I can cover my ears. The next thing I know, I am lifted off the ground, as if an angel has flown by and picked me up. Only instead of carrying me, the angel tosses me like a football. I land hard, and it hurts. I cry and scream because I'm scared now. People run at me, past me, into the street. The truck driver stumbles out of his cab. I see his face, looking like he's just seen that angel and doesn't know what to make of it. "I tried to stop! I tried to stop!" He says this over and over. And Rita is screaming, and I want her to quit, but she won't. She keeps screaming and screaming and never stops.

I gasp for air. I'm sitting in the living room, staring at the empty couch. I am light-headed, and I think I'm going to be sick again.

Rita is right. I caused my father's death.

What's wrong with us? Are we all killers? Murderers? Is Rita? Is Jeremy?

Am I?

35

After the weekend, the prosecution takes two days to sum up its case and for Keller to give his closing argument. Chase and I sit through all the explanations. Keller brings in his whole team and puts on a grand finale. A short, chubby lab guy uses four-color art to reexplain diagrams of the blood evidence found at the scene and on the bat, in spite of whatever Jer did to wash it off. A gorgeous assistant prosecutor, with long black hair and a body that three of the jurors can't stop staring at, sets up a miniature stable, complete with horses and a baseball bat, just to show the jury who stood where and what the prosecution has been claiming all along took place, that Jeremy Long willfully bludgeoned to death his father, John Johnson.

Life is as miserable out of court as it is in court. Rita and I aren't speaking, which isn't such a big loss. I've tried to put myself in her shoes and imagine what it might do to a person to see her husband crushed by a truck. She's apologized for blurting out something she kept to herself all these years. In her own way, I guess, Rita has tried to take back what she said about me killing my father.

But T.J. was right. Some things you can't take back.

And sometimes you can't go back to the way things were. I saw T.J. again. He was standing on the sidewalk outside my house when I left for work Saturday morning. We stared at each other for a minute or two. He didn't scare me this time, but I still found nothing to say to him. Finally, I kept walking, passing him without looking back.

"Hope?"

I stopped but I didn't turn around. I waited, wanting him to say more. I yearned to hear the old T.J. and know he was still there. But he didn't say anything else. So, after a few seconds, I walked off again. I didn't stop until I got all the way to the Colonial. And when I looked back, I saw that T.J. hadn't followed me.

But the worst is that something's happening between Chase and me, and I don't know what it is, unless he can sense that I killed my own father. Of course I haven't told him. When he's dropped me off after court, I haven't asked him to stay, and he hasn't asked me to go with him. Maybe we're both just too tired.

I've thought about my father and what happened the day he was killed. I've gone over and over it enough to be as depressed as I've ever been. Then I started writing about everything to Jeremy. I wrote *for* him too, still in my chicken-scratch penmanship, pretending I was writing his fancy, swirling letters. We argued. "Jeremy," I said, "I killed my own father!" And Jer said back, "You were three, Hope." And I said, "But if I hadn't run into the road, he wouldn't have run after me. It was my fault!" "You were three," Jeremy replied. "How much fault could you have had in you? You didn't mean to hurt anybody." We argued more, and finally Jeremy got in the last word: "Fault, schmalt. You're forgiven because God says so. He's got your back. He's your father too, you know." So even though he wasn't really there, my brother got me through the worst of it.

Still, it's not something I want to tell Chase. Could that explain the distance I feel growing between us?

Chase and I text at night—he's positive Rita isn't the murderer. I think he's wrong, but I don't want to fight him. I'm pretty sure neither of us wants to risk arguing. So we guard our words. We're careful with each other. If I've moved away from Chase, he's moved away from me, too. Maybe it's just that we both know the trial is almost over and things will never be the same.

More than anything, I want to talk to Jeremy. I want to tell him about my father, about what I remember. I want to talk to Jer about Coach. My brother lost his father, and he's had to grieve all by himself.

The night before Raymond's closing, I can't sleep. As I pace the living room, an August moon pushes its way inside the house so I don't need to turn on lights. I miss Jeremy so much that it hurts my chest, my arms, my throat. I didn't know missing could do that.

I wander into Jeremy's room. The moonlight is even brighter here when I open the curtains all the way. I gaze around the room. This is the room of a little boy—baseball curtains, comic books, and his jars. The only poster is pinned to his door, one he made himself. It says: BEYOND HERE, THERE BE DRAGONS. Jeremy told me that's what mapmakers used to write on unknown spaces on maps so travelers would know where they shouldn't go.

Jeremy has been gone from this room for so long, but it still smells like him, like late-season grass and cherry Kool-Aid. I crumple to the floor, then lie on my back and peer up at his shelves of jars. Tomorrow that jury may decide whether or not my brother will ever come home. I want to pray. I know that's what Jeremy's doing. Only he never calls it praying. He just talks to God in his head. He doesn't have to write. Maybe that makes it easier for him to talk to God than to talk to people.

It's not that easy for me, but I close my eyes and try:

Dear God, this is me, Hope, talking to you in my head like Jeremy does. I guess I've clammed up on you like Jer has with the rest of us. Maybe we both got slapped somewhere along the way. You know he didn't do this. You must have seen who actually did. If it's Rita, then I don't know what to say about that. Look, I know Jeremy hears you—you loaned him your song that once. I'm not asking for a whole song—but maybe just a note or two would be good. Thank you. Love, Hope.

Feeling a little better, I sit up too fast and bang my head on Jeremy's bottom shelf. I spin around in time to see Jeremy's glass jars wobble. One jar tips in slow motion and topples off the shelf before I can catch it.

Crash! The jar shatters into pieces that skid across the wood floor. I'm horrified. Jeremy would freak out if he saw this.

I drop to all fours and scramble to pick up the lid. It's

rimmed with broken glass, and my finger slices across it, mingling blood with jagged shards. The bottom of the jar lies upside down at my feet. I can make out writing there, something scrawled on the glass in black marker. Carefully, I examine the bottom of the jar. It says: **9:23 a.m., May 4.** The date is there too, faded and harder to read. But I make it out—it's three years ago, about the time Rita moved us to Ohio.

I'm stumped. Was Jeremy dating the time he got his jars? I guess it makes as much sense as anything else in this room. I think I may have seen him scribbling on the bottom of a jar a couple of times. Since he's always been so private about his collection, I never paid much attention.

I start to clean up the mess when I see a piece of paper wedged underneath the lid of the broken jar. I pull it out and unfold it, careful not to drip blood from my cut finger onto the paper. The writing is Jeremy's tight, controlled calligraphy, the only thing controlled in his life. I hold the slip of paper up to the moonlight. It says: **Air on the day Rita smiled and Yellow Cat purred.**

Yellow Cat. The old yellow cat that was living in this house before we rented it, the cat Rita made us turn over to the animal control people.

Why would Jeremy write that?

I pick up another jar, a tall, skinny one that once held olives for Rita's martinis. I remember the night—about a year ago?—when Rita caught Jeremy dumping out an almost full jar of olives. He needed a jar, and we were all out of empties. If Rita hadn't been so drunk, I think she would have killed him. I hid him under my bed until she got over it.

My mind is already flashing images at the speed of light.

Jeremy, his arms raised above his head, like thin branches against a black sky. While his bony fingers clasp a lid in one hand, an empty jar in the other, he sweeps the sky like he's catching fireflies . . . or maybe stars. Then, with angel eyes and a devilish grin, he twists the lid on tight, like the earth might stop spinning if he didn't do it right.

On the bottom of this olive jar is a date, close to a year and a half ago, and the time: 10:22 p.m. I open the jar and turn over the lid. I knew it. There's a piece of paper stuck there, under the lid. I can't unfold it fast enough. It reads: **Air on a perfect starry night, sprinkled with Hope's laughter.**

Air? That's it. Air. My brother didn't collect empty jars. He collected air. Did this jar contain the air from one of our stargazing nights a year and a half ago? Had Jeremy trapped that night in an olive jar, saved that moment? I can almost feel a chill in the air and those stars loosed in his room, mingling with atoms of Kool-Aid and grass.

I look around at the dozens and dozens and dozens of glass jars filled with Jeremy's collectible moments. *Air.* My mind is a slide show on speed: Jeremy, his jar sweeping air above his head as he rides that pinto around the pasture; air captured as the church choir sings "Amazing Grace"; air gathered from the top of a slide when I took him to the park. Jeremy taking a canning jar from a store in Salina, Kansas, and running straight to the middle of a wheat field. Did he capture the scent of grain and the feel of dust and sunshine? In Chicago, Jeremy grabbing jars from the fridge and dumping their contents on the floor . . . to fill the jars with memories.

How long has he been collecting air? When did he start? I try to remember.

There's a system to the jars. If I know my brother at all, he's ordered this world of glass and air. Where I'm standing, the jars are three years old. I want to know when he started. I follow the shelf all the way back to the door. First shelf, first jar, a peanut butter jar. I turn it over and check the bottom. It's hard to make out, but I can read the month, February, and the year—a decade ago, the year my brother stopped talking. I remember we came home to our shack in Minneapolis, and Jeremy scooped out the last drop of peanut butter, eating it right from the jar and not giving me any. I thought he was mad on account of Rita hitting him for no reason.

I know I shouldn't open this jar. I have no right. Jeremy has saved the air of that day for over ten years. He wouldn't want that day to show up in his room now. But I can't help myself. I can't keep my fingers from turning the lid, from lifting it off, from stripping the yellowed paper away from the lid, from unfolding the secret message: **Air from the day Jeremy Long stopped talking.**

"Jeremy, Jeremy, Jeremy." I hug the jar and slide to the floor, where I rock back and forth. Tears blur the air swirling in Jeremy's bedroom. How could I have missed it? I should have known the jars meant more than empty glass.

I survey the walls of shelves, all full except for one, the bottom shelf across the room, where half a dozen jars have started a new row. The last row? My heart speeds up. Jeremy was collecting jars, collecting air, right up to the day of the murder. He always had his pack with him and empty jars in the pack. Did he collect air that morning?

I get to my feet so fast that I almost drop the jar I'm

holding. I set the peanut butter jar back down, right where it was. Then I hurry to the other side of the room, to the shelf farthest away from the beginning shelf. I want the end, the last jar.

There are four jars dated the morning of the murder. I want to rip off the lids to the jars right now and see what Jeremy collected that morning. Did he save air when he learned Coach was his father? He would have. He wouldn't have let that moment escape. Did he keep collecting air as things kept happening? He couldn't stop the events, but he could capture them. Four jars. Four jars with the date of the murder, and the last one has a dark smear on the side of the lid. A smear of dried blood.

I have to know. I put one hand on the first lid. I am set, ready to turn, to release that air and see what he wrote.

But I can't. What if this is evidence now? It might prove beyond a reasonable doubt that Jeremy knew Coach Johnson was his father. It might prove he was there. What if this is bad evidence, *incriminating* evidence?

Slowly, I let go of the lid. I know Jeremy didn't murder Coach. I know it without a shadow of a doubt. But I think he saw it happen. And I believe what he saw might be captured in these jars of air. Did he see who murdered his father?

Was it his mother?

I am holding living witnesses, air particles that were there the day of the murder. These jars could prove that my brother is innocent.

I don't remember Raymond's number, so I have to look it up in the phone book. It's past midnight.

Mrs. Munroe answers. "Yes?"

"I'm sorry to call so late, but it's an emergency. Could I speak to Raymond, please?"

"Just a minute, Hope. I'll get him."

It's way more than a minute before I hear Raymond on the phone. "Hope, what's wrong?"

"I'm sorry. I didn't mean to wake you up, but—"

"You didn't," Raymond says. "I've been working on my closing argument. I think we're going to have to stick with the insanity plea."

"No!"

"I know you don't want to go that way, but you heard Keller's closing, didn't you? I'm afraid your mother gave them the missing piece, motive. Coach was Jeremy's father, a father who refused to acknowledge him. No, I'm sorry, Hope, but—"

"But I have something to show you, Raymond! Something the jury has to see. I think it will prove Jeremy didn't kill Coach, and I think it will prove who did."

"Hope, it's too late to—"

"Just hear me out, Raymond. Please?" I can tell he thinks I'm making it up. There's a silence over the phone. Then Raymond sighs. "Okay. But make it fast, Hope. I have to close tomorrow, no matter what."

I tell Raymond about the jars, the air, the dates, everything. I read him the notes from the three jars I opened, one accidentally, two on purpose. And I tell him about the four jars, the murder jars.

He doesn't say anything until I'm done. Finally, he says, so soft-like that I barely hear him, "Imagine that boy collecting air like that, seeing moments and saving them."

I'm proud of Jer for that. "I know."

Then Raymond's tone changes, from awe to something else. Fear? "Hope, what do the jars from the murder date say? Read me the notes."

"I didn't open them, Raymond. I don't think I should. Do you? Won't Keller say that I did it myself? That I made it up to save Jeremy? This way, I can prove I didn't write the notes. I didn't even know what was in them. And the jars, they could do tests on them, right? They could tell they haven't been opened?"

"Wait. Hope. You haven't opened the jars?"

"Not the ones from *that* day."

"Hope, what if one of the jars, the jar with the blood, says: **The day I killed my dad**? Did you think about that?"

I swallow hard. I know Raymond doesn't mean to hurt me. If Jeremy killed his dad, that's exactly how he'd have labeled that jar. "It won't say that. He didn't do it, Raymond. It will be okay. I know Jeremy didn't do it." What I don't want to add is that I think I know who did. I can almost see Rita's name on that note: **The day Rita killed my dad.** Rita's done a lot of bad in her life, but she's the only mother I've ever had.

"Hope, even if those jars clear your brother, I can't use them. I don't even know if I could get any of this before the judge. Trial practice precludes introduction of new and unsubstantiated evidence in a closing argument."

"Raymond, you're smart. You're smart enough to get these jars in. You have to give Jeremy's jars a chance to save him. Please?"

"I don't know. . . ." But I can tell he's thinking.

"You can do it, Raymond. I have faith in you."

There's a long silence, but I can hear Raymond breathing, thinking. "Maybe I can't introduce the jars," Raymond says slowly, ". . . but maybe you can."

"Huh?"

"Why not? The prosecutors took two days for their show-and-tell. Keller brought in half his office for their closing. Why couldn't the judge let me have my one assistant?"

"Raymond, do you think it would work? I'm not that great talking, even just to one person, you know? And I'm horrible when I have to speak in front of my class at school." I close my eyes and try to imagine standing up in that courtroom and talking to the jury in front of all those people. It's horrifying.

But Jeremy's in that courtroom. And Jer needs me more than he's ever needed anybody. "If that's what it takes, I'll do it."

"Good. I'll give it a shot if you will," Raymond says.

Raymond and I stay on the phone and talk about the best way to show the jars to the jury and to re-create the crime with them. I scribble notes and ask Raymond questions until I can't think of any more.

Finally, Raymond says, "Hope, we better hang up now. I have a closing to finish, and you have a demonstration to prepare. So, see you in court?"

"See you in court."

I stay up the rest of the night, working on what I'm going to say to the jury. Pulling out my old school note cards, I write something for each jar. I try saying everything out loud over and over.

When I notice the moonlight has switched to sunlight, I jump into the shower and smile to myself, remembering what I told Chase about morning versus night showerers. I guess this shower counts for both.

Rita's still out cold, so I'm on my own for wardrobe selection. I end up picking out the gray skirt and white blouse I wore the first day I testified in court, but adding a wide black belt and my favorite sea glass necklace. The glass is green, shaped like a tear.

When I check myself in the mirror, I still don't look much like a lawyer's assistant, but I'll have to do. I'm all Jeremy's got.

36

I wait until the last minute to wake Rita. She stumbles out of her bedroom, looking like death warmed over. She's sober, but that's about all I can say in her favor. We don't speak to each other, except for me trying to hurry her up. I put ten jars into my backpack, wrapping them in towels. She doesn't even ask what I'm doing, or why I'm taking a backpack to court. Would she try to stop me if she knew?

It takes me twenty minutes to pass through the courthouse turnstile because the guard insists on searching my pack. It isn't easy to convince her that the jars don't have anything deadly in them. Rita doesn't wait for me.

"Where've you been?" Raymond asks as soon as he sees me. He must have been pacing because he's worked up a sweat.

We only have ten minutes to iron out our plan, and Raymond spends most of it on how to convince the judge that the jars are our way of re-creating the crime scene. That's his "legal premise" for bringing in the jars and me.

"I have a bad feeling about this," Raymond says as we enter the courtroom. His feeling is contagious. The room smells like stale pond water and cigars, although it's against the law to smoke in here. Heads turn when Raymond and I walk by the rows. We set off low conversations, tiny buzzes, like bumblebees in our wake.

I'm relieved to see Chase is already here, sitting in the front row, right behind the defense table. As we pass that row, I risk a glance at him. His hair, uncombed, makes him look wildly handsome. His head is in his hands, so I can't see much of his face, but enough to tell he hasn't shaved. I try to catch his eye as we walk toward the judge, but he doesn't look up.

I can't think about Chase now. I can't worry about anything except Jeremy.

My brother is already sitting behind the table, looking like his skin won't hold him, like everything he's knotted up inside is fixing to bust out.

The courtroom grows silent as Raymond and I stand in front of the judge. It's a packed house. I scan the back row, and there's T.J., sitting with his mom. He nods at me, and I nod back. I'm not sure if I'm glad to see him or not. I think I'm a different person than I was when we were best friends. Is it possible to change so fast? All I know is that the old Hope wouldn't be standing here, fighting for a chance to speak in front of everybody. But I am.

Prosecutor Keller strolls up, shoving between Raymond and me so he's closer to the judge than I am. I watch Keller's eyebrows arch up and down, like a couple of woolly worms doing calisthenics. Raymond talks fast. Keller interrupts. Raymond talks louder, waving his arms almost like Jeremy.

"Your Honor, this is ludicrous," Keller says. I think he also says something about Raymond trying to bring elephants into the courtroom, but I'm having trouble focusing. I want to go sit down with Chase and Jeremy. "The defense's entire request is absurd."

"Absurd?" Raymond shouts back. "Absurd is you bringing in half your staff for your high-tech show-and-tell performance and then having the unmitigated gall to accuse *us* of wanting to put on a circus!"

"Mr. Munroe makes a good point, Mr. Keller," the judge observes calmly.

"All I'm asking, Your Honor, is to be allowed one assistant and a few glass jars for demonstration and re-creation," Raymond finishes.

"With glass jars?" Keller mocks.

"Unopened jars," Raymond explains. "And the prosecution is welcome to test each jar for fingerprints and age to ensure they've not been opened by the defense or the defense's assistant, if—"

"Ridiculous!" Keller throws back his head in a fake laugh.

"If it's so ridiculous, then you have nothing to worry about," Raymond says.

"Worry? Who says I'm worried?" Keller snorts. "I just don't want to waste the court's time with a—"

"That'll do," says the judge. "I'll be the *judge* of what wastes the court's time. I've heard enough." She takes her time leaning back in her chair. "I'll allow the defense's request." She turns to Raymond, who is beaming like he's won a gold medal. "But, Mr. Munroe, let me remind you that I'm paying close attention. Be careful out there. And tell your *assistant* to do the same."

I smile up at her, but she doesn't smile back.

It doesn't take long for the trial to officially start up again. This time it's Raymond's turn to talk to the jury. He starts off his closing argument by recalling the nice things people said under oath about Jeremy. I'd like to listen, but I can't. I block out everything except Jeremy and his jars. As quietly as I can, with my back to the jury, I put my backpack up on the defense table and start taking out jars. One by one, I set them in front of me, straightening them, arranging each jar in chronological order. I have notes that go with each jar, if the judge lets me get that far. So I set out all my notes.

Only then do I let myself look at Jeremy. Jer isn't looking at me. He's staring at the jars, his eyes soft, his mouth open, lips turned up slightly, like he's just run into old friends he hasn't seen for years and missed something awful. When I'm all finished lining up the jars, I take Raymond's seat next to Jer.

Raymond is still repeating testimony of the character witnesses, but the jury isn't looking at him. They're watching me. Me and Jeremy. Raymond must see this too, because he stops suddenly. Then he says, "I could go on and on and tell you what you've already heard, but I don't want to do that. Instead, I've brought with me my assistant. I think you'll remember her from when she testified before you in court: Hope Long, Jeremy's sister. I'd like Hope to walk you through what we believe really happened on the day John Johnson was murdered." He comes over and waits for me to get up so he can sit down.

My knees wobble when I stand. Something that doesn't belong in my throat is pounding there. I cough a couple of times as I step around the table and face the jury on the other side of the courtroom. "You guys may be wondering why I brought these empty jars to court this morning," I begin. "These are just a few of over a hundred glass jars my brother has on shelves that go all the way around his room. Jeremy collects them. You already heard that in court." I hate my voice. It's weak and shaky, but I make myself keep going, like I rehearsed. "Collecting empty jars is a weird hobby, but so's collecting stamps or aluminum foil, or string, or Barbies, or glass fairies, or sea glass, right? My whole life, I thought these were empty jars, that Jeremy was collecting the jars them-selves. But I found out different last night when I accidentally knocked into a shelf full of these jars. One fell off and broke." I glance at Jeremy. "I'm sorry about that, Jer."

"Louder, Hope," Raymond whispers.

Out of the corner of my eye, I glimpse Keller, itching to stand up and object. I clear my throat and try to speak louder. "Anyway, that's when I discovered that these jars aren't empty at all. And that's why I brought these here—to demonstrate and re-create that day of June eleventh, when somebody mur-dered John Johnson." Raymond told me to work those words in, so now I have. "See, each jar is labeled on the bottom with a time and a date." I hold up the first two jars, one in each hand, and walk them over to the jury and back. "There are labels on the inside, on bits of paper tucked under the lids, so you can't see them. That's what I discovered when I broke that jar last night. And I discovered something else too. My brother didn't collect empty jars. He collected air. Air and moments and memories."

I let that one sink in while I set down the two jars. "I brought a few jars from different years so you could get an idea of how Jeremy stored things, all in perfect order. Some days, he collected moments that meant a lot to the whole nation or world, like this one, dated **November 4, 2008.** I can read the date on the bottom of the jar, but I can't see the inside label unless I take off the lid, which I don't want to do, if it's all the same to you. I'm pretty sure the label will read something like **Obama is elected president.**"

I pick up a Mason jar, and it strikes me that the glass is the color of Chase's eyes early in the morning. "The date on this one is five years ago, July second. I have no idea what's in here. But if Jeremy doesn't mind, I'd like to find out the same time you do, just to give us a better idea how this all works."

I glance back at Jeremy. He doesn't give me a go-ahead nod, but he doesn't freak out either. I take that as a yes and twist the lid. It takes muscle, and for a second I'm afraid I won't be able to get it off. Then it gives. As I lift that ridged silver lid, I imagine a whoosh of air in my face, and I blink.

"Yep. There's a piece of paper wedged in here." Fingers trembling, I dig out the note and read it, my voice breaking: *Air of a sunlit afternoon in Enid, Oklahoma, when Hope and I write funny notes.*

I bite my lip hard enough to keep back tears. I have no

idea which afternoon that was or why it meant enough to my brother to save. "I can do another jar like this, if you want," I say to the judge. "But I'd rather skip to these last ones. They're all dated June eleventh, the day of the murder."

"Why don't you move on to that day, then, Hope?" The judge widens her eyes at the jury, then turns back to me. "I think the jury understands the collection."

I'm relieved, but I can't remember what's supposed to come next. "Um . . . could you hold on just a minute, please?" I thumb through the note cards I've made up until I get to the right one. "Okay. Got it."

Raymond leans up and whispers, "Talk to the jury, Hope."

"Right." I step closer to the jurors and begin at the beginning. "That morning of June eleventh, Coach Johnson got up early. It was a cloudy morning, but nobody expected rain. He walked to the ballpark, like he did every game day, so he could post the team roster for the day's game." My mind flashes me a picture—not of Coach or the ballpark, but of the roster again, the one I saw in Coach's office, the one with *Chase Wells* crossed out and *T. J. Bowers* written in. I make myself keep going. "Then he went to the barn to do chores. He might have started mucking stalls before Jeremy arrived, just to help him out. We'll never know that."

I go back to the defense table because I need the right jar. "I think that brings us to this next jar. The date is the morning of the murder, and the time is seven-ten a.m." I take the jar over to the jury box and walk it along the rail while each juror leans forward and studies the date, written with black marker on the bottom of the jar. Juror Number Three pulls her glasses out of her purse and puts them on. Juror Number Eight waves me away as soon as I get to him.

"Seven-ten in the morning," I repeat. "That means the air in this jar was collected by Jeremy a few minutes after Rita got to the barn. Remember how Rita was so sure she got there at seven minutes after seven? Seven-oh-seven."

I study the lid of this jar that I think may have held grape jelly once. "I haven't opened this jar before," I tell the jury. "But I'm going to do it right now." I twist the lid in one turn and pick out the label from the underside of the lid. My heart is jumping in my chest, making my hands shake. I can barely unfold the jagged paper. I read: *A fortress of gray clouds as I walk to the barn on game day.* My heart stops thundering. I try not to show how relieved I am, but I shoot up a Jeremy-style prayer of thanks.

"We know that Jeremy got up really early too because he always did. He couldn't wait to put on his Panther uniform. Jer loved game day. He was so excited about the game that he must have stopped to write this note and collect air on his walk to the barn.

"Jeremy makes it to the barn and parks his bat, like always, and maybe his batting gloves—we don't know for sure. He starts to look for Coach, but he hears voices. Arguing. Screaming—at least Rita was. Maybe he'd seen Rita's car, and maybe he hadn't. It doesn't matter. He walks toward the shouting, but Jeremy hates arguing, so he stops, maybe hides.

"And that's when Jeremy hears something he never thought he'd hear. His own mother shouts, 'Jeremy is your son! You better pay up.' Or something like that. Those words would ring in Jeremy's ears. *Your son. Jeremy is your son. Coach's son!* Can you imagine what went through Jeremy's mind? He had a father, the best father in the whole world. Coach was already the best man in Jeremy's world. Now he had a father who was kind and good to him, who loved him."

I can't look at Jeremy. I won't look at Jeremy. He'll make me stop. Or he'll cry, and I'll want to stop.

"So what does Jeremy do next? He does not want to hear his parents argue. He wants to let those words play in his head: *Jeremy is your son.* So he races out of the barn, grabbing his pack with his jars in it—he has to record this day, this moment of all moments. He stumbles to the pasture, and there's old Sugar. He's ridden her bareback with the halter a dozen times before. So he jumps on that old pinto and rides. Beside himself with joy, he circles the pasture on Sugar— people saw him. Pretty soon, the old horse slows down and goes back to grazing, with Jeremy on her back.

"Maybe that's when Jer gets off the horse. Maybe he rolls in the grass, or twirls in the pasture, or dances a jig—who knows? Having a dad feels too good to be true."

I walk back to the defense table and take up the next jar, a honey jar, dimpled on the sides. "This is a day that Jeremy Long . . . Jeremy Johnson . . . never wants to forget. His world has changed in one moment. He has a dad. A daddy. And he already loves John Johnson. So he takes out this honey jar from his backpack. He writes the date on the bottom of the jar with his special pen that writes on glass, the pen he always carries with him. And he writes the time, 7:44 a.m."

I walk the jar over to the jury, showing them the flat bottom with the date and time in black calligraphy. "Can't you see him, waving the jar high above his head and snapping on the lid, capturing the glorious air on the day he found out he had a father, a kind and loving father?"

I pop open the jar. I'm dizzy, woozy with the air in this jar, or the lack of it in the courtroom. I wish I'd read the note first. I unfold the note and read it to the jury. "It says, **Air on my first Father's Day.**" Tears try to squeeze up my throat. My mouth fills with them, and I have to swallow so hard it hurts.

I go back to the table and trade jars, choosing the next one in line. I've already read the time written on the bottom of this one. "This next jar is labeled only three minutes later, three minutes after the last jar filled with air of a special 'Father's Day.'" I show the date and time to the jury. "I think there was too much joy in Jeremy for only one jar. So he had to use another." I'm pretty sure this note will be filled with more hallelujahs about having a dad, but I open it anyway. The courtroom has gone quiet, not even a cough. I read the note out loud: **Chase runs toward the sun on my Father's Day.**

I stare at the slip of paper in my hand, Jeremy's tight calligraphy still dancing on the paper. I read it again, to myself this time.

But Chase didn't run that day.

I don't understand. I try to catch Chase's attention, but his head is down. My stomach cramps. Tiny claws pinch my insides. How could Jeremy have seen Chase if he didn't run that day? Chase said he didn't run on game days.

"Hope," Raymond whispers, loud enough for me to hear, "open the last jar."

I don't move.

307

"You want me to do it?" Raymond asks, reaching for it. When I don't answer, he picks up the jar and stands. Numb, I watch as he turns the jar upside down and faces the jury. "This jar is dated the same day, June eleventh, the day of the murder. The time written on the bottom is 8:01." Raymond turns to me, frowning. "That's right before Mrs. McCray came into the barn and found John Johnson dead." Slowly, he rolls the jar in his hands until it's right side up. He walks toward the jury, his hand on the lid of the final jar.

I can't let him do it. I run after him. "No! Don't!" Grabbing the jar from his hands, I beg him. "Please? Please, Raymond. I'll read it."

He nods and sits back down.

I hold the jar gently, the glass cool in my hand. At last, I turn to my brother. I'm still afraid he'll shout at me with his eyes, scream for me to stop. But he's not even looking at me. Instead, he's gazing up, smiling, taking deep breaths of the air I've released into the courtroom, his father's air. He closes his eyes and inhales so long I half expect him to float away.

I move in closer to the jury and hold up the jar so the jurors can see the lid, the dark red dried in the ridges of the rim. "You can see this is blood that—"

Keller objects, and the judge sustains.

But I know they've seen it, the blood. "Jeremy has been happier than he's ever been in his life. A father. A loving father. With that air tucked away in his jars, he goes back to the barn. We may never know what he planned to do. Maybe he'd just watch John Johnson in a new light from now on. Maybe he'd hug his father and draw him pictures to tape to his refrigerator. Maybe my brother would have spoken, called him Daddy.

"But Jeremy never gets the chance. Instead, when he walks into the barn, he doesn't see his father. He searches the stalls for him. Then Jer spots him, his father, lying in a muddy red pool of sawdust and blood. Does he scream? Does he cry? Whatever else he does, he runs to his father and kneels beside him. The blood soaks into his uniform. He hugs this man who has been his father for less than an hour. Hugs and rocks him.

"And then what does he do? Jeremy Long does the only thing that's ever put order in his world. He takes out his last jar, writes the date and time on the bottom: *June 11, 8:01 a.m.* And he captures this air." I open the jar and think I feel a rush of stale air, scented with blood and death. Behind me, Jeremy moans as the death air mixes with the Father's Day air, with the air of game day, with Chase running, and with a father's breath leaving his body. Then I pull out the slip of paper tucked away inside the lid, and I read it: *Air of blood and my dead father.*

I'm not the only one crying in this room. I hear sniffles from the spectators. In a blur, I see T.J., and he's standing up, crying. And Rita, in the very back row. Sobbing.

But I have to finish. I don't want to. But it's the only way left. "Poor Jeremy. There he is—no father. Only a mother, a mother he last saw arguing with the man lying on the ground. A mother Jeremy loves, no matter what she's done. He has to protect her. He stands up, grabs the bloody bat, and races home, where he'll try to hide the bat . . . to save his mother."

These are the words I rehearsed all night. I couldn't let

myself think of what might happen to Rita because of them, because of my words. I believed those words. I'm not sure Raymond did, but I did.

Only now, they don't sound right. They don't ring true in this courtroom. *The truth, the whole truth, and nothing but the truth.*

I have to keep going. "My brother didn't kill John Johnson. He was protecting someone he thought did, someone he loves." As I say this, I'm meaning for them to understand that Rita did it, that Jeremy didn't. This is what I've rehearsed, what I've believed. And yet, something nags at me inside. The air I'm breathing swirls in my head, making me dizzy— death, fathers, sons, baseball, and Chase running. Why was he running toward the sun, away from the barn? He said he hadn't gone near the barn that morning. Why would he lie?

"She's right!" Rita stands up at the back of the courtroom. "I did it. It was me!"

37

The courtroom goes crazy. The judge bangs her gavel and tries to get order.

I stare back at Rita, and I know that this is the best thing she's ever done. And in that same instant, I also know she's not telling the truth. Rita's best moment, and it's a lie.

Because of Chase. Because he lied about being there.

Because I keep seeing Chase's name crossed out. Because I can't get the crime scene photos out of my head. A crumpled long strip of paper beside the body in at least one crime photo. I've seen those long, narrow papers before. And then I see them again, in my mind, on Coach's desk, in his drawer. Rosters. And I see the name crossed off: *Chase Wells*.

Not wanting to see the truth I know I'll see, I turn and look at Chase. He's staring back this time, and the truth is all there on his face, his gorgeous face, and in those eyes. "Why?" I whisper it, but it feels louder than the commotion going on all around me. I think everybody in the courtroom may be going crazy, declared insane, everybody except Jeremy.

But it feels like Chase and I are the only ones here. We're three feet apart, separated by a table, a railing, and people passing between us. But all I see is Chase. Chase and the dozens of images in my head of us together.

"I'm so sorry," he says. "I never meant for Jeremy to be blamed."

Behind us, Sheriff Wells's booming voice rises over the courtroom. "You better adjourn this trial, Judge! This whole thing's out of order. You want me to take the kid's mother into custody?"

"Hope," Chase continues, as if I'm the only one here, "you have to know I wouldn't have let Jeremy go to prison. I'd have—"

The sheriff wheels around and is on Chase in two strides. "Shut up! Don't say another word!"

Chase flinches as if he's been slapped. "You knew, didn't you?"

I don't know which face shows more pain, Chase's or his father's.

"That's why you tried to scare Hope off the case, to keep us apart." Without taking his gaze from his dad's face, Chase says, "You knew all along that Jeremy didn't kill Coach . . . and that I did."

His words take away what's left of my breath.

"I said, shut up!" Sheriff Wells cries. His face is cartoon red, like faces in those animated shows Jeremy loves to watch. "I told you not to try to dig up trouble, but you wouldn't listen. Everything would have been okay if you'd just listened to me! I had it all under control."

Crime scene photos are flashing through my brain. I knew all along something was wrong with them. And now I see it. The photos of Coach with the stuff from his pockets spread out on the ground—the picture I saw in the sheriff's crime scene file had a long strip of paper that wasn't in Raymond's photo. I didn't know what the paper was then, but I do now. The roster. Probably the roster Coach had posted at the ballpark that day . . . with Chase's name crossed out, just like it had been on Coach's copy, the one he kept on his desk. That roster wasn't in the photo they gave Raymond . . . because Sheriff Wells took it away. He must have seen it and figured out everything right then and there.

Chase turns his back on his dad and stares at me. "I am so sorry. I didn't mean to. I didn't—please, Hope?"

I don't know what he wants from me. Arguments leap like flames around us, but they don't reach me. My head shakes back and forth as I stare at Chase, *my* Chase. I'm piecing together the lies. I still feel the air, full around us, slicing apart, then coming together, like air through vents. "I don't understand."

"We're not saying another word!" Sheriff Wells shouts.

"*I* am." Keeping his gaze on me, Chase grips the rail and gets to his feet. His voice is loud enough for the judge and everyone else to hear him. The crowd quiets as if their volume has been turned off, like the night crickets Chase and I listened to a million years ago.

Still looking only at me, he says, "I didn't mean to do it.

313

You have to believe me. And I didn't plan for Jeremy to get arrested for the murder. I wouldn't have let them send Jeremy to prison. I just thought—or at least I convinced myself at first—he'd be better off wherever they put mental patients, and I wouldn't have to go to jail for something I didn't mean to do."

I hurt inside, in places I didn't know I had. I'm aware of people moving around Chase, talking to him. I think they're reading him his rights, like on television. Somebody's handcuffing the sheriff, then Chase. The judge is talking to Chase, and he's listening to her. T.J. has pushed his way in closer, and his lips are moving. But the words are floating over me, like this air, circling above me but not letting me breathe it in.

"I didn't plan it, not any of it," Chase continues. "I think, with time, I could have convinced myself I didn't really do it, not even the murder—if I hadn't spent time with you, Hope, if I hadn't gotten to know Jeremy through you."

"Why?" I can't ask the things I really want to ask. *Was it all a lie? Was I totally and completely fooled? Were you spying on me the whole time? Did you ever care about me? Is everything hope-less?*

Chase takes in a big breath of air, Jeremy's air. "I went out for my jog, like I always do . . . even on game days." He looks down before admitting, "I always check the roster on game day. Only I couldn't believe it. Coach had scratched out my name and put T.J. in as starting pitcher. I wasn't even on the roster. I'd told Dad I was starting pitcher. He'd rounded up his buddies to come and watch me pitch. He'd bought fireworks.

I'd never seen him so proud of me. For weeks, it was all he could talk about—his son was going to pitch in the biggest game in all Ohio, to hear him tell it. Coach Johnson had promised me I could pitch. And I wasn't even going to play?"

"All this over a stupid game!" Sheriff Wells shouts.

Chase glances back at his dad. "Couldn't disappoint you, could I, Dad? I couldn't let you down. *I* keep my promises."

"You're a fool," Sheriff Wells mutters, but he looks broken, not angry.

"I know. I'm a screwup, okay? Don't you think I know that better than anybody? I just couldn't stand to see that look, the look you give me when I've disappointed you . . . again."

Chase turns back to me, as if I'm the one he's explaining everything to, not the judge, not his dad, not the court reporter taking down every word. "I knew there had to be a mistake. I yanked down the roster and ran to the barn. Coach was always in the stable early. I found him in the back stall, brushing one of the horses. He didn't want to come out, and when he did, he seemed tired. The sun was peeking through the clouds, making an orange glow inside the barn.

"'What is it, Chase?' he asked, like I was just another inconvenience to him. That's me. Mr. Inconvenience.

"I shook the roster at him. 'What's with this?' I demanded, trying to control my temper. I was already breathing hard from the run. All the way to the barn, I'd been imagining the scene when Dad would show up at the park and discover I wasn't pitching. I'd gone over it in my head, over and over.

"'That looks like the roster I put up this morning, Chase,' Coach said. But he knew what I meant.

315

"'I'm supposed to be the starting pitcher. You promised I could start the game this afternoon!' I was shouting.

"He shook his head. 'Maybe your dad promised you that. *I* didn't. I thought you could get your swing under control, but you're not there yet. This is a big game, Chase. You ought to know that by now. I want to beat Wooster.' He was so calm. And the calmer he got, the angrier I got, like I had to turn up the heat so he'd understand how important this was.

"'So you're pitching T.J.?' I screamed. 'You've got to be kidding! He doesn't even have a curveball.'

"'Chase, you've got a lot of talent,' Coach admitted, 'and I think you're going to be a strong pitcher. But pitchers bat in our league. You know that. And your swing has been way off.'

"I told him how hard I'd been practicing. I told him over and over.

"'That's good,' he said. 'You keep it up, and we'll see.' Just like that.

"'No! You can see *now*!' I told him. I'd spotted Jeremy's bat leaning against the wall when I came in. I ran and got it. His gloves were there, so I put those on too. I took a couple of practice cuts and ran back to Coach. He was heading into the stall. 'Wait! I want you to see. I've evened out the swing like you told me. I have, Coach!'

"'It's over, Chase,' he said.

"But he'd promised. He'd *promised* me!

"'Go on home and tell your dad, son. It's about time he learned how to lose too.' Then he turned his back on me. He was breaking his promise. He shouldn't have done that. I was

316

counting on that game. My dad was counting on it. Everybody would be there. He couldn't take that away from me.

"Something went off inside me. It felt like an explosion. I swung the bat. Just like I'd been doing in the batting cages. One swing. I only wanted to show him. That's all. He dropped to his knees, like he was praying. Then he toppled to the ground. I stared down at him. Blood poured out of his nose, his mouth. So much blood.

"I dropped the bat, and I ran. I ran fast so the whole mess got farther and farther away from me. I couldn't believe what I'd done. Had I really killed him? It wasn't possible. It was too horrible to be real. So maybe I hadn't done it. When you run far enough, fast enough, all thoughts leave your head. It's a running high. You can imagine things. Maybe I'd imagined this.

"I was all the way home before I realized I was still wearing the batting gloves. Nobody was there. I put my shoes and shorts and the gloves into a garbage bag and set it out with our trash. Then I waited for Dad to get home and arrest me.

"Only it didn't happen. I got a phone call from one of the team mothers—all the players on the team got it." Chase makes a move toward me, and the guard closes in, stopping him. "I didn't even know they'd arrested Jeremy until that afternoon. I thought they'd let him go the next day. Then the next. Then it was weeks.

"At first I figured they'd see right off it wasn't Jeremy. How could they find evidence when he didn't do it? When they didn't let Jeremy go, I convinced myself that he'd get off. Dad kept telling me the jury would just put Jeremy in a kind of home, that he'd be happy there."

I remember all the questions Chase asked me about Jeremy and how surprised he'd been when I told him why a mental hospital would kill my brother. He'd wanted to believe Jeremy could live happily ever after in one of those places.

As Chase has been talking, I've pictured everything—Chase arguing with Coach, Chase picking up the bat, swinging. . . . But I've pictured other moments too—Chase wrapping me in a blanket, bringing me hot chocolate; Chase, his arms around me, his hand lifting my chin, his lips brushing mine.

I have two hearts. One is jumping for joy because I know my brother can come home. Everyone will know he's not guilty, not crazy. But the other heart is broken, shattered in pieces because I think I loved Chase. "Why did you pretend to help me, to care?"

"I wasn't pretending, Hope. Do you think I wanted to get involved? I tried to quit, to keep away from you . . . but I couldn't. I wanted to help you, to be with you. Then when you talked about Jeremy, I wanted to help you get him off. Remember? Reasonable doubt?"

I want to believe him. And I don't want to believe him. I want the truth, but it's trapped in between horrible facts, out of reach, like air in a bottle. "Was everything a lie? You? Me? Us?"

"No!" he shouts. "God, no!"

God hangs over the courtroom, echoing in the air.

"Hope?" the judge says. And for a minute, I think it's a question: *Hope?* I burst into tears, sobs that shake the earth. I have to lean on the defense table or I'll fall to the floor and never get up.

Things happen fast. Reporters are shouting questions. The judge pounds her gavel. Keller agrees with Raymond about releasing Jeremy. One of the officers takes Chase by the elbow. Another one struggles with Chase's father. T.J. and his mother come up, both offering help, friendship.

Something touches my shoulder. I know that touch. It's my brother. His stiff fingers press something cool and hard into my palm. It's the aspirin bottle. He's printed on the side in tiny, curled letters: **Hope's tears—Psalm 56:8.** When I smile up at him, he wipes the tears from my cheek.

Rita edges in close, closer than she's been for a long, long time. I look up at Jeremy. He's smiling at her, the lines in his face soft with relief that his mother didn't kill his father.

Rita starts to say something to me, but she stops and turns back to Jeremy.

And then I hear it. It has been ten years since I heard that sound, but I recognize it as clearly as if I'd been listening to it just this morning. I close my eyes and take in the single note that swallows every other noise in the courtroom. It drowns out shame and anger and lies. Then it slides into more notes that mingle with the words blowing around us, in the air, filling the room.

I open my eyes and see that Chase isn't looking at me anymore. He's staring at Jeremy because that song, of course, is coming from Jeremy's mouth. From his heart. His soul.

When my brother stops singing, the courtroom stays silent. We look from Jeremy to one another. Nothing will ever be the same for anyone in this room. I think we all know that.

When we finally leave the courthouse—Raymond, Rita, Jeremy, and me—the air outside has changed. We stop on the top step and breathe in the moment, clear as sunshine, right as rain, and true as song.

Epilogue

"Hope! Hope!"

I don't answer right away. It's Saturday morning, nearly eight months since Jeremy started talking again, and I still get a rush hearing my brother say my name. I make him say it again. Then I join him on the front lawn. Our dog, a black-and-white mutt we rescued from the shelter, trots over to greet me, then races back to Jer. Jeremy named the puppy Maple, but only he knows why.

Outside, a white fog hangs over the budding treetops. A car door slams, and I see Raymond getting out of his car, followed by his wife and daughter. Jer and I run to meet them. "How's my Christy?" I ask, checking to see if the baby's grown hair yet. She's dressed in pink so we'll know she's a girl anyway. Her whole name is Christina Hope Munroe. Raymond says you can't have too many Hopes.

"Want to hold her, Jeremy?" Becca Munroe offers up her prize.

My brother shakes his head. He loves that baby, but he's afraid to hold her. "We sing tomorrow," he says, grinning.

"I know," Becca says. She and Jer sing in the choir, and tomorrow is their Easter cantata.

I glance back at the house, and Rita waves from the window. She won't come outside. Hangover. At least being drunk embarrasses her now. She and Bob spend a lot of time together, and not just at the Colonial or at night. They went to the zoo last week, and they took Jeremy with them. Rita was sober for almost three weeks after the trial. Maybe she will be again.

"So," Raymond says, picking up Maple and scratching his ears, "did you get enrolled at Wayne County okay?"

"Yep. Thanks." Raymond tried to get me to apply to Ohio State, but I'm not ready to leave Jeremy. I'm going to commute with T.J. to Wayne County Community College for now. Raymond wants me to major in prelaw. I might. But right now I'm leaning toward being a private investigator. Anything's possible.

I still think about Chase. At the weirdest moments, a picture will flash to my mind, and I'll see his green eyes, tanned face, and that smile—and I'll miss him so much it hurts. He's in a juvenile facility, where he'll be for a long, long time. I haven't seen him or spoken to him. I wrote him once, but I didn't mail it. He could be in prison the rest of his life.

Jeremy tears into the house and comes back with a quart pickle jar I washed for him over a month ago. He writes the date on the bottom of the jar, then folds a slip of paper and tucks it under the lid. I don't ask what he's written. I think I can guess.

The fog moves in, rushing to get a part in my brother's memory. As Jeremy raises his arms, I can't take my eyes off him. In the instant he sweeps the air, his face changes from gawky—too much gum, too big ears—to handsome and wise with secret knowledge. And in that instant, he captures in his jar the fog of spring and the promise of hope.

*You have collected
all my tears in your bottle.*
Psalm 56:8 (New Living Translation)

Acknowledgments

I love acknowledgments, although mine should really be called "Thanksgivings"!

A million thanks to Allison Wortche, my gifted editor, whose sensitivity and insights have strengthened this book, and whose gracious spirit makes the work fun. I'm so grateful to Alfred A. Knopf Books, a house I've admired my whole life, for welcoming me into their family.

As for Anna J. Webman, my magnificent agent, thanks for taking such great care of me. I'm proud to be part of Curtis Brown Ltd.

For such an intricate mystery, I needed help! Thank you to the experts who answered all my questions and often came up with better ideas than I did:

- Patrick G. Lazzaro, prosecuting attorney, Cleveland, Ohio, and former administrative judge in Ohio (we must do this again!)
- Rick Acker, deputy attorney general in the California Department of Justice
- Assistant prosecutor, Ashland County, Ohio

And on the home front, thanks to my amazing family for letting me steal so much material from your lives. I hope you realize how very thankful I am for all of you.

About the Author

Dandi Daley Mackall is the award-winning author of many books for children and adults. She visits countless schools, conducts writing assemblies and workshops across the United States, and presents keynote addresses at conferences and young author events. She is also a frequent guest on radio talk shows and has made dozens of appearances on TV.

Dandi lives in rural Ohio with her husband, three children, and their horses, dogs, and cats.

SilenceofMurder.com
DandiBooks.com